THOREAU
IN
PHANTOM BOG

B. B. OAK

KENSINGTON BOOKS
www.kensingtonbooks.com

KENSINGTON BOOKS are published by

Kensington Publishing Corp.
119 West 40th Street
New York, NY 10018

All Kensington titles, imprints, and distributed lines are available at special
quantity discounts for bulk purchases for sales promotion, premiums, fund-
raising, educational, or institutional use.

Special book excerpts or customized printings can also be created to fit spe-
cific needs. For details, write or phone the office of the Kensington Sales
Manager: Kensington Publishing Corp., 119 West 40th Street, New York,
NY 10018. Attn. Sales Department. Phone: 1-800-221-2647.

Kensington and the K logo Reg. U.S. Pat. & TM Off.

eISBN-13: 978-0-7582-9028-1
eISBN-10: 10-0-7582-9028-4
First Kensington Electronic Edition: September 2015

ISBN-13: 978-0-7582-9027-4
ISBN-10: 0-7582-9027-6
First Kensington Trade Paperback Printing: September 2015

10 9 8 7 6 5 4 3 2 1

Printed in the United States of America

Praise for *Thoreau at Devil's Perch*

"A favorite literary figure shows an unexpected flair for detection in this historical mystery. Original and charming."

—Laura Joh Rowland

"A promising debut . . . Thoreau is just as you'd expect him: erudite, eccentric, waxing philosophical about his love of nature, and a natural detective."

—*Publishers Weekly*

"Well researched, captivating and compelling until the very end, *Thoreau at Devil's Perch* is both mystery and love story during a time that appeared deceptively simple. Through their diaries, the main characters, Adam and Julia, become to feel like old friends you want to revisit again and again. I've never been a fan of using historical figures in fiction— B. B. Oak has changed my mind. Well done!"

—Anna Loan-Wilsey

"Ambitious . . . the research and fresh take on Thoreau make for an admirable start."

—*Library Journal*

"B. B. Oak brings Thoreau's nineteenth-century world to vivid life in this intriguing puzzler that will keep you guessing to the terrifying end."

—Victoria Thompson

Books by B. B. Oak

THOREAU AT DEVIL'S PERCH

THOREAU ON WOLF HILL

THOREAU IN PHANTOM BOG

Published by Kensington Publishing Corporation

The only free road, the Underground Railroad, is owned and managed by the Vigilant Committee. They have tunneled under the whole breadth of the land.

—Henry David Thoreau

Nearly every week some fugitive would be forwarded with the utmost secrecy to Concord. Sometimes they went by [railroad] cars from Concord, and then Henry Thoreau went on escort, probably more often than any other man.

—Mrs. Ann Bigelow, a founder of the
Concord Female Anti-Slavery Society

JULIA

When I called on Henry Thoreau's mother this afternoon, she was affable enough, but hardly forthcoming. And the same could be said of her two daughters. Mrs. Thoreau ushered me into her small parlor to meet them, and I found their resemblance to Henry quite striking. His elder sister Helen has large, deep-set eyes like his, and his younger sister Sophia has an aquiline nose just as prominent. So familiar and endearing were their features to me that I felt as if I already knew them. They did not reciprocate my warm feelings of friendship, however. Their manner toward me remained polite but wary throughout my short visit, and rather than be frank with me, they outright lied. But with so much at stake, I do not fault them for their subterfuge. Nor do I resent their hesitancy to include me, a complete stranger, in their clandestine operation.

Even Henry, to whom I have proven myself trustworthy and even doughty when the situation required it, was not very forthcoming when I broached the subject with him last week. I had requested that he come to Plumford to advise me on a structural change I wished to make to the house I'd inherited from my grandfather.

"I hope you do not intend to destroy the elegant proportions of this fine old construction with gables and fretwork," he said immediately upon arriving. Dressing up the plain fronts of eighteenth-century houses with Gothic Revival motifs had become all the rage, even in small towns like Plumford and Concord.

"Of course not, Henry. You should know me better than that," I replied. In truth, although we have shared some rather harrowing experiences during the last few years, we did not know each other all that well, for Henry is most reserved around women. I showed him the rough plan I'd drawn up, and he understood its purpose immediately.

"This looks to be a drawing of a hidden compartment beneath the stairs," he said. "I surmise its use would be to conceal runaway slaves from the eyes of the law."

"Exactly. I would like to offer you the use of my house as an Underground Railroad Station, Henry."

He kept his expression impassive. "Why make such an offer to *me?*"

"Come now, Henry. It's common knowledge that the Thoreau family is active in the Railroad."

"The more common the knowledge, the less it can be trusted," Henry said in a dismissive tone and went back to examining my plan. "Your measurements are slightly off," he concluded. He took a pencil from his coat pocket and made some corrections. "There. That should work."

"Now all I need is a carpenter I can trust. Will you take on the job, Henry?"

"I might."

"And will you link my house to the Railroad?"

"I might," he said again. For a man who speaks his mind so freely and eloquently, Henry can be very tight-lipped when he so chooses.

"Pray be less ambiguous," I implored.

"The configuration of the network we speak of is intentionally kept ambiguous," Henry replied. "I freely admit that I conduct fugitives from one Station to another, but I leave the organization of Station routes to others."

"And who might they be?"

"I reckon you'll find out soon enough, Julia." And with those parting words, off he went. Shortly thereafter I received an invitation from Mrs. Thoreau to take tea with her and her daughters this afternoon.

And so here I was, cup in hand, sitting betwixt Helen and Sophia on a worn horsehair sofa, across from Mrs. Thoreau on a straight-back chair. After we had all expressed our pleasure in the fine weather we were having, Mrs. Thoreau got down to the purpose of my visit. Or so I thought.

"Thank you for volunteering to help in our Cause," she said. "Your offer could not have come at a better time, Mrs. Pelletier."

I inwardly flinched, as I always do, when I am addressed by my married name. Outwardly I smiled.

"Henry tells me you are a most accomplished portrait artist," Mrs. Thoreau continued.

Rather than modestly demur, I nodded my assent. My talent and skills, after all, are all I can lay claim to in my present situation.

"The Concord Female Anti-Slavery Society holds a fair on the Common every summer to raise money," she went on to inform me, "and we are hoping you will agree to make portraits of the attendees for us to sell. Nothing elaborate, of course. Just quick pencil drawings."

I'd come with the expectation of being asked to take part in the Underground Railroad, not some humdrum fair. But I have vowed to do anything I can to help free the four million slaves in my country, so I swallowed down my disappointment and told her I would be most happy to oblige.

"Excellent!" Mrs. Thoreau said. "Your participation will give us the opportunity to get to know you better, Mrs. Pelletier. And once we are on more familiar terms, we might discuss your participation in . . . other activities related to the Cause. All in good time."

When I heard the phrase "all in good time" my face fell, for that usually means a good *long* time.

"Do not look so let down, my dear young woman," Mrs. Thoreau said. "The fair is a most important endeavor. All the proceeds we earn from it pay for the printing and dissemination of antislavery literature."

"Members of our Society work on handicrafts to sell at the fair all year round," Helen added.

As if on cue, Sophia pulled from her pocket a hook and a bobbin of white thread and commenced crocheting. "God in His providence has placed this Cause in the hands of women," she declared.

"It is left to us to agitate this nation's conscience if men are not willing to do it," Mrs. Thoreau stated firmly. "Even if we must step out of the bounds of our womanly sphere to do so."

"It's high time we extended the limits of those bounds!" I put in.

All three Thoreau ladies voiced their enthusiastic agreement, and I anticipated a rousing discussion concerning women's rights to follow. Instead the conversation turned to mundane matters concerning the fair, and I confess that my attention waned. Gazing out the front window I observed a man in rough farm clothes ride up on a sturdy dray horse. He tied the horse to the gatepost and hurried to the Thoreaus' entrance door. Mrs. Thoreau left us to answer his vigorous knocking, and, after a brief conversation with him in the dooryard, she returned to the parlor, looking rather concerned.

"Is something amiss, Mother?" Helen asked her.

"So it seems. The Plumford cargo did not arrive in Carlisle last night."

"Henry will get to the bottom of it," Sophia said. "I'll run to the Emerson house and inform him."

"No need to do that," Mrs. Thoreau said. "He's helping Father in the pencil manufactory right now. I'll go tell him myself." And with that she hurried to the house's back annex.

I looked from Helen to Sophia in the ensuing silence, waiting for them to speak. "What sort of cargo has gone missing?" I finally made bold to ask them.

"Oh, just a crate of Thoreau pencils," Helen replied.

I could not be put off by such a clumsy lie as that. "Why were pencils made in Concord dispatched from Plumford?"

Helen stared back at me blankly. "Why indeed."

"No delivery wagon was available in Concord," Sophia said, apparently more adept at invention than her sister.

Realizing further questions would only result in further fabrications, I left off my inquiry and looked out the window again. Henry and his mother had joined the farmer waiting in the dooryard. They talked awhile, and then the farmer shook hands with mother and son and rode away. Henry headed off on foot in the opposite direction, and Mrs. Thoreau returned to the parlor. Conversation concerning the fair resumed, and nothing more was said about the undelivered cargo. I took my leave shortly thereafter, and no one protested my hasty departure. I am sure they could not wait to talk frankly and openly amongst themselves. That they did not feel free to do so in my presence was disappointing but understandable. Trust is won through actions rather than words.

When I left the Thoreau home on Texas Street, I walked briskly but decorously down Concord's bustling Main Street, but as soon as I reached the open road north, I lifted my skirts and broke into a run. I sighted Henry as he was crossing a bridge over the Concord River and called to him to wait. He looked surprised to see me.

When I drew up to him, I was panting more than a little. As a girl I could run like the wind without getting winded, but that was before decorum required I wear stays. "I've just been visiting your mother," I explained to Henry as soon as I caught my breath. "She told me nothing concerning your mission, but I have deduced you are going to Plumford to see about a fugitive slave."

Henry remained silent.

"I can help you, Henry!"

"How?"

"By offering my house as a safe haven for the runaway if need be."

Henry did not accept my offer, but neither did he turn it down. "Come along then," he said in a brisk tone. "Since we're both going in the same direction, we might as well walk together."

We continued over the bridge and up Lowell Road to Plumford, three miles away. Most men would have slackened their pace or at least offered a supporting arm to a female walking companion, but Henry did not. That's one of the traits I like best in him. He treats me as a comrade with little regard to my gender. Nor does he make any effort to engage in polite conversation with me. His long silences are contemplative rather than brooding, and I do not mind them.

When we reached the base of Wolf Hill, Henry suggested that we take a path that traversed it rather than continue on the road, and I agreed that would be the more efficient route. The path turned out to be steep and rocky, but I made no complaints as pebbles bruised the undersurface of my feet through the thin leather soles of my cloth gaiter boots. The left boot soon tore along the side, leaving my poor little outermost toe exposed to very rough treatment. On we trudged through groves of birches and beeches unfolding new leaves and stands of tamaracks sprouting fresh needles. Purple-trumpeted trillium and fragrant lily of the valley bloomed on the forest floor, but Henry did not suggest we stop to admire their show. Nor did he hark to the calls of the spring birds, disregarding the ovenbird's sweet refrain of *teacher, teacher, teacher* and the insistent *pit-pit-pit* of the wood thrush. He didn't even remark, as he usually does with wry amusement, that the oriole was saying *eat it, Potter, eat it.* His concern for the slave who'd gone missing pushed him forward, and he ignored my stumbling effort to keep up with him. When the path narrowed, however, he held back branches so I could pass unscathed. He may not be gallant, but he is always considerate, and if I could conjure up a big brother, he would be just like Henry Thoreau. But at my ripe old age of four and twenty, I reckon I no longer need a big brother to guide me. I have gone my own wayward way for too long now.

Back on the Lowell Road, about half a mile from the Plumford Green, Henry came to a stop and took off his broad-brimmed straw hat to wipe his brow. His thick crop of hair stood up like a patch of unruly weeds. "I think it best for me to go alone from here," he told me.

"Why can't I continue with you?"

"Allow me to remind you that it's against Federal Law to aid and abet fugitive slaves, Julia. You could be severely fined, even arrested, for taking one into your home."

"I am willing to risk it!"

"I have found that most people who say that are just spouting off their moral or political convictions and have not considered the consequences long and hard enough."

"Well, I assure you that I have. I am not like most people, Henry. My reasons for wanting to aid and abet fugitive slaves are deeply personal rather than merely theoretical."

"Personal?" He regarded me closely. "In what way?"

I would have preferred to keep it to myself but saw that Henry needed further convincing. Therefore I divulged the wretched truth about the man I was bound to for life. "I am married to a man who was once a slave trader."

Henry does not often look surprised, but he did at that moment.

"My husband, Jacques Pelletier, made his fortune shipping captured Africans to the French West Indies," I continued. "When I learned of this I immediately left him, for I could not abide living off the profits of his trade."

"You were right to renounce a life that went against your moral sense," Henry said. "Once you learned the truth, leaving such a man was the only honest thing you could do for yourself, despite the marital vows you made."

"And if I am to stay true to myself, how can I now abide living by the unjust laws that support slavery in my own country?" I asked him. "It seems so selfish and wasteful for me to live alone in the big house my grandfather left me when I could harbor fugitive slaves in it. Indeed, I have come to believe that is the very purpose of my inheritance."

Henry was silent for a long moment. "I will not stand in the way of such a high and earnest purpose, Julia," he finally said. "Let us go on together."

We left the main road and took an overgrown byway called Drover's Lane that cut through poor fields and rocky pasture. Henry told me it used to be a well-traveled route to the town of Carlisle ten miles away but had fallen into disuse when a more direct highway was built twenty years ago. Eventually a ramshackle homestead that I assumed was abandoned came into view. "That's the Station," Henry said.

The dilapidated house was set a good ways back from the lane, but as soon as we set foot on the drive leading to it, a dog started barking. The closer we got, the more furiously it yelped, but it held its position on the sagging porch. It was a very large mongrel, and I hoped it was tethered. It was not. Just as it was about to bound off the porch and charge us, a woman came out of the entry door and gripped it by the scruff of the neck.

"Ripper doesn't like strangers," she warned us as we drew near. She did not appear to like strangers either as she glared at us, eyes furrowed into slits.

"I am not a stranger to Ezra Tripp," Henry said. "Is he your husband, ma'am?"

She nodded and raked a hand through her snarled, graying tresses, attempting to put them in some semblance of order. She had my sympathy, for no female likes to be caught with her hair down.

"I would like a word with him," Henry said.

"He's not home at present."

"Where is he?"

"What business is it of *yours,* sir?"

"Your husband and I are both in the same business," Henry said.

"Are you a farmer?"

"No, a Railroad Conductor. I come from the Stationhouse in Concord. We have been alerted by another Conductor that your husband did not deliver his shipment to the Carlisle Station last night. Do you comprehend my meaning?"

"Oh, I get your meaning all right. But I got nothing to do with my husband's unlawful undertakings," Mrs. Tripp replied.

"Could you at least tell me if he left for Carlisle last night?"
She nodded.

"By way of Drover's Lane?"
She nodded again.

"Alone?"

"No, with that shipment, as you call it, in the back of his wagon under the cover of a blanket. I reckon the master she ran from would call her his rightful property."

"We should simply call her a human being, Mrs. Tripp," I put in. "Same as we are."

"But for her *skin!* And that makes a world of difference, as you know as well as I do," she replied.

I opened my mouth to argue, but Henry gave me a silencing look and addressed Mrs. Tripp. "What time did your husband leave for Carlisle?"

"A few hours before daybreak."

"Aren't you concerned that he has not yet returned?"

"Not at all. He is no doubt having himself a good time with his drinking cronies in Carlisle. He'll be back when it suits him and no sooner. Now Good Day to you. I have told you all I know, and I have chores to attend to." She turned and tugged the dog inside the house with her.

"I must go find Tripp," Henry told me. "I hope I'll meet up with him along the byway as he is returning home, but if I don't I'll walk all the way to Carlisle and seek him out there."

"I'll go with you."

He gave my damaged boot a disparaging look. "Time is of the essence, and you would only slow me down."

I didn't argue with him, for I knew he was right. "I'll go home then. If you locate the fugitive, and she is in need of a place to stay, pray bring her to me."

"I will," Henry said. "It is obvious that she would not be welcomed back by Mrs. Tripp."

We parted and went in opposite directions on Drover's Lane. But I did not get very far before further walking became near impossible. Realizing I would never make it to town unless I mended my boot, back I limped to the Tripp homestead.

The front door was ajar, and I called to Mrs. Tripp. She did not respond, but I heard Ripper's toenails scratch against the bare wooden floor as he ran across it. He came charging out and cornered me on the porch before I could retreat down the stairs. His barking and snarling terrified me, but I challenged him by stamping my feet and yelling. This went on for a long moment or two until Mrs. Tripp finally came out. Her face was wet with tears.

"Ripper," she said softly. "Settle down now, boy." And he did!

"Forgive me for disturbing you again, Mrs. Tripp," I said, "but my boot is in need of mending. Would you happen to have a large needle and strong thread or string? Even some rags would do. I could wrap them around the boot to keep the sole from flapping."

With a sigh Mrs. Tripp motioned me to come inside. It was a humble place, with little in the way of decoration, but for a daguerreotype of two boys framed in cheap pasteboard upon a simple shelf.

"Your sons?" I said, indicating the picture.

She nodded.

"Fine looking boys."

"They take after their father. Billy is ten. He's at school now. And Jared is sixteen. He went to Ohio to work on his uncle's farm." Mrs. Tripp turned and looked me in the face as tears continued to run down hers. "He left two weeks ago."

She obviously missed him a great deal, and I hoped he was not the sort of boy who would forget to write home to his mother. "Well, at least he didn't go off to fight in that horrible Mexican War."

"Oh, he wanted to! And he would have too, if not for his brother." She blotted her eyes with the edge of her apron. "But never mind about Jared. Let me hunt you up a darning needle and yarn."

I set to work mending my boot at the kitchen table, and Mrs. Tripp put on the kettle. She said very little over tea, and I did not stay long. But I could not help thinking she was not a bad sort despite the ignorant prejudices she'd expressed concerning slaves. Perhaps she resented the time her husband devoted to helping them escape to freedom. The farmstead was in sad disrepair and certainly could have used more of Mr. Tripp's attention.

When I reached the end of the rutted drive I was surprised to see Henry running down Drover's Lane from the direction whence he'd gone. As he neared I saw that his countenance was most grim. I rushed to him and asked what had happened.

"Tripp has been shot dead," he told me. "I found his body by a bog less than half a mile up the lane."

"No! What about the fugitive?"

"Vanished," Henry said. "I was on my way to Plumford to report the murder, but if you would do so instead, I'll return to the bog to look for her."

"Yes, I'll inform Constable Beers."

"Best inform our good doctor first, Julia. I would like Adam to have time to examine the body without Beers's interference."

I did not question Henry's instructions, for I have come to trust his judgment completely in matters concerning murder.

ADAM

Wednesday, May 17

As I stood on my office doorstep gazing across the road at the Green this afternoon, every living thing before my eyes seemed to mirror my desire for Julia. The songbirds clad in gaudy mating colors were singing with an ardor that near matched my own, and the coronas of the narcissus were opening wide to the swallowtail butterflies hovering above them. Finally Julia came into view, running across the Green as fleet of foot as the goddess Atalanta, her pale blue dress billowing like a cloud. When she reached my doorstep I pulled her inside, slammed shut the door, and threw the bolt. Ere she could utter a word I curled my arms around her waist and pressed my lips to hers, greedy to taste her nectar. Although we'd had our customary tryst at cockcrow this morning, my hunger for Julia is never satiated, and I would have taken her right then and there if she'd allowed it. She did not. Instead, she broke away from me, breathless and flushed from my kiss or, more likely, from running.

"We're quite alone," I assured her. "Molly went home early to help her mother dig a garden, so we have the whole house to ourselves." I grasped her hand. "Come. We'll go up to your chamber." She shook her head and pulled back her hand. Her reluctance confounded me. She had been my ardent lover for five blissful months. "What's wrong, dearest?"

"A man has been shot dead, Adam. A farmer named Ezra Tripp. Henry Thoreau found his body on Drover's Lane near a bog, and he awaits you there."

"How did Henry get involved? Or more to the point, how did *you,* Julia?"

Her brief explanation confirmed my belief that she should take no part whatsoever in the Underground Railroad. But now was not the time to resume our ongoing argument concerning this. I hastened to the barn, hitched Napoleon to the gig, and drove off to the bog. I had learned from experience that it is best to examine a corpse before Constable Beers and the Coroner's Jury gathered around it and mucked up evidence. I knew the murder victim, but not well. I had treated him only once since he and his family had become tenants of a farm off Drover's Lane last year. And I was familiar with the bog up the lane from the farm, having had a few boyhood adventures there. We locals called it Phantom Bog, and as I drew closer to it, I saw four redheaded vultures circling above, ominous portents in a cloudless blue sky.

And then I saw a man of middle height and solid build in the center of the bog. It was Henry David Thoreau, and he was walking on water. Now I have witnessed Henry perform a number of athletic feats, but this was a new one. Of course he was not actually walking on the water itself but upon the sphagnum moss that covered its surface. As he raised a hand in greeting and continued toward me, he had to keep shifting his body weight this way and that to maintain his balance on the spongy, decaying vegetation that quaked and undulated beneath his feet.

There was a horse hitched to an empty wagon near the

edge of the bog. A body lay beside the wagon. I climbed down from the gig and identified the dead man as Ezra Tripp. Last month he'd fallen from his hayloft, and I'd popped his dislocated shoulder back into place, much to his great relief. And now he was staring up at the vultures with unblinking eyes as a whirl of flies danced on the clotted blood of the wound in the center of his chest. I knelt beside the body to inspect it more closely.

Henry joined me. His clothes were soaked through. Assuming he had taken a misstep and fallen into the water before I arrived, I did not remark upon it.

"Tell me what you see, Doctor," he said. It was not the first time he had given me this directive over a corpse.

I attempted to flex the dead man's arms and legs to no avail. "Rigor mortis has taken hold," I said. "That indicates he has been dead for at least ten to twelve hours." I unbuttoned Tripp's waistcoat and shirt to examine the wound. "He was shot through the heart with a rifle, not a fowling piece," I continued. "The entry hole of the ball is clean and small as my thumb. He died instantly. And since he is lying on the ground I assume he was standing beside his wagon when he was shot."

"I think not," Henry said. "Note the blood spatters on the dashboard. And see there." He pointed at hoof marks gouged deeply into the soft soil a dozen feet from the body. "I hypothesize that the shot was fired at close range just to the left of the horse, and the animal reared at the sound, yanking the wagon to the right. This caused Tripp to fall out of the wagon rather than tumble straight back into it."

The horse, now peacefully grazing on spring grass, cast looks back at us, curious at the sound of strange voices.

Henry led me a few rods up the road and pointed at a set of boot prints. "Here the shooter waited, turned sideways as the wagon approached, and raised his gun. The back foot, as you can see, dug more deeply into the ground when the recoil of the gun against his shoulder drove his weight backwards onto that foot."

"But who would kill a poor farmer in cold blood?"

"Perhaps someone who wanted his precious cargo," Henry said.

"A slave catcher?"

Henry nodded. "The killer could have followed the runaway's trail to Plumford, accosted Tripp here, and when Tripp refused to hand her over, shot him."

"And then dragged the poor slave off with him," I said with a sinking heart.

"I see no signs of that," Henry said as we walked back to the wagon. "It looks to me that when she heard the gunshot she threw off the blanket she was hiding under, jumped from the wagon bed, and ran for her life. You can clearly see shoe prints in the dirt here. Their small size indicates a woman. And look how they become more widely spaced as she sprinted down the road, toes digging deeper into the dirt."

We followed the prints until they veered off the road and disappeared into a tangle of red maple shoots and blueberry bushes. "And here is where you lost her trail," I said.

"Not quite." Henry guided me into the undergrowth to show me where the runaway's feet had pressed down the maple shoots and broken twigs of the bushes. "Beyond here, the trail disappears altogether as she ran onto the bog sphagnum. And over yonder are the shooter's tracks going from the road into the bog as well."

The boot prints were easier to follow, but they too disappeared altogether on the pond's mossy cover. "The killer pursued her," I said grimly.

"So it appears."

"It's no easy feat to get across a bog without falling through the sphagnum," I said. "Especially in the dark of night."

"I have already examined the bog's perimeters and could find only one set of prints coming out of it."

"Which ones?" I dreaded the answer.

"The shooter's," Henry said, confirming my fears. "He went due west until he gained the road toward Acton. I lost his tracks on the busy turnpike."

"Then the poor runaway most likely drowned."

"That's why I went probing beneath the sphagnum," Henry said, explaining his sopping clothes. "But I did not come upon her body."

"Unfortunately, that doesn't prove she's still alive."

"Yet my instincts tell me she is," Henry emphatically declared.

It has never ceased to surprise me that as much as Henry values the science of deduction and analysis, he trusts his intuition as much as empirical evidence. He claims we all have this inborn knowledge, and it irks him how few of us use it.

We returned to Tripp, and I rolled him over to see if the bullet had passed through his body. There was a small but decided bulge in the fabric of his coat at the center of his back. I took out my pocketknife and sliced through the material. A lead ball of a large caliber tumbled out.

"The bullet punched right through his backbone," I said. "That's what slowed it enough to be caught and held by the fabric of his coat."

Henry took the bullet and eyed it closely. "There's a triangular nick on one of the grooves. Do you think it was made passing through his body?"

"No bone is hard enough to nick a bullet so neatly."

"Then no doubt a small defect in the barrel of the gun marked it so." He slipped the bullet into his pocket.

We covered the corpse with the blanket from the wagon, led Napoleon and Tripp's horse out of the sun, and sat ourselves down under a cedar to await the constable and the Coroner's Jury.

"I confess I love the smell of decaying vegetation," Henry said, inhaling deeply. "It is the strong, wholesome fragrance of the very earth itself."

"Strong for certain," I replied. "But fragrant? I think not."

Henry smiled. "Fortunately, most folks don't find bogs as pleasant as I do. Hence, they remain undisturbed and continue to be sanctuaries for scarcely seen plants such as leatherleaf and sheep laurel."

"Well, this particular bog is also the sanctuary for a phantom," I informed him.

"That makes it richer and wilder still! Is there a legend attached to this phantom?"

"Yes, a sad one that goes back more than a hundred years."

I related to Henry that a couple named Jacob and Charity Stiles had lived in a cabin near the bog back in the seventeen hundreds. Jacob beat his wife unmercifully when he was drunk, but the town fathers, respecting a man's right to discipline his wife and fearing Jacob's vicious nature, put off calling him to task for his abuse despite pleas from those who pitied the poor young woman. It was known she often fled into the bog to escape Jacob's fists and boots until he regained control over his drunken bouts of fury. Then one day she disappeared altogether. Jacob claimed she had just run off, but it was feared that he had murdered her. No one would have anything to do with him after that, and he eventually moved away. But Charity's ghostly presence remained. More than a few townsmen traveling past the bog at nightfall saw her rising up from it. Hence, it became known as Phantom Bog.

"Guilt caused them to see the apparition because none had lifted a finger to help the poor woman," Henry said.

"Yet long after those men were dead and buried," I said, "there have been sightings of a beautiful water wraith hovering over the bog in the twilight mist. In truth, as a boy I would come here at nightfall with my mates to wait for her to emerge from the water, for it was said she was clothed in nothing but a cloud shroud. Of course all we got for our trouble was countless mosquito bites."

"And that's all you deserved," Henry said and went back to regarding the bog with renewed interest.

Soon after that Constable Beers arrived on horseback. When he dismounted I breathed a sigh of relief for his sway-backed horse. To carry about such a heavy load as Beers cannot be easy.

We three gathered over the body. The constable visibly bridled at Henry's disclosure that Tripp was killed in the act of conducting an escaped slave, now gone missing, toward freedom.

"I am surprised that a citizen of Plumford was involved in slave smuggling," the constable said. "I thought such law breakers and trouble makers as that only resided in your town, Mr. Thoreau."

"The Underground Railroad has stations from the Deep South all the way up to the Canadian border," Henry told him.

"Well, I would like to know who else in Plumford is breaking the law. And it is your obligation to tell me."

"The only obligation I have is to do what I think right," Henry stated firmly. "The reason I informed you of Mr. Tripp's involvement in the Underground Railroad is because you should know that he might have been killed by a slave catcher."

"That's the last thing we need in our peaceful town— escaped slaves and the murderous hunters that come after them!" Beers sputtered.

Henry ignored his indignation. "Here's the bullet that killed Tripp," he calmly said, extracting it from his pocket.

Beers, whose stomach is most delicate despite its girth, put his hands behind his back rather than touch a piece of metal that had gone through a man's heart and bone. "Since it cannot tell us who fired it, why bother me with the bullet?"

Henry returned it to his pocket. "Very well, Constable Beers. Let us focus on the facts at hand." He described how he had tracked the two sets of footprints into the bog and the one set out of it.

"Well, she must have drowned," Beers said.

"I explored the bog as well as I could and did not find a body," Henry said.

Beers shrugged. "Very well then. She didn't drown."

"To be certain of that, you should form a search party and conduct a more exhaustive investigation," I told him.

Frowning, Beers waved his hand to ward off mosquitoes. "I doubt I can drum up much concern for a missing runaway. What business is it of ours?"

"Is not the injustice of slavery every man's business, Constable?" Henry said.

"It is every man's business to mind the law," Beers retorted. "And slavery is still lawful in this country." He glanced down at the corpse and then quickly averted his eyes. "If Tripp had minded *his* business, he would still be alive."

"What do you intend to do about his murder?" I asked him.

"What can I do? I am sure Tripp's killer has traveled well beyond my jurisdiction by now."

"Always ready to do nothing, aren't you, Constable?" I said.

Beers glowered at me, and I glared right back at him. I had little respect for the man. Not only was he as thick as the soles of the shoes he cobbled, but he was lazy to boot. Yet he continues to get reelected Town Constable, most likely because he is such a popular tavern denizen.

"I have done my duty and informed Coroner Daggett to convene a jury here," Beers told me coldly.

That was doing very little indeed, for it was up to the Town Coroner to collect six townsmen to comprise a jury and bring them to the body. In less than an hour Fred Daggett, who was busy enough running his general store, arrived in his chaise with two of the jurymen, and after that came a horse trap with the other four. Mr. Jackson followed in his undertaker's wagon. I affirmed that Tripp had died of a gunshot wound, and the jurors concluded that he had been murdered. Coroner Daggett declared he would inform Justice Phyfe of the verdict when he returned from a business trip in Lowell, and that was that. The proceedings did not last more than five minutes. Undertaker Jackson suggested that he take the body back to town and clean up the blood before letting Mrs. Tripp view it, and Coroner Daggett agreed.

"Who here knows the Tripp family?" Daggett asked us.

"My farm is the closest to theirs, but neither I nor my family are acquainted with the Tripps," one of the jurors said. "My wife will do the neighborly thing and pay a condolence call on Mrs. Tripp this afternoon, but someone should tell the poor woman of her husband's demise beforehand."

"I will do it," I said when no one else spoke up. I didn't know Mrs. Tripp very well, but at least I had briefly conversed with her the time I took care of her husband's dislocated shoulder.

"And I'll drive the wagon back to the farm," Henry said.

"You should accompany them," Daggett said to Beers.

"Whatever for?" Beers replied. "No need for *three* men to bear the bad tidings to the poor woman."

"It is your constableship duty to investigate this matter,"

Daggett reminded him sharply. "And if Justice Phyfe were present, he would tell you the same."

Without further protest Beers hefted himself upon his long-suffering horse and followed my gig and Tripp's wagon to the farmstead. Except for a few scraggly chickens in the front yard, there were no signs of life at the Tripp house, but when I knocked on the door a dog's frenetic barking erupted from within. Mrs. Tripp came out to the porch, quickly closing the door behind her before the dog bounded out.

"Good Day once again, Mrs. Tripp," Henry said and took off his hat.

I too removed mine. "I am Dr. Walker if you recall, ma'am."

"And I am the Plumford constable," Beers announced with a curt bow of the head. "We have come to tell you that your husband was murdered last night less than a mile from here up Drover's Lane. He was shot in the chest by a slave catcher."

Henry and I exchanged a look of dismay. For someone who did not wish to tell Mrs. Tripp the tragic news, Beers had done so most abruptly, holding back nothing.

"A slave catcher," Mrs. Tripp repeated hollowly. "Did you catch *him?*"

"No, he plumb got away," Beers said. "And the slave your husband was carting has gone missing too."

"Did you hear a gunshot last night?" Henry asked Mrs. Tripp.

"I heard nothing," she said. She could barely move her pale lips, so frozen with shock was she.

"Let us go inside, so you may sit down," I said.

She shook her head, and then jerked it toward the door. Behind it the dog was scratching and barking. "Better not come in. My dog bites."

We told her that Undertaker Jackson had taken charge of

her husband's body, and that a neighbor lady would be coming over shortly.

"I must make myself presentable then," Mrs. Tripp said. And with that she went inside and closed the door firmly behind her.

Satisfied that he had done his duty, Beers waddled to his horse and rode off. Henry and I were reluctant to leave Mrs. Tripp alone, however. After we unhitched, watered, and barned Tripp's horse, we sat on the porch steps to await the juror's wife. The dog had ceased its infernal barking, and all was quiet within the house.

"Left to Beers, there is little chance Tripp's murderer will ever be found," I said in a low tone. "Nor will he make any effort to search the bog for the fugitive."

"Then we will have to conduct our own search," Henry said, and we made plans to meet at the bog tomorrow with as many men as we could each round up. "My hope is that she did not perish in the bog and has continued toward Canada on foot, keeping to the woods and following the North Star."

"May God protect her," I said.

"The government certainly won't," Henry said angrily. "And I cannot recognize as my government that which is the slave's government also."

"I am an abolitionist to the marrow," I told him, "and I do not countenance any law that supports slavery. Nevertheless, I am totally against Julia using her house as an Underground Railroad station. That is far too dangerous a situation for a woman who lives alone."

"I would never ask Julia to do anything that would endanger her," Henry said. "However, the Railroad is sorely in need of new Stations right now, Adam. The established ones in Concord, such as my family's house, have become known to slave hunters and are being closely watched."

"If I could do so in good conscience, I would offer Tuttle Farm as a Station," I said. "But I am away all day and many nights seeing to patients, and Gran is much too ill to take on the responsibility of sheltering runaways."

"Mrs. Tuttle is ill? I am most sorry to hear it," Henry said. "Your grandmother has always seemed indomitable to me."

"In spirit she is," I said. "But not in body. Gran has a fatal tumor of the glands and has been slowly wasting away since the New Year."

"I wish you had told me sooner, Adam. I would have come to her bedside."

"Except for family, she does not care to have people see her in such a weakened state."

"Nonsense. Is not disease the rule of existence? Why, there is not a lily pad floating on the river but has been riddled by insects. And I shall tell your grandmother just that when I call on her."

"She may not take too kindly to your comparing her to an insect-riddled lily pad, Henry."

"Mrs. Tuttle has not taken kindly to a number of my notions. But I think it would do her good to get riled up over them once again."

He was probably right. If there was one thing Gran always enjoyed, it was getting all riled up. "Why don't you ride back to Tuttle Farm with me after the bog search tomorrow, Henry? I'll tell Gran to expect you."

Henry agreed to this plan, and shortly thereafter the juror's wife arrived at the Tripp house as promised, carrying a basket laden with food. She had a kindly face.

"How did Mrs. Tripp take the sad news?" she asked us.

"Like a Stoic," Henry said.

"I do not think she has let it sink in yet," I said, having oft seen such a numb response from kin when I delivered a dire diagnosis or pronounced a loved one dead.

When the neighbor lady rapped on the door the dog inside started barking madly again. "He does not like strangers," Henry said. "Stay here whilst I go in and tether him."

"No need," the lady said. "Although I am not well acquainted with Mrs. Tripp, I do know the dog. His name is Ripper, and he often comes to our farm to chase the chickens. But his bark is truly worse than his bite, for he has never harmed a one of them. I eventually made friends with the beast by throwing him scraps of food."

And sure enough, when Mrs. Tripp opened the door, and Ripper got a sniff of her visitor, he became quiet as a lamb and began thumping his tail against the jamb. Mrs. Tripp invited her neighbor inside but did not include Henry or me in the invitation, so we took our leave.

Henry headed back to Concord on foot, his favorite mode of transportation, and I drove back to town, sure that Julia was anxiously awaiting a report concerning Tripp's murder and the runaway. When I entered the house the first person I came across was Julia's house helper, Molly Munger, crawling about the parlor carpet.

"Have you lost something, Molly?" I asked her.

She sat back on her heels and smiled at me. "Not my mind, if that's what you're thinking, Doc Adam."

Her pert answer amused me, but in truth she really had come close to losing her mind about two years ago, after an unfortunate affair with a scoundrel that resulted in a pregnancy and miscarriage. A strapping, rosy-cheeked girl of eighteen, she looks the very picture of health now, and her cheerful disposition conveys to me that she has put past regrets well behind her.

"I am hunting out stains to remove with my potion of ox

bile and water," she went on to explain, gesturing toward a bucket on the floor beside her. "Pa always gives Ma the gall bladder of any ox he butchers, and she squeezes out the juice and stores it in a corked phial. She let me have a dram of it to spruce up this old Turkey rug. I aim to spruce up this whole house for Julia. She was a good friend to me when I most needed her, and I am mighty glad to be of help to her now."

I left Molly to find Julia in the room across the hall that she had transformed from Doc Silas's cluttered study to her equally cluttered studio. Instead of journals and books scattered about, there were paint pots and canvases and sketch pads. Julia was peering into a large looking glass when I walked in but turned her attention to me. "Tell me everything, Adam!" she demanded.

Since Julia has never been one to flinch at gory details concerning murder, I did tell her everything. She expressed great concern about the missing slave girl and volunteered to help in the bog search.

"It will be an arduous and somewhat hazardous enterprise," I said.

"One I am willing and able to take on," she insisted.

"Your skirts will get caught up in the overgrowth and soaked in the pond water beneath."

"I'll hitch up my skirts."

"Then every man's eyes will be on your limbs instead of attending to the business at hand."

"I'll wear trousers then."

"Don't be ridiculous, Julia."

"I am just being practical."

"No, you are being just the opposite. Your presence in the bog would be a hindrance, not a help."

She considered this a moment. "If simply being a woman is considered a hindrance, then I withdraw my offer." She went back to gazing into the mirror.

"Why do you stare into the glass so intently?" I asked her. I'd never known her to be vain.

"I am looking for imperfections," she said.

"You have none!" I assured her.

She rolled her eyes at that. "Imperfections in my painting." She gestured toward a canvas set on the easel beside her. "When I study the work in reverse, I can better spot the flaws in it."

I positioned myself behind her and saw that the painting she was assessing was a portrait of Mrs. Easterbrook, the deacon's wife, a woman of upright character and advanced years. It was so lifelike that I expected it to start speaking to me in the very voice of the sitter.

"I see no flaws in your rendering," I told Julia.

"Then what *do* you see?"

I saw Mrs. Easterbrook's pale visage beneath a starched white cap, just as she has always appeared to me in church, on the Green, or wherever I have come upon her in Plumford. Yet I saw something more. "Goodness," I replied, surprising myself.

Julia nodded. "That is exactly what I tried to capture. The goodness of Mrs. Easterbrook's spirit. I would never tell her that though. It would only embarrass the modest old dear. Indeed, all Mrs. Easterbrook thought worthy to capture in her portrait was the fine workmanship of her lace collar. Her daughter made it for her, and 'tis her most cherished possession."

"She will cherish this portrait far more, I should think. It is very fine, Julia. As fine as any portrait hanging in the Athenaeum."

"*My* work will never hang there," she said ruefully. "Nor anywhere but a house or two in Plumford. I am but a country limner, after all, with commissions few and far between."

"That will change when we leave Plumford." I kissed the

top of her head, where the golden waves parted. "Just be patient, my darling."

"Patience has never been my strong suit."

I could not disagree, for Julia is a creature of impulse, spontaneity, and willfulness. I would not wish her to be any other way, for I love her just as she is. Yet I cannot help thinking how much easier our life together would be at present if only Julia had acted less rashly in the past. Under the false assumption that she and I could never marry, she'd married a man whom she'd known for little more than three weeks, only to discover that he'd made his fortune in the slave trade. That much Julia has told me of Jacques Pelletier but little more, except that he is elderly and coldhearted. To make matters worse, she was married in France, where divorce is forbidden. According to Boston lawyers well-versed in French marital laws, as long as Monsieur Pelletier is alive, Julia and I cannot be legally recognized as husband and wife. For us to live openly as a married couple, our only choice is to remove ourselves from Plumford and settle where we are unknown. I cannot leave now, when my grandmother so sorely needs me, hence Julia and I must either stay apart (impossible!) or continue our liaison in secret.

We regarded each other's image in the mirror, a study of contrasts. Julia is all lightness and grace, and I am of stolid physique and blunt features. Not one feature or trait do we share in common, and it is hard to believe that we used to think we were closely related. If you are raised up on lies, however, they become your reality. Yet even being under the misapprehension that Julia was my first cousin did not stop me from falling in love with her near two years ago. Or maybe I was in love with her since first we met as children. What a delicate little fairy princess she had seemed. But in the months that followed I saw her for what she truly was—a hellion of a girl, as much a daredevil as any boy. So of course I loved her even more.

"Hitch up your skirts for me, why don't you?" I suggested softly into her ear. "I would be most happy to admire your limbs in the mirror if not in the bog."

"No, Molly might walk in on us, and we must keep to the rules we've laid down for the sake of propriety," Julia said. "But you may admire my limbs all you care to in my bed tomorrow morning. I shall be waiting for you there, as always."

She kissed me and sent me off to Tuttle Farm.

JULIA

It was well past midnight when I put aside my sketchbook and turned off the lamp in my studio. I paused at the window and drew aside the curtain, intending only to look out at the Green before retiring. But the full Milk Moon called to me, and I could not resist going out. I went no farther than the dooryard gate, of course. A man may roam through the night as much as he pleases, be he a ruffian or a gentleman, but no woman dares do so if she wants to be considered both sane and a lady.

Am I either? My conduct would indicate otherwise. I have deserted my husband and become an adulteress. Furthermore, I am unrepentant. My only regret is that Adam and I cannot live together, and as I gazed at the stars I longed for him so much I near fainted. Or maybe 'twas just looking up at the sky with my head thrown back that caused me to feel dizzy. I grabbed onto a fence picket to steady myself, and the sensation passed.

I went back to my stargazing, searching for the star that Henry told me helped guide runaway slaves north. To find it, I first located the seven stars that formed the Big Dipper. The two stars farthest from the dipper's handle pointed to the bright North Star, and when I located it I sent up a prayer that the end of slavery would come soon.

Across the road the Town Green was full of moonlight but empty of people. All the shops were closed; all the homes in darkness. Plumford folk go to bed early. I believed myself to be the only one in town stirring until I saw Mr. Chadwick, who lives on the other side of the Green, exit his house and make his way to his barn to visit his cow Cora. His daughter claims he walks in his sleep, but perhaps he just longs for some warm companionship. He recently lost his wife of seventy years, poor man. Or lucky man, to have had a partner in life for so long. I hope Adam and I will still be together in seventy years. Since we are only in our twenties, it is entirely possible. Even so, we do not have endless time to bide. With each passing day I grow more and more restless to go away with him! Far, far away!

This restlessness of mine makes sleep difficult. So rather than go up to my chamber to toss and turn in my lonely bed after I'd had my fill of moon gazing, I took a stroll around my property. The backyard affords me privacy, being long and deep, with overgrown shrubbery separating it from my neighbors' yards on the north and south sides. A tumbled stone wall marks the western border, and beyond that lies woodland. When I reached the wall I paused, recalling how Adam and I used to explore the woods for summer days on end as children. It had seemed an enchanted forest from a fairy tale to me in those days. Indeed, a dozen years later, I could still imagine it thus. The mountain laurel branches extending over the low stone barrier seemed like bony arms stretching out to pull me into the thicket, and the blossoms on the dogwood trees, glowing in the moonlight, beckoned to me like waving ghost hands. More eerie still were the smooth, pale trunks of the beech trees, which might as well have been the legs of mythic giants. And calling me from deeper within the woods were the trilling songs of trolls and hobgoblins, or perhaps just toads and frogs.

Feeling a chill in the damp night air, I turned away from the woods and started back to the house. The white clapboards shone in the moonlight, but the windows, five across on both stories, were black holes. I wished I had left a lamp burning, for there is nothing more dreary than to walk into a big, dark, empty house. I heard a rustling behind me but did not look back, discounting it as the sound of nocturnal woodland creatures scurrying through dried leaves. All the same, I did quicken my pace a bit. And when I heard what sounded like human footfalls gaining fast behind me, I broke into a run. Suddenly a strong arm wrapped around my waist, and a hand pressed tight over my mouth.

"Have no fear," my assailant whispered. "I am your friend Henry." I relaxed, and he released me. "I have runaway slaves with me, Julia. Will you give them shelter?"

"Of course," I whispered back.

Henry waved over two figures waiting in the shadows at the edge of the yard. When we went through the back door and stepped into the kitchen, I lit a lamp and saw that in addition to a young male and female Negro, a baby made three. All had much lighter skin than the only other Negro I knew, a man who had come directly from Africa named Mawuli. Indeed, this couple and child had nearer my own coloring, and if I were to paint their portraits I would blend yellow ochre, vermilion, and white with only a smidgen of burnt sienna to capture their skin tones. The man's eyes were large and thickly lashed, of a dusky umber hue, and the woman's eyes were gray tinged with viridian green. The baby's eyes were closed. It was sleeping peacefully in the woman's arms but appeared rather thin and frail.

Henry introduced me to the couple as Mrs. Canvas. "In the Underground Railroad, we go by the names related to our occupations for prudential reasons," he explained. "It's safer for all concerned."

"If we don't know the real names of folks that help us," the man said, "slave hunters can't make us give 'em up if we get caught."

"And it's best that runaways don't use the names they were called by their owners," Henry said. "Those names are posted in notices offering rewards for their capture."

"My wife and I go by the name Cooper now," the man said. "I was made to cooper casks and barrels on the plantation and hope to make my living by it when we get Canada under our feet."

"What name do you go by in the Underground?" I asked Henry.

"I call myself Mr. Measure," he said.

"Most apropos," I said. Not only does Henry use measurements in his work as a land surveyor and carpenter, but he has a natural aptitude at estimating weights and measures by eye. I have heard it said that he can take the measure of a man at a glance, too.

"Mr. Measure met up with us on a lonesome lane tonight," Mrs. Cooper said.

"And Mr. Cooper near brained me when I came out of the woods and approached them," Henry added with an amused expression.

"We thought you was a slave hunter!" Mr. Cooper said.

"But when they saw I had no weapons or shackles," Henry continued, "they realized I meant them no harm."

"It was when we saw your kind eyes, sir," Mrs. Cooper said.

"They were headed for the farm near Phantom Bog," Henry said, giving me a pointed look. "I told them that the Conductor who lived there could no longer help fugitives, and I had been sent to take his place. I dared not take them back to

Concord, however. The Stations there are being watched. So I brought them here."

"I am so glad you did!" I turned to the Coopers. "You are welcome to stay for as long as need be."

"I shall return tomorrow night to escort them to Mr. Mill's house in Acton," Henry said. He paused, held my gaze, and then spoke in a low, confidential voice. "Mr. Mill has a goat named Capricorn." He then bade us all farewell and went off into the night.

I invited the Coopers to sit down at the kitchen table and fetched bread and cheese and dried fruit from the pantry. They ate this simple fare with such eagerness and appreciation that I wondered how long they had been without sustenance. Between bites they told me a bit of their history. They had been raised on the same plantation on the Eastern Shore of Maryland and had loved each other since childhood.

"It was just a matter of time afore we jumped the broom together," Mrs. Cooper said. Seeing my puzzlement she explained that because slaves weren't allowed to marry legally, a ceremonial jumping over a broom in front of witnesses was their way of sealing their vows. Their master, however, did not recognize such a union. As far as he was concerned, slaves had no right to any family ties, and the children they bore were just part of his stock. Being hard-pressed for money, he meant to sell Mrs. Cooper and the babe to a slave trader who would auction them off in Georgia.

"Both my wife and my child would be lost to me forever," Mr. Cooper said. "I could not let that happen."

"And I could not bear never seeing my husband again," Mrs. Cooper said. "So off we ran! If we get caught and returned, we will be flogged for sure and most likely imprisoned, but it is worth the risk to stay together."

"I understand how you feel," I told her.

She shook her head. "How can you, ma'am? You are a free-woman."

Free? Little did she know that I was bound as if by manacles and chains to a man I abhorred. But Mrs. Cooper was right to question my assumption that I could understand a slave's feelings. I had not been born a human chattel, and my own dismal situation was of my own making entirely.

"I only meant that I too would be willing to risk everything to stay with my man," I said. "We too have loved each other since childhood."

"Where is your husband tonight?" Mr. Cooper asked, assuming he was the man of whom I spoke.

"Away," I replied and hoped he would not take offense at my curt answer. I turned my attention to the sleeping babe in Mrs. Cooper's arms. "Girl or boy?"

"A girl! Can't you tell?" Mrs. Cooper drew back the blanket so I could fully appreciate her child's feminine features. "She is but three months old. Would you like to hold her?"

I had not considered doing so, but it seemed rude to refuse. I held the babe stiffly at first, but then, when she opened her big brown eyes and stared up at me, every muscle in my body softened and a heavenly warmth radiated through me. I had dandled a baby once or twice before, but never had I experienced such bliss whilst doing so. But then, no doubt upset to see a strange visage instead of her dear mother's, the Cooper baby began wailing most furiously. Mrs. Cooper took her from me, and Mr. Cooper shook a wooden rattle to quiet her. But it did not.

"She be hungry," he said to his wife. His tone sounded scolding, but his expression was gentle and concerned.

"I will try to satisfy her." Turning from me, Mrs. Cooper unbuttoned her calico bodice.

"My wife is not making enough milk for the poor mite," Mr. Cooper told me. "Do you have a cow?"

"No, but a neighbor across the Green does," I replied. "I'll go ask him for milk tomorrow morning. To do so this late at night would draw suspicion, I'm afraid."

Mr. Cooper nodded and moved his chair closer to his wife's, wrapped his arm around her shoulders, and pressed his cheek against her turbaned head as she suckled their child. Not wishing to intrude on their intimacy, I left them alone in the kitchen and went upstairs to ready a bedchamber for them. When I returned about ten minutes later, Mrs. Cooper was pacing the room with the squalling baby, and Mr. Cooper was nowhere to be seen.

"Has your husband gone out to the backhouse?" I asked Mrs. Cooper, thinking it would have been more prudent for him to have availed himself of a chamber pot.

"He has gone to find a cow," Mrs. Cooper said, patting the baby to soothe her.

Less prudent still! I held my tongue but could not prevent a groan from escaping my mouth.

"It will be all right," Mrs. Cooper assured me. "He has done this a number of times since my milk started drying up."

But it was not all right. When Mr. Cooper returned with a bowl of milk he looked most anxious. "I fear I was seen," he told us.

"By whom?" I said.

"An old white man who looked a bit balmy."

"Mr. Chadwick," I said. "Did he say anything to you?"

"No. He just rubbed his eyes and shook his head."

"Let us hope he thinks you were just part of his dream. He walks in his sleep."

"From the look on his face, he thought me a nightmare." Mr. Cooper turned to his wife. "We should flee from here right now."

"No!" I said. "You cannot go running off into the night."

"We'll head for the next Station. Mr. Measure mentioned that it was in a town called Action."

"Acton, not Action," I said. "Do you even know where it is?"

"We will ask along the way. And when we get there, we will seek out Mr. Mill."

"All that asking and seeking will make you far too conspicuous," I made haste to point out. "You might as well wear a signboard declaring yourself a runaway slave."

"Then what should we do?"

How I wished Henry were there to give us the answer! But Mr. Cooper apparently expected *me* to. "If need be, I will guide you to Acton tonight," I said as calm as you please. "But if Mr. Chadwick does not report what he saw to anyone and just goes back to bed, which is entirely possible, you are far safer to stay the night here. Keep watch at a front window through a slit in the curtain if you please, Mr. Cooper. And you, Mrs. Cooper, please wait in the pantry with the baby so her cries won't be heard if someone comes to the door."

Relieved that they both followed my instructions, I ran up to the attic with a lantern, and from a storage trunk pulled out a pair of pantaloons, a jacket with brass buttons, tasseled boots, and a wide-brimmed hat that had belonged to Grandfather Walker. He was a slight, slender man, and his garb fit me well. Before departing my chamber, I left a quickly scrawled note for Adam on my bed and returned downstairs disguised as . . . well, as a most unfashionable lad, I suppose.

The baby was no longer crying, and when I looked in the pantry I was happy to see her peacefully sucking milk from a dishcloth. Mrs. Cooper smiled at me, and for one brief moment I thought all would be well. But then Mr. Cooper ran into the kitchen and told me he had espied a very fat man dressed in a night shirt and britches approaching the house. Immediately thereafter came a pounding at the front door.

"Let me in, Mrs. Pelletier," bellowed Constable Beers.

"What do you want?" I shouted back through the door.

"I want that shlippery thief of a shlave you are hiding," Beers replied, his speech slurred. "Mr. Chadwick roused me to report that milk has been stolen from his cow. He saw the culprit, a Negro, run to your house. I am here to arrest him for thievery, and if he turns out to be a fugitive I will do my best to return him to his rightful owner. That is the law!"

"There is no one here but me," I loudly avowed. "And you have frightened me most terribly, Constable Beers. I am trembling in my nightdress as I stand here."

"Open the door!" he demanded.

"I pray you, allow me to make myself decent first. My nightdress is exceedingly thin."

This gave Beers pause for a moment. "Very well then. I give you permission to go dress yourself properly."

"Thank you, sir. You are a true gentleman."

Leaving him to await me at the front door, out the back door I slipped with the Cooper family. Mr. Cooper took the baby from his wife, and we ran down the yard toward the woods. The branches of the mountain laurel bushes poked and scratched at us as we clambered over the stone wall, and Mr. Cooper covered his child with his jacket to protect her. I glanced back, half expecting to see the rotund figure of Beers bowling down the yard toward us in pursuit. There was no sign of him.

When we were on the other side of the wall I led the Coopers through the stand of beeches and deeper into the woods.

"Do you know where we are going?" Mr. Cooper asked me.

"Of course," I replied. "The road to Acton lies on the other side of this woodland. We will get there easily enough if we head due west."

"Have you a compass?"

"Yes, right here," I said, tapping my forehead.

I was not half as sure of myself as I attempted to sound, however. Although Adam and I had explored the area often, we had never done so at night. And the terrain I'd been familiar with as a child had changed over time. Indeed, nothing looked familiar to me as I led the Coopers onward until I spotted an old friend standing still in the moonlight. Hugo the Elephant! Or so Adam and I had dubbed this particular boulder because of its size and configuration. I recalled that the section of the rock formation shaped like an elephant's head faced west and noted that when I too faced west the moon was over my right shoulder. I let that serve as my compass for the rest of our trek through the dense woodland, and we eventually reached the road.

We picked up our pace. Behind us we heard dogs howling, but I doubted Beers would have had time to gather together a hunting party to chase after us. I doubted too that he would have had the inclination or energy to do so. He had no warrants for anyone's arrest, for one thing. And he had sounded quite drunk, for another. It was far more likely that he had fallen asleep on my front stoop as he waited for me to open the door.

Even so, when I heard a wagon coming fast toward us I told the Coopers that we must run off the road and hide behind a large elm tree standing in a field. The wagon passed us right by, the driver looking from side to side as he whipped his horse to urge more speed. Was he on the outlook for us? Or was he carrying word ahead to Acton to alert the constable there to be on the lookout for fugitives? Perhaps neither. When there is danger we see everything through the distorting lens of our fears.

And fear can be exhausting. The Coopers looked completely fagged out by now. I told them that we must all rest for a moment and catch our breaths. Mrs. Cooper leaned against her husband, and I leaned against the elm. The solidity of the tree trunk seemed to give me strength. My breathing evened out, and I felt a connection to the Divine Intelligence at the center of my being. I released my fears and doubts, trusting this Intelligence to guide us to safety. We regained the road and continued on our way. We saw no one for the next few miles, but then a lame man appeared, staggering toward us from the opposite direction. I told the Coopers to keep the width of the road between us as we went past the man. As we drew closer I saw that he was not lame but quite drunk, in an animated argument with himself punctuated with bursts of profanity. We came abreast of him, and I looked directly in his face, ready to stare him down or stand up to a challenge. But he did not even look at us! It was then I realized that he was so hammered as to be near sightless, and even if we'd been a trio of bellowing hippopotamuses parading past him he would not have remarked us. He staggered out of sight.

Forward we marched down the road, three abreast under the descending moon. The eastern sky began taking on a rosy tint from the coming dawn when we at last approached Acton. I spotted a thickly wooded area a hundred yards to the side of the road and told the Coopers to hide themselves in it whilst I went to town to find Mr. Mill. I did not know how I was going to find him, only that I must.

I walked into Acton, a pleasant place of some prosperity, with a millpond providing water power to turn the saws, looms, and equipment at small manufactories that bring employment beyond farming. Disguised as a boy, I attracted hardly a glance. It gave me some small pleasure to meet passing men's eyes with a bold and direct look, which for a woman would be thought pert or even saucy. I lengthened my stride and gave it a bit of swagger. For all I know I looked quite the fool, but no one laughed and called my bluff, so I was satisfied.

As I came on the row of mill buildings the air was full of the rumble and clatter of machinery. I strode inside the first, a sawmill, and walked right into a hefty brute, his beard and hair and eyebrows stuffed with wood shavings and sawdust.

"Blind, are you?" he barked at me as he rushed past. The collision sent me back hard against a beam, and I felt a jolt of pain in my shoulder and well nigh yelped in pain.

The mill rumbled with activity as a double pair of up-and-down saws chomped through long logs. I espied a man who looked to be the owner or manager sitting behind a desk strewn with papers and made my way to him, my tread kicking up sawdust. I had to shout to get his attention.

"What is it you want?" he hollered back.

I told him I was seeking work for want of anything better to say.

He glared at me with narrowed eyes and impatiently tugged at his white, scraggly chin beard. "Ever swung a cant hook, boy?"

I shook my head.

"Do you know how to use a crosscut to square up logs?"

I shook my head again.

"Well, can you at least use a race knife?"

Another head shake.

"Off with you then," the mill boss said. "You can be of no use to me."

"Perhaps I can," I stalled. "Would you like me to foretell your future?"

He drew back in his chair. "You claim to be a fortune-teller?"

"An astrologer," I said. "And just by looking at you I can tell you were born under the sign of the goat."

"You think I look like a goat?"

In truth, he rather did, but of course I did not say so. "The *goat* represents the sign of *Capricorn* in the zodiac," I stated with a conspiratorial look and waited for him to signal me that he understood the code.

He did not. "Get away from me with your Black Arts!" he shouted. "I am a good Christian."

Apparently I did not move fast enough, for he sprang up, came around the desk, grabbed me by the back of my collar, and half-lifted me off my feet as he hustled me outside.

"Be gone, you gypsy imp! Be gone!" he shouted after me as I ran down the street. Other men stopped to glare at me, and I felt something hit me between the shoulders. A stone? A horse turd? I did not pause to look.

The next mill I entered was a carding establishment with piles of raw wool just inside the door. The air was full of wool fluff as the needles on the rotating carding engines pulled and aligned the raw wool fibers to make them ready for spinning. An elderly man approached me, and, before I could say a word, he told me to show him my hands.

I was reluctant to do so, sure they would give away my sex. "I ain't got all day," he said.

I stuck out my hands, thankful they did not tremble under his scrutiny. "You're hired," he said. "Smallish hands like yours suit this work."

"Thank you, Mr. Mill," I said. "I need to earn money to feed my goat Capricorn."

"My name is Mr. Tomkins, and I don't give a fig about your goat. Come along. I'll show you how to work the combing machine but once. Then you're on your own, young fellow."

He headed toward the back of the mill, but I did not follow him. I would not have minded learning how to operate a combing machine, but could not afford to waste any more time in the wrong mill. If the Cooper family was kept waiting in the woods for too much longer, they would likely strike out on their own. So out the door I went, without so much as a fare-thee-well to Mr. Tomkins. I could not help but be pleased, however, that I had passed muster and been hired by him. How much easier it is to earn money as a male!

The air inside the next mill I entered smelled deliciously of fresh flour. Two enormous millstones ground round and round against each other, making a thunderous noise, and the thickset miller standing beside them had such a peaceful smile on his rosy face one would think he was listening to a lullaby. I waved to get his attention from the doorway, and as he came toward me he regarded me most attentively.

"Whom are you looking for, young woman?" he said.

That he had immediately seen through my disguise yet did not question my reason for one indicated to me that he might well be part of the Underground Railroad. "I believe I am looking for you, Mr. Mill."

He registered no surprise at being addressed thus. "What have you been told about me?"

"That you have a goat named Capricorn."

He motioned me to follow him to his office in a far corner of the mill. When he closed the thick door it muffled the sound of the grinding millstones. "Who revealed this information to you?" he demanded.

I almost blurted out *Henry Thoreau*. "Mr. Measure. Do you know him?"

"Yes. And his value to the organization is immeasurable," the miller said.

"Last night he delivered some very precious cargo to Plumford, a young black couple and their babe, and I have brought—"

"But you are not the Plumford Conductor," the miller interrupted. "I know him too."

"I am sorry to inform you that he was murdered yesterday."

The miller's jaw dropped open, but no words came out of his mouth for a moment. "Who murdered him?" he finally managed to ask.

"Possibly a slave hunter. He was transporting a runaway when he was shot."

"What happened to the runaway?"

"She has gone missing."

"More terrible still! What is being done about it?"

"The murder is under investigation by the Plumford constable, but he is both inept and unsympathetic to the Cause. So Mr. Measure has taken matters into his own hands."

"Thank God for that at least," the miller said. "Measure is the most capable man I know. Young but wise. Intellectual yet practical. And as careful as he is fearless."

I agreed on all points and could have added a dozen more admirable traits regarding Henry, but there was no time to spare at present. "As I was saying, I have brought the fugitive family Mr. Measure left in my safekeeping to Acton and—"

"*You* conveyed them?" the miller interrupted again. "I assumed you were just acting as a messenger. Why did you take it upon yourself to be a Conductor? That is not a job for a woman."

"Well, it fell upon me to take on the job despite my sex. I led the Coopers here by foot and left them hidden in a wooded area whilst I came for you."

"Highly irregular," the miller said huffily, and for a moment I feared he would refuse his help. But the goodness in his nature overcame whatever petty concerns he had regarding my gender, for in the next breath he said, "Let us make haste! We must get that dear family out of the woods before they are discovered. From what you have just told me, there may well be one or more dangerous slave hunters about the area."

We went down a set of stairs, climbed onto a wagon loaded with bagged flour, and off we went to collect the Coopers. We found them not too far from where I'd left them. They'd moved to a sunny spot, and Mr. Cooper had made a bed of ferns for his wife and child. The miller had them lie on the soft bags of flour and covered them with burlap. Back at the mill, he led them into a simply furnished storage room to wait until he made arrangements to put them on a train heading north. His wife, he assured them, would bring them food and milk for the babe in short order. The Coopers and I embraced and parted forevermore.

After briefly stopping by his house to tell his wife about the Coopers, the miller drove me back to Plumford. Rather than have him drop me at my front door, which would surely attract attention, I had him let me off by the new cemetery a little ways from town.

"Good Day to you, miss," he said. "What name do you go by in the UGRR?"

It took me a second to appreciate that the initials stood for the Underground Railroad. "Mrs. Canvas."

"Missus? You were widowed young then."

"What makes you think I am a widow, Mr. Mill?"

"No husband in his right mind would allow his wife to be a *Conductor*. And just look at you, dressed in male clothing. No husband with half a backbone would allow that neither."

I smiled. "For one so devoted to gaining civil liberties for our black brethren, you do not seem eager to give any liberties to women, sir."

"There is no place in this free country that slavery should be tolerated," he said. "But women have a proper place in the world as well as men have. And that has been true since Adam and Eve."

I was far too weary to argue with him. I just stuck out my hand.

"Nonetheless, you did right good, Mrs. Canvas," he said as he shook it.

I kept both my head and the brim of my hat turned down as I strode into town and was not recognized by the few people who were already about. No one paid me any mind whatsoever, but they well might have if I had entered the house. (Who was that young man calling on Mrs. Pelletier at such an early hour?) Patients called on Adam at all hours, so I went into his office instead. He was writing down something at his desk in a rather agitated manner when I stepped through the door.

"I require your attentions, Doctor," I said in as deep a voice as I could manage. "Let us start with a kiss."

He looked up with a surprised expression. It turned to one of joy at the sight of me. And then to anger, and he leapt up from the chair and came toward me.

ADAM

As I have done almost every morning for the past five months, I came to town a few hours before my posted office hours, barned Napoleon and my gig, entered my office, dashed through the passageway that connected it to the house, and ran upstairs to Julia's bedchamber. There she has always awaited me, her lithe body naked beneath the covers.

But not this morning. A sheet of notepaper lay on the pillow where her head should have been resting, and I snatched it up. What I read was hardly a billet-doux. *Must deliver precious cargo to another Station. Shall try to be back by midmorning. Do not worry.* I crumpled the paper in my fist and threw it to the floor. Do not worry!

I searched the house from attic to cellar, looking for clews that might tell me where this mad mission had taken her. All I found were two plates with bread crumbs and cheese rind upon them that had been left on the kitchen table. I then investigated the barn and found nothing out of the ordinary. From there I aimlessly explored the back property and even went a little ways into the woods. There I found a wooden baby rattle. Odd. But of no help whatsoever.

I reckoned that if anyone could enlighten me, it would be Henry. Although we had arranged to meet at Phantom Bog later in the day, I could not wait that long to question him and considered driving to Concord immediately. But what if Julia returned home whilst I was gone? Better to find someone to deliver a note to Henry post haste and await his reply. I returned to my office, and as I was writing my inquiry concerning Julia's whereabouts, she walked in.

"Where have you been?" I demanded, rising to hover over her. I wanted to grab her by the shoulders and give her a good shake. "And why are you dressed like that? You look absurd!" In truth she looked quite fetching in trousers. She also looked exhausted. Rather than shake her, I took her into my arms. "I have been near crazed with worry, Julia."

"I am sorry for that," she said. "But pray hear me out, and you will understand why it was necessary for me to go away."

I did indeed hear her out, never once interrupting her as she related the details of her adventure to me. And I continued to hold my tongue even after she stopped speaking.

"You are angry," she said, drawing back to regard my countenance.

"I have not expressed a word of anger, Julia."

"But I can read your face like an open book."

"Then you have misinterpreted what you have read there. It isn't anger you have aroused in me by your reckless actions, but concern for your safety."

"I don't consider my actions reckless," she said. "What else was I to do but guide the Coopers to Acton? Wouldn't you have done the same in my situation?"

"Yes, but *we* are not the same, Julia!"

"If you are referring to our difference in sex, pray do not call mine the weaker one."

"I do not claim that women are weaker in mind or spirit than men, but it is a fact that they have less muscle mass, hence less physical strength. How could you have defended yourself if you'd been attacked by a slave hunter last night? It's risky enough to hide fugitives in your home, but far riskier still to conduct them to the next Station. God help us, Julia, a Conductor was murdered just yesterday!"

"And that is why I was called to do my part last night."

"Must you always heed your adventurous spirit when it calls you to danger?"

"It was not my desire for adventure that I acted upon, but my desire for justice! I could not let the Coopers go back into bondage."

"Henry should never have brought them to you."

"Of course he should have, Adam. Mine is one of the safest houses in the area right now. Don't be angry with Henry for what happened next. He fully expected to take the Coopers to Acton himself tonight."

"I'm not angry with anyone," I insisted. But of course anger is a reaction to fear. And I fear losing Julia more than death itself.

She reached up to stroke my hair, a gesture that usually soothes me. Her hand trembled with fatigue, and her lovely countenance was drained of its usual vitality. I decided that she needed rest more than she needed further reproofs from me at the moment.

"Go to bed, Julia, before you fall asleep on your feet. We will talk of this later." For once she did not put up an argument.

Soon after she left, the stable boy who works at the Sun Tavern came bursting into my office. Sam Ruggles had sent him to fetch me quick. A guest staying in one of the upstairs bedchambers Ruggles lets out to travelers seemed to be in great pain and in dire need of treatment. I took up my bag and hurried to the Sun.

Mrs. Ruggles was waiting on the stair landing when I got

there, and she led me up to the distressed man's chamber. I could hear his groans through the closed door and went in to find a slender but wiry fellow half-sitting, half-lying on the bed. He looked to be in his middle twenties, a year or two older than me. His bright, nervous eyes scanned me with suspicion.

"I am a doctor," I said, "and have been called in to help you."

"Then I welcome thee. I am a Quaker far from my community and feel most awful."

The Wideawake Hat hanging on the bedpost confirmed that my patient was indeed a member of the Society of Friends. He appeared feverish, yet he had wrapped a blanket about himself and shivered as if cold, although he was fully and somberly dressed in a black frock coat, black trousers, and black boots. His pale, smooth hand was moist to the touch when I took his pulse, which was two hundred beats per minute.

I asked him what was the matter, and he pointed to his right leg. "Pitched off my horse in the dark and fell on a sharp rock. It tore right through my trouser leg and cut my shin. Tied my handkerchief around my shank to close the cut and rode on. Pain was shooting up my leg something fierce, so when I saw this place I figured I would get a room and rest awhile. Just fell into bed without even taking off my boots. I guess I slept a good long time. I have no notion what day it is."

"It's Thursday morning. What day did you come here?"

"Wednesday at dawn. Had to pound on the door a good while to wake up the innkeeper."

"So it has been over twenty-four hours since you were injured. Let's have a look at the wound."

He lay back, and I first removed his boots to make him more comfortable. He was wearing red stockings, an unexpected ostentation for a Quaker. I then rolled up his right pant leg and cut away the blood-soaked handkerchief he'd tied around his lower limb. I saw that the injury he'd sustained was most severe. His flesh had been sliced right down to the tibia and into the adjacent calf muscle. There was considerable swelling, and virulent infection had taken hold, for pus was seeping from the wound.

I asked Mrs. Ruggles, who was hovering in the doorway, to fetch me up some clean linen cloths, a pan of hot water, and a bottle of cheap whiskey. She did so most speedily, and, without inquiring if I needed her further assistance, she departed just as swiftly.

I know that Quakers eschew liquor and all stimulants but did not hesitate to give the man a good dose of laudanum to quiet him and help with the pain. He surprised me with the alacrity with which he drank it down. I then poured the whiskey into a bowl and soaked my instruments in it. I washed my hands in the basin in the room, laid out my tools, pulled up a chair, and got to work. The amount of pus worried me greatly, although some of my profession call it laudable pus and believe the body produces it to rebalance the humors. I believe no such thing, for I was taught at medical college, by none other than Dr. Oliver Wendell Holmes, that pus is the result of infection and the source of that infection must be got out. What's more, the more the pus, the more serious the infection. My main concern was gangrene.

Told my patient to be as still as he could bear to be, spread open the lesion, and laid some linen strips inside the border of the gash to sop up the blood that began to flow afresh. I really could have used a good assistant to do the sopping up, one who did not blanch at blood and gore and had a gentle touch and compassionate nature. In a word, Julia. Whenever she had assisted me in the past, we had worked as a team of the same mind and heart.

The poor man moaned as I probed down into the wound with my forceps. It took me a good quarter hour to pick out what looked to be fibers from his pants, and gritty dirt. This took some patience as such work gets slippery and messy with the blood and pus and the patient's shifting about.

Finally satisfied I had gotten out all the offending foreign bodies I could reach, I doused the wound with whiskey, which brought a howl and a stream of profanity from the man that would have scorched the ears off a pagan seaman, much less his fellow Quakers. Gave him another dose of laudanum, mixed with whiskey this time, and he fell back, so white you would have thought I had purged all the blood out of him.

After I let the wound drain, I told my exhausted patient I had to use a needle to stitch him up and it would cause him considerable pain. I trebled up a short piece of linen and gave it to him to bite down on, and he took it and used it.

Smeared the sides of the lesion with honey and pressed it closed, and with the first thrust of the needle he moaned and bit hard down on the linen in his mouth but kept his leg steady. He was then most fortunate to lose consciousness. I sewed up the wound with catgut, making sure the ten stitches were evenly spaced and not too tight. I left a half-inch opening to allow for drainage, smeared more honey over my work, and sat back, satisfied that I had done everything in my power to prevent gangrene from setting in.

My patient came awake as I cleaned my instruments in the whiskey and to my surprise asked in a low mumble when I thought he could travel.

"You don't want to rip open the stitches, so not for several days at least," I said, hoping he managed to live that long. The infection either winning or losing would decide his fate. "Eat all you can, drink plenty of water, and rest."

"How about leaving me a bottle of that red poppy juice you been giving me, doc?" he said.

I refused, for I had already given him more than I should have so he would not suffer too much during the operation. I told him this and assured him I would check in often, as my office was right down the street. He waved a dismissive hand, more irritated with my refusal than grateful for my medical aid. I bid him farewell, and when I exited his room I heard a most terrible screaming coming from down the hall. Assuming that yet another guest was in dire pain and in need of my medical attentions, I hurried forth. The door to the chamber was open, and I paused at the threshold, my concern dissolving into amusement.

The screams, it turned out, were emanating from Mrs. Ruggles's red and purple parrot. The cause of the bird's excitement seemed to be the feather duster Mrs. Ruggles was waving about the chamber she was cleaning, and they both seemed to be having a fine time of it. As the bird flew overhead, Mrs. Ruggles pranced around the room, merry as a pixie, be it an oversized one. But when she noticed me in the open doorway she stopped abruptly, and the parrot settled on her shoulder, becoming just as still.

"You have caught me acting foolsome, Doctor," she said. Her English is heavily accented and less than fluent.

"You weren't acting foolish at all," I told her, but in truth I was rather amused that one so staid and plain as Mrs. Ruggles would carry on with such a sense of abandon and frivolity in private. I liked her more for it.

"Did you fix up the man?" she asked me, putting on a serious demeanor.

I told her I'd done the best I could and would come back to change his dressing tomorrow. I prescribed a light diet of easily digestible food for him and plenty of fresh water to drink. She assured me she would see to it.

I'd never had occasion to be in the upstairs quarters of the Sun Tavern before and hadn't realized how extensive the guest accommodations were. Now I saw that there were narrow halls running hither and thither that connected the original structure to the many additions that had been tacked onto it over its many years of existence. Like most of the houses and shops that surrounded the Green, the tavern had been built well before the War for Independence. The date etched in a stone of the taproom fireplace is 1710.

I proceeded to the taproom to find Mr. Ruggles. He took ownership of the Sun when I was a boy, and I cannot imagine any but him as its proprietor. Indeed, he looks the very image of the Old Sol face painted on the ancient signboard hanging in front of the tavern, for he too has heavy brows, wide-set eyes, full cheeks, a flat nose, and a wide, benevolent smile. Ruggles pours drinks with a generous hand and allows a great deal of raillery and revelry to take place in his taproom, but he has never let the horseplay get too much out of hand. It is his duty to keep his business reputable, else the Plumford Selectmen would advise the county authorities to revoke his license. If there is one thing a Massachusetts taverner must be, it is respectable. And Samuel Ruggles is certainly that.

One thing the men in town most liked about Ruggles was that he had done very little in the way of sprucing up the Sun during his two decades as taverner. So when he came back from Boston with a Dutch bride two months ago, we felt a high degree of trepidation. But things have turned out pretty well for all concerned. Especially for Ruggles. He looks a good twenty years younger and radiates happiness.

Mrs. Ruggles has made the Sun glow too. Every piece of copper and pewter on the bar shines from her vigorous polishing, and she and her little army of hired girls have cleaned all of the inn's hundreds of crown glass window panes to let in the light. Even the chestnut beams overhead, long blackened with the smoke and dust of years, have been wire-brushed clean so their wooden pegs and adze marks are visible. And all the whale lamps burn clean and bright at night, without a trace of smoke, with their reflectors as bright as mirrors. As far as I'm concerned, the Sun has been enhanced by this industrious woman's loving touch and attention to detail, and I wager eight out of ten patrons of the place would say the same.

I found Ruggles behind the taproom bar eating pancakes. The shelves in back of him held an array of gleaming decanters and tumblers, along with flasks, jugs, demijohns, and bottles of various spirits. His regular customers would be coming in for their daily drammings soon enough, but at present the dark, cool room was empty of customers. I came in and stood up to the bar.

"How's Friend Haven?" Ruggles asked me.

"Is that his name?"

"Yep. He signed the registry book Jerome Haven."

"He has a bad cut and infection, and he'll be laid up for at least a few days."

"Well, I hope the folks waiting on him in Amesbury don't get to worrying too much," Ruggles said.

"He told you that's where he was headed?"

"Yep. To a Friends community there, he said. That's all I got out of him. Poor man looked mighty exhausted. And no wonder. He'd been riding all night. Pounded on my door at dawn on Wednesday. He was limping, but I never guessed he would get so sick on me. Guess I'm stuck with a teetotaling Quaker now. Not much profit in that."

"I think he should stay put as long as possible, Sam."

"Don't worry. I won't rush him on his way. I am a great admirer of Quakers for their brave stand against slavery." Ruggles's round face became grim. "And now Plumford has its own martyr to the Cause, shot dead whilst transporting a slave. It was the talk of the tavern last night."

"No doubt Constable Beers was the one doing most of the talking," I said.

"Well, the more rum he swigs, the more his tongue wags," Ruggles allowed. "And he was kept well supplied with free drinks by his curious audience. None of us had any notion that

Ezra Tripp was a Conductor in the Underground Railroad. To be honest, I never thought he had much gumption. Now I regret never offering him a drink on the house. I did let him drink on credit, though. I don't suppose Tripp's widow will appreciate settling his sizeable booze bill."

"From the look of it she hasn't a penny to spare, Sam."

"Guess I'll tear up Tripp's tab then. It's the least I can do for such a hero. It's a damn terrible thing what happened. Last night Edda and I got down on our knees and prayed that the poor runaway got away safe and sound."

"If we don't find her body in Phantom Bog, there's a good chance she did," I said. "Henry Thoreau and I have organized a search party today. I've enlisted hands from Tuttle Farm, and he's bringing volunteers from Concord."

"Well, on such a warm day like this you boys are apt to get mighty hot in that bog, so I'll drive over with a keg of cold cider. I'm too heavy to take part in the search myself. Good chance I'd sink right through the mire. I weighed myself on the platform balance at Daggett's store the other day and found out that I'd gained fifteen pounds in less than three months. That's what I get for marrying such a good cook, I reckon. There's nothing pleases Edda more than cooking. Except cleaning, I suppose. And canoodling with me. But I guess I shouldn't say more about *that*." His big, satisfied smile said it all.

"Guess you weren't such a confirmed bachelor after all, Sam."

"Oh, I always intended to marry. I just hadn't found me a suitable mate until Edda come along. The minute I set eyes on her in Boston, I knew she was the gal for me, so I wasted no time hitching up with her. I thank my stars I met her fresh off the boat from Holland, before she was grabbed up by some other fellow. She is one handsome woman, is she not?"

"Indeed she is," I readily agreed. If Ruggles thought Edda handsome, then so she was. In his eyes, anyway.

"I have a notion to get her likeness done on canvas by that

limner cousin of yours, Adam. I heard she painted Mrs. Easter-brook, and if she is good enough to paint the deacon's wife, I reckon she is good enough to paint mine."

"Good *enough?*" I said indignantly. "Why, Julia could well be one of the finest portraitists in the country, Sam. She was trained by her father, Ellery Bell, who has painted royals and grandees all over Europe, and Julia equals if not surpasses him in talent. It's just a fluke that Plumford has such a fine artist in residence at present, and anyone who sits for her should feel very fortunate indeed."

"Well, that settles it," Ruggles said, slamming his palm on the bar. "Edda must *sit* for her, as you put it, as soon as possible. When might she be free to paint my darling wife, Adam?"

"That is not for me to say."

"I reckon she is in great demand."

"To be sure," I said. "But you may be able to catch her be-tween commissions."

"I'll go see her as soon as I can, and bring Edda along with me. How could any artist resist the opportunity to paint such a beautiful subject?"

Fortunately, no reply was required of me, for at that mo-ment Edda's parrot swooped into the taproom like a flaming comet. Ruggles made a cooing sound, and the parrot flew over to him and perched on his bald head. Ruggles did not seem to mind this at all. "Does Roos want a special tidbit?" he said. The parrot replied in a stream of gibberish, or so it sounded to me. "Roos only speaks Dutch," Ruggles told me. "But I'm teach-ing her English." He rolled his eyes upward. "Does Roos want a tidbit?" he repeated. "Say 'tidbit,' Roos."

And strike me down if she didn't! The word came out of her black beak quite clearly, albeit in a shrewish tone. Ruggles chuckled and extracted a bouquet of dandelions from his apron pocket. Roos flew off his head and settled on the bar to deli-cately nibble on the buds as Ruggles held each stem out to her betwixt his forefinger and thumb. Edda came into the taproom and beamed at the sight of them together.

"Roos just said 'tidbit,' " Ruggles informed her.

Edda caught her breath, clapped her hands together, and opened wide her pale eyes and small mouth. "I cannot this believe!"

Ruggles tried to get Roos to squawk out 'tidbit' again for Edda. Ruggles kept repeating the word in the most coaxing of tones, but the parrot remained stubbornly silent. My own fascination with its talking skills had reached its limit, and I bid Sam and Edda farewell. They hardly noted my departure, so engrossed were they in their beloved pet.

After making a few patient calls, I drove my gig to Phantom Bog. My Tuttle Farm volunteers had gathered there already with apple-picking poles, and soon Henry and his Concord men came along, equipped with long ice-cutting pikes. With the methodical care of the surveyor, Henry explained to us how we were to line ourselves up at the edge of the bog, fifteen feet between each man, and slowly proceed across the sphagnum looking for rents in the moss through which the fugitive could have fallen. Upon finding a rent, we were to carefully plunge our poles into the tea-colored water and poke about the soft muddy bottom.

"In this orderly fashion we will find her body if it is there to be found," Henry concluded grimly. "Let us begin."

We had to get through a thick border of blueberry bushes and maple saplings to reach the bog, and, as we slowly made our way into this snarly, boot-catching tangle, we roused up battalions of mosquitoes and green-headed flies. Slaps and curses were heard up and down the line as thousands of humming and buzzing vampyres feasted upon us, but we did not break formation. And I wager not a man amongst us thought once of turning back.

Onto the quaking sphagnum we marched, far enough apart from each other to prevent our combined body weight from sinking it. Even so, there was always the fear that one's foot would plunge through the mat of vegetation, resulting in a bodily plummet into the icy bog water beneath. If a man slid under the mat he could quickly drown. So as we walked we kept an eye on each other, left and right. This was no easy matter, as there were spruce and tamarack and laurels growing out of the sphagnum, reaching heights up to six feet and restricting our vision. And we kept tripping on cranberry and leatherleaf stems, so that more than a few of us pitched forward on our faces and got a cold soaking, myself included.

As we probed the rents in the sphagnum with our poles, Phantom Bog began to give up her morbid secrets. Up came so many skunk, possum, raccoon, and rabbit carcasses that we ceased to comment on the discoveries and just returned the pale, slimy flesh and white skeletons to the tannic brew that had claimed their lives.

On we trudged in silence. I looked up into the gnarled, dead branches of a spruce tree and met the unblinking, yellow-eyed stare of a roosting great horned owl. It might have been the very devil himself observing us, so malevolent did the creature's gaze seem to be. But I am a man of science, not superstition, and did not allow myself to think the owl a bad omen. Even so, when it dropped from its perch in eerie silence, slowly flapped its three-foot-long wings, and then glided like a flitting shadow into the distant trees, I was relieved to see it go. In the next instant there came a shout from a fellow up the line who was working his ice pole in a hole several feet across. "I've found a body, I fear," he said, hauling up on his pole.

We gasped as we glimpsed a backbone and a clump of flesh come out of the churned water. But then we saw antlers and realized it was the hairless carcass of a buck. We shouted relief and then gaped at the antlers—a six-pointer, one of the men said in amazement. None of us had ever seen a deer in the area. They'd been hunted out over sixty years ago.

"Let it sink back to its watery grave intact," Henry said. And his order was followed without protest, although I am sure a few of the men coveted those antlers.

On we wobbled and labored until the sky suddenly went from bright sun to a foreboding, angry, roiling black. We stared up at a thunderhead that rose straight above us for thousands of feet as a hard, cold wind chilled us to the bone.

"Crouch down!" Henry shouted.

Every man squatted on his haunches and made himself small whilst the thunderstorm unleashed a torrent of water down upon us. All the hair on my body began to tingle, and an instant later a bolt of lightning hit right into the bog, striking a tree less than fifty yards away with an earsplitting crack. The tree burst into flame, and through the mist I saw the shapely, swirling figure of a young woman with long, flowing hair suspended just above it. I wasn't the only one who saw her.

"The phantom!" one man after another cried out.

We none of us dared stand to get a better look, for the thunder was rolling above us like logs rumbling down a mountain and the singed air smelled of the blacksmith shop. Sure enough, another bolt of blue-white lightning struck the bog, blinding us all. As soon as my eyes cleared I looked back toward the tree. The driving rain hissed and sputtered as it pelted the scorched trunk and began to douse the flames. The figure was gone.

The storm retreated as quickly as it had attacked, and the sun emerged once again. Henry was the first to speak. "Let us resume our search," he said softly.

We reformed our line and proceeded to examine the remainder of the bog. Finding nothing, we concluded that whatever else might have happened to the runaway, she did not drown in the bog.

When we returned to terra firma Sam Ruggles was waiting for us with a keg of cider as promised, and one of beer, even more appreciated. As we stood around his wagon quenching our thirst, we talked of the violent and sudden storm. But not one of us mentioned seeing the phantom. I reckon we were all waiting for someone else to risk making a laughingstock of himself first. It is one thing to tell stories about the phantom sightings of our superstitious ancestors, but quite another to claim a personal sighting. After all, we are modern men living in an age of scientific discovery and invention, an age of railways and steamships, of gas lighting and rubber vulcanization and anaesthesia. Phantoms have no place in such a world as this, and, as Henry and I drove away in my gig, I expressed this opinion to him.

"The world is but a canvas to our imagination, Adam," he replied. "We all observed a meteorological phenomenon on the bog today, and we can make what we choose of it. If some think they saw the phantom, then that is what they saw."

"Do *you* believe that's what we saw, Henry? Or was it just a mirage?"

"I believe that Nature is a personality so vast and universal that we cannot limit our beliefs concerning her," he replied.

We said no more about it as we continued on our way to Tuttle Farm.

JULIA

Thursday, May 18

I found Molly Munger in the dining room when I came downstairs after a few hours' sleep. She was standing before an assemblage of brass candlesticks and oil lamps that she had collected from all round the house and arrayed on the table. The strong scent of rum emanated from her person. Although I have never known my hired girl to be a tippler, I sniffed ostentatiously and raised my eyebrows as I regarded the open liquor decanter on the sideboard.

Molly laughed and shook the flannel cloth she was holding at me. "I soaked it in spirits. Ma told me it's the best way to clean brass."

"As good a use as any for Grandfather's blackstrap rum," I said. "What a fine housekeeper you've become, Molly dear!"

"You sound mighty surprised."

"I meant to sound mighty pleased," I said, although in truth her diligence does surprise me. When Molly kept house for Grandfather, she'd been rather lackadaisical in her domestic duties, to put it kindly.

"You feeling all right?" she asked me. "You kept to bed much later than usual this morning."

"I didn't get much sleep last night."

"You had over company, didn't you?"

"What makes you suppose that, Molly?"

"Well, considering that you eat like a bird, it would have taken more than you alone to gobble up all the bread and cheese that was in the pantry. And there were two plates on the kitchen table." Molly gave me a sly sideways look. "I guess I know who came calling last night."

"You shouldn't guess about such things, Molly."

"Don't fret," Molly said. "You and Doc Adam have always kept my secret, and I will keep yours."

Rather than tell her the truth, I let her assume that it was Adam whom I'd entertained last night. As Henry has made clear to me, the fewer people who know about my involvement with the Underground Railroad, the better.

Unfortunately Constable Beers knew about it. He had no proof, but if he chose to make his suspicions public, my house would no longer be a safe Station. I would have to somehow bluff him into silence. I put on my best bonnet and freshest white gloves and went to his cottage shoe shop, my damaged boot in hand. I found him alone, and, when he looked up from his lapstone, he did not return my smile.

"Have you come to make amends, Mrs. Pelletier?"

"Actually, I hoped you would make some mends." I waved my boot at him. "Will you be so kind as to repair this?"

"What is in need of repair is the law you have broken," he replied without budging. "I will not allow you to continue harboring a fugitive slave, and I intend to search your house as soon as I obtain a warrant from Justice Phyfe. He is due back in Plumford this afternoon."

"You need not wait for a warrant, Constable. I invite you to come to my house directly and look anywhere you please."

"Do not play me for a fool, Mrs. Pelletier. Now that you

are so willing to allow me entry, I wager that black thief you were hiding is long gone."

"Then why bother getting a search warrant? Best we forget all about it."

"You defied my authority last night, young lady. And I will not forget about it." He pounded his hammer against the piece of leather on his lapstone a few times. "Oh, no. I will not forget."

"Do not force me to register a complaint against you, Mr. Beers."

His hammer paused midair. "Against *me?*"

"I am sure Justice Phyfe would be scandalized to hear that you came to the door of a helpless lone female in the middle of the night and demanded that she let you in."

"I made clear to you that I was investigating a theft, madam."

"In fact, you were not at all clear, sir. Your diction was slurred, and I believe you were drunk. That alone was reason enough not to open my door to you. Never mind your absurd accusation that I had gone and milked Mr. Chadwick's cow."

"Not you!" Beers shouted. "The Negro!"

"What Negro?"

"The one Mr. Chadwick saw!"

"I wager Mr. Chadwick sees many apparitions during his habitual walks in his sleep. And I dare say he won't even recall reporting that particular hallucination to you, Constable. Even if he does recall it, who would believe him?"

"I believed him," Beers said.

"But we have already established that you were not sober, sir."

Beers threw down his hammer and rose from his cobbler's bench, his face red and angry as he came toward me. "You think yourself a clever minx, don't you?"

I took a step back, but my gaze did not waver as I faced down the man. His small eyes had a hard malice in them, but his other features were weak, and he was the one to blink first.

I took care not to show him the smallest sign of triumph and held up my boot. "Can you fix this, please?"

He snatched the boot from my grasp and gave it a cursory look. "You women and your silly fashions," he said with the utmost disdain. "A cloth boot is not worth the trouble to repair."

"But I cannot afford to buy a new pair," I said most piteously.

"Oh, very well. I'll stitch it back together properly." Returning to his bench, he did so in a thrice, using wax-coated thread and a hog's bristle as a needle.

He charged me two cents, and we said no more about last night. I believe I have convinced him that it is better for all concerned if he does not pursue the matter and involve Justice Phyfe. Beers has always avoided trouble like the Plague, and it seems likely he will continue to do so.

Upon leaving the shoe shop I noticed an enclosed red wagon on the Green. It was stationed by the town pump, and the piebald horse that had pulled it was being led away by the Sun's stable boy. I strolled across the plush spring grass to get a closer look at the contrivance. The words DAGUERREOTYPE SALOON were painted on it in gold letters, and leaning against it was a slender young man I took to be the itinerant daguerreotypist. He wore tight striped pantaloons, a jaunty cap, and a gold hoop earbob in his right earlobe.

"Why, aren't you a fine looking young lady," he drawled, giving me an impertinent smile above a bristle of reddish chin beard. He had freckles sprinkled all over his face like stars. A grouping of them on his cheek was shaped like the Big Dipper. "Have you been taken already?"

"I'm married, if that's what you're asking."

"I'm sorry to hear it. But I was inquiring if you've ever had your likeness taken, ma'am."

"No, and I doubt I ever shall. I have no desire to have a frozen-faced image of myself."

"It will not look frozen, I assure you."

"Most daguerreotype portraits I have seen make the subjects look like corpses."

"Not the ones I take. Except, of course, when the subject is in fact dead."

"You take pictures of dead people?"

"Yes, upon request."

I pretended a shiver. "How macabre."

"Not really. Some find it comforting to have a final image of a loved one before the casket is sealed. Indeed, I could make a good living just taking funeral portraits, but I much prefer my subjects to be lively ladies such as yourself. Wouldn't your husband be delighted to be presented with your likeness?"

"Only if it were that of my corpse in a casket."

The daguerreotypist looked stunned by my reply for an instant and then laughed. "Aren't you the droll one?"

"I was being *dead* serious."

He laughed again. "You're a sight more amusing than most people I come across up North. Why do Yankees maintain such a stiff upper lip?"

"To cover bad teeth, I suppose."

"I wager your teeth are perfect, ma'am. Smile for me, won't you?"

"Why should I?"

"If you smile for me whilst I take your likeness, I'll give it to you free of charge."

In truth, I was most curious about the process and could not pass up the chance to learn about it at absolutely no cost to myself. So I suppose, despite my European rearing, I am a true Yankee after all. "I accept your offer, Mr. . . ."

"Just call me Rusty, ma'am. Rusty from Delaware." He

swept off his cap and gave me a low bow, showing off his bright red hair.

"Well, aren't you the Southern gentleman."

His open, freckled countenance became wary. "Have you a prejudice against Southerners?"

"What makes you think so?"

"Your mocking tone just now."

"I didn't mean to mock you. But in truth I do have a prejudice. Not against all Southerners, of course. Only slaveholders."

"Well, I own nary a slave and never have."

"Yet you tolerate slavery in your state."

"That peculiar institution is tolerated by *all* the states in this great Union, ma'am, for it is tolerated by the federal government." His tone was weary. No doubt he had made this point many times before during his travels in the North. "But if you no longer wish to pose for me because of where I happened to be born, so be it."

"I am not so intolerant as that," I said. "Pray take my likeness, Rusty. I want to see how it's done."

He bowed again. "Please step into my saloon, my lady."

The interior of the refitted wagon, or "saloon" as 'twas Rusty's pretension to call it, was about twenty feet long and brightly lit thanks to a large skylight. Swaths of pale silk covered the walls, and the scent of chlorine and other unidentifiable chemicals permeated the atmosphere. Rusty had me sit in a velvet "visitor's chair" and went behind a heavy curtain at the end of the wagon. After a moment he returned with a slender box that he told me contained a copper plate coated with silver. He inserted it in the camera obscura that stood like a vigilant Cyclops in front of the chair, and instructed me to smile and hold still whilst he counted to ten. At the count of one he slid open the box in the camera to expose the plate to light, and at the count of ten he removed the exposed plate.

"Care to join me behind the curtain and watch me work?" he said with a sly smile.

As tempted as I was to observe the process, I did not think it wise to be alone with him in such a small, intimate space. "I will stay here," I said, "and you can tell me what you are doing from back there."

He made a big show of looking disappointed, but he obliged me. "First thing I'm doing is putting the plate in a container that holds a cup of heated mercury," he called through the curtain. "The mercury vapor will amalgamate with the silver and develop the picture." After a short time of silence he spoke again. "Now I am immersing the plate in a hyposulfite bath to remove the silver coating." And then, a moment later: "I am now dipping the plate in a gold-chloride solution to gild and varnish the image. And now I am rinsing and drying the plate. It's about ready to seal under glass. Which would you prefer to have it set in, ma'am—a case or a frame?"

"Whatever is cheaper," I said, keeping in mind that he was giving me the image free of cost. "How does it look?"

"Wait and see for yourself." A moment later Rusty pulled back the curtain and extended to me, most dramatically, the framed daguerreotype. "I initialed and dated it in back," he said. "Does the image please you?"

I glanced at the flat facsimile of my face. There was no art in it. No magic. "It pleases me no more or less than my image in a mirror."

"I should think that would please you very much."

"Ha! The camera may not be a flatterer, but the camera operator certainly is."

"I'm being most sincere," Rusty insisted.

"If you were sincere you would admit that the fixed smile on my face makes me look like a simpering idiot. A smile that is forced instead of spontaneous is rarely attractive. That's why I do not demand smiles from my own subjects."

"Your subjects?" Rusty gave me a wry look. "What are you, a queen?"

"A portrait painter."

"Aha! Then you are even more prejudiced against me than you let on. You must regard daguerreotypists as rivals who will eventually replace limners like you."

"Indeed I do not! The stilted black-and-white replicas you make with your infernal device can never replace an artistic creation that captures both the subject's features and essence."

Rusty smiled. "Time will tell, ma'am. Time will tell."

I removed my gloves, wrapped them around the rather fragile glass image of myself, and stuck it in my reticule. We exited the wagon, and I saw that a collection of curious townspeople had gathered around it. They eagerly asked Rusty how much it would cost to make a likeness, and the price he quoted was so low that they began to line up to be taken.

I would have been happy to capture the visages of each and every one of them on canvas. But of course I would have taken weeks rather than minutes to do so and charged far more than most of them could afford. Perhaps Rusty was right. We limners were on the way out. Never mind artistic skill and talent. Never mind years of training and discipline. We might soon be replaced by one-eyed mechanical monsters and their operators. But even as this dire realization sank in, up floated ideas of how I might use this newfangled invention to my own advantage as an artist.

Musing upon this as I headed home, I did not notice Granny Tuttle's ward, Harriet Quimby, standing at the door of Adam's office. She waved to get my attention, which surprised me, for I am accustomed to Harriet running the opposite way whenever she spots me. The girl has always made it clear that my very presence in Plumford is obnoxious to her. And I have always hoped she might come to accept me or at least outgrow her childish animosity toward me.

"Where is Adam?" she demanded as soon as I was within hearing distance.

"Out on the bog, no doubt," I replied. "He and Henry Thoreau organized a search for a runaway slave who went missing when—"

"Yes, yes," Harriet interrupted impatiently. "Adam told Granny and me all about that last night. But I was hoping he hadn't left yet. Now what am I to do?" She began wringing her hands.

"What's wrong, Harriet? Has Granny taken a turn for the worse?"

"No, but she very well might if she leaves her bed," Harriet said. "She is all in a biver about Mr. Thoreau's expected visit this afternoon and means to be downstairs when he calls. She wants me to help her, for she is weak as a kitten and cannot manage on her own. I have never gone against her wishes, but it seems this time I must. The least exertion might do her harm, and I promised Adam I would keep her abed. I came to fetch him to talk some sense into her. Granny always listens to Adam."

After such a whoosh of words, Harriet had to pause to catch her breath, and I took the opportunity to make a suggestion. "Perhaps I could reason with Granny."

"You?" Harriet looked most doubtful, and no wonder, for Granny Tuttle has disliked me for even longer than Harriet has.

"Come along," I said, grasping Harriet's hand. "I haven't visited the old dear for a while, and now's as good a time as any."

Off we went to Tuttle Farm, a brisk twenty-minute walk from town on a road that rose and dipped between orchards and pastures and was quietly shouldered by the Assabet River. Farmers were out in the fields plowing whilst their wives were out in their kitchen gardens hoeing. Many a folk hallooed to us along the way, and Harriet and I called Good Day back at them. Nary a word did we speak to each other, however. I gave my silent walking companion an occasional sidelong glance, but her yellow straw bonnet shielded her countenance from me as much as it shielded her complexion from the sun's rays.

It was such a fine spring day that I threw off my own bonnet for an unhampered view of my surroundings. Everywhere I looked I saw Nature's abundance and beauty. Hedgerows enclosing the fields were chock-full of flowering hawthorn, nannyberry, and pin cherry shrubs, and velvety violets bloomed along the road. The meadows were studded with sunlit dandelions, and the tall tulip trees showed off gigantic yellow and orange blooms. Long yellow catkins hung from the poplars, releasing cotton puffs that floated in the soft air like fleecy snowflakes. The hill pastures had turned a rich, thick emerald green, and a herd of brown cows driven by a flaxen-haired boy trotted down the road toward us, most likely on their way to the pastures to graze. Harriet and I stepped aside to watch them pass, and we both laughed at the sight of the frisky calves gamboling alongside their mothers. I heard wild screeching above us and looked up to see a pair of red-tailed hawks dipping and rising and circling each other.

"Look, Harriet! Two hawks a-courting!" I said, pointing to them. "They are dancing together in the air and screaming out their passion for each other. It's their way of canoodling."

Harriet looked at me instead of the hawks, her round, young face pinched with disapproval. "I do not care to hear you talk of such things! It is unseemly."

It should have vexed me, I suppose, to be reprimanded by a mere girl of sixteen, but I found her misdirected prudishness rather amusing. "Pray what is so unseemly about pointing out two lusty birds performing a mating ritual, Harriet? They are doing what nature compels them to do, and there is no sin in it."

"But there is sin in it if you are a married woman," she muttered.

That surely took me aback. Why would Harriet say such a

thing unless she knew of my intimate relationship with Adam, which was indeed sinful in the eyes of state and church? In the eyes of Miss Harriet Quimby too, if I had heard and interpreted her remark correctly. Rather than ask her to repeat what she'd said, I did what many a woman in my dubious position would do—I pretended I had not heard her.

On we continued in silence, and soon the Tuttle farmstead could be seen from the road, poised on a level piece of ground in the center of a grassy field halfway up a hill. We took the long lane that led up to it. It was overhung by maple trees and bordered on either side by low stone walls thrown by Tuttle settlers who began clearing the land over two hundred years ago. Adam, a Tuttle on his mother's side, is the last surviving male descendant in the line, and his grandmother never lets him forget it.

As we drew closer the sight of the Tuttle apple orchard frothy with pink blossoms filled me with delight. I recalled the first time Adam had brought me there in the spring. A city child, I had never been in a blooming orchard before, and I had wept, overcome by the beauty. Adam had laughed at my mawkish gushing, as most boys of nine would have. But then he had taken my hand and given the back of it a big, wet smack of a kiss.

Upon reaching the farmhouse, I saw that the enormous chestnut tree that stands in front of it was already in full leaf. The tree is most impressive, but the house itself is not. Its roof is slightly swaybacked, and its rough, uneven clapboards have been left in their natural state, rather than painted white or yellow as is the current fashion. It is a most comfortable abode, however, and trailing back from it are a succession of attached buildings of varying sizes, making it possible to walk under cover of roof from kitchen to buttery, woodshed, cow barn, henhouse, wagon shed, and sheep barn. The Tuttles gave up raising sheep years ago, and Adam has converted the end barn into living quarters for himself.

Harriet and I entered the house through the kitchen door, and the moment I stepped inside I felt the difference. Yet nothing had changed. Dried herbs still hung from the heavy ceiling beams, and the old flintlock musket that Adam's great-grandfather had fired in the War for Independence still hung above the fieldstone fireplace. Granny's footed pots and blackened three-legged skillets, along with her hodgepodge collection of hefty ladles, skewers, and skimmers, were still gathered around the yawning hearth, and a small bed of coals glowed within it, as always. However, no pot of simmering stew hung from the swinging crane above the coals, the brick chimney oven was cold, and there was no rising dough or freshly baked bread on the bleached oak table. What felt so different in Granny Tuttle's kitchen was her absence from it.

We went up the narrow flight of stairs to her bedroom. The windows were open, and a warm breeze puffed out the homespun linen curtains and carried the scent of lilacs into the room. Granny lay on the four-poster bed she had shared with Eli Tuttle for forty years. She was covered with a blue and red counterpane that she'd most likely knitted herself, using wool she'd sheared from a sheep she'd raised up from a lamb; wool that she'd dyed with crushed plants from her garden and spun into yarn on her wheel. Now these ever-busy, nimble hands lay motionless atop the cover, fingers so twisted with arthritis they looked like claws. Her bright eyes, however, moved quickly enough when she swung her gaze from the window to me.

"Well, if it ain't Julia Bell," she said, calling me by my full maiden name as she has done since I was eight. "High time you paid a visit to a poor, sickly old woman."

"I came last week, ma'am." I would never call her Granny to her face, for she has never given me leave to do so.

"Last week? Then what in tarnation are you doin' back so soon? Ain't you got better things to do than bother a poor, sickly old woman?"

I had to laugh. Granny was as contrary as ever, despite her illness. But then I saw that the effort of being ornery had cost her dearly, for she closed her eyes and lay still and silent, her thin, drawn face white as the pillowcase.

"Yes, she is far too weak to get out of bed," I whispered to Harriet.

Granny's eyes flew open. "No, I ain't!"

"Nothing wrong with your hearing, though," I remarked dryly.

"Nothing wrong with me at all exceptin' I am dyin'!" Granny said. "And since you are here, Julia Bell, you can help Harriet carry me downstairs."

There was no reasoning with her, I realized. Hence, I saw no point in further depleting her energy by trying to. "Very well," I said, ignoring Harriet's reproachful look. "Where would you like us to put you?"

"On sich a fine day as this, I wish to be brought outside."

And so she was. But we could not very well lay her on the ground, so first Harriet and I lugged the heavy, humpbacked sofa from the parlor and set it under the chestnut tree. Moving Granny proved to be a far easier task, for she is near as lightweight as the anatomical skeleton in Adam's office. But before we carried her down from her bedchamber she insisted upon being properly attired in her yellow-checked gingham frock and a fresh white neckerchief and cap. It would shame her, Granny said, to receive company in a nightgown in the middle of the day.

Once we'd settled her upon the sofa, propped her up with pillows, and covered her with a quilt, Granny asked Harriet if she would kindly go to Daggett's store and fetch some pekoe tea for Mr. Thoreau.

"Henry doesn't drink beverages containing caffeine," I helpfully interjected.

Granny scowled at me. "Don't you think I know that, missy? But I mean to offer it to him anyway out of common courtesy, and 'twould be deceitful to offer what I don't have on hand."

"No one is more truthful than Granny Tuttle," Harriet added.

I, for one, could debate that. Hadn't Granny lied to Adam about his parentage for twenty-four years? I threw her a glance, but she avoided looking at me and kept her eyes on Harriet.

"Off to town with you then. You are a dear, sweet girl to do my bidding." Granny smiled at Harriet with the warm affection she reserved for a chosen few.

I, needless to say, was not one of the chosen. Indeed, I belonged to another category entirely—those Granny had no regard for whatsoever. Therefore I became wary when she told me, as soon as Harriet departed, that she wanted to have a frank talk with me. But I could not very well refuse to listen to the old dame, so I sat myself down at the opposite end of the sofa and waited for her to speak. She pushed herself up on her elbows and looked at me a good long moment but, without uttering a word, she sank back into the pillows and closed her eyes.

I gazed at her deeply etched, sunken face and thought it no wonder Granny looked so worn out. When she married Eli Tuttle half a century ago the farm had not been near as gainful as it is now, and she had worked as hard as her husband to make a success of it. In addition to that, she had borne six children. It is said that there is no greater pain than having to bury a child, and the Tuttles buried all six of theirs. Three died in childhood, of whooping cough, scarlet fever, and diphtheria. The eldest son died of blood poisoning caused by a cut from a fish hook, and one daughter died in childbirth. Adam's mother, the last of their offspring to survive, fell to her death from a tree twenty years ago, and ten years ago the influenza took Granny's husband. Yet never once have I heard Granny rail against God or even Fate. And I very much doubt she has ever felt sorry for herself, either.

She opened her eyes and sat up with a start. "Lors me! I clean forgot about the dandelions. They must be bloomin' right about now."

"They are," I told her. "They popped up overnight as if from fairy dust sprinkled over the meadows."

"Fairy dust." Granny sniffed. "You was allus full of fancy and nonsense, Julia Bell. Dandelions come up same time every year to feed hungry little critters like cottontails and goldfinches. And to supply me with the fixin's for my Ladies' tonic."

"Ladies' tonic, indeed," I said wryly. The fermented brew Granny made from dandelion blossoms, sugar, water, and yeast had quite a kick to it.

"If dandy heads ain't gathered as soon as they blossom, the tonic don't taste as good," Granny said anxiously.

"Why don't I go pick you some right now?"

"It's too late in the day," Granny said. "They should be picked whilst the dew is still on the grass. So you just stay put. We need to have us a private talk."

I shook my head. "If you had been honest with me the last time we talked in confidence, Adam and I would be married now."

"You can't lay all the blame that you two ain't married at my feet, missy!"

"Are you blind to your own culpability, ma'am?"

"Oh, I see clear enough where I was at fault. And don't think I haven't suffered over it," Granny said. "But when I finally twigged how much Adam cared for you, I told him the truth. And he went to France as quick as he could to fetch you back, but you had already gone and married someone else. Is that *my* fault?"

Yes! I wanted to shout back at her, but I pushed down my anger and held my tongue. What possible good could come from quarrelling with this weak old lady? She closed her eyes and drifted off to sleep again, much to my relief, for I needed time to regain my equilibrium. I gazed out at the newly plowed fields and fresh green meadows and contemplated what had led to the unwarrantable situation Adam and I now found ourselves in.

I'd come back to Plumford two years ago to nurse my maternal grandfather, Dr. Silas Walker, who had badly broken his leg and was being treated by his grandson, my cousin Dr. Adam Walker. Adam and I had grown attached as children, but we'd been abruptly separated when my mother died and my father took me off to France at age eleven. I had not laid eyes on Adam for twelve years when I returned to Plumford, but in a matter of weeks we had fallen in love—deeply and irrevocably. And most imprudently. In the Walker family history, the offspring of first cousins had always been born with birth defects too severe to sustain life. Therefore, I had listened to Granny Tuttle when she'd advised me to go back to France before Adam and I gave in to temptation. I listened because I wanted for Adam exactly what she did—a happy life with someone who could give him the family he so desired. Someone like her darling ward Harriet Quimby, for instance, who bore no blood relation to him.

But as it turns out, neither do I! Adam and I are not consanguineous cousins, after all. His biological father was not his legal father, Owen Walker, who was my uncle. And Granny Tuttle always knew this. Her daughter Sarah, Adam's mother, had confided in her before Adam was born.

To her credit, Granny did eventually inform Adam that he

was a Walker in name only. Alas, she told him too late. I had already married an elderly, seemingly kindhearted man whom I'd met on the ship back to France. Admittedly, I had acted hastily and as it turns out most unwisely, but my motive for doing so was based on a lie Granny had led me to believe. Therefore, who is to blame for this quandary Adam and I now find ourselves in? I turned my head to look at Granny. She had awakened and was regarding me intensely with her gimlet eyes.

"You got somethin' to tell me, Julia Bell?" she said.

"I thought you had something to tell *me*, ma'am."

"I intended on tellin' you to get the blazes out of Plumford."

The wind had picked up a bit, and I tucked the quilt around her scrawny neck. A neck, I admit, I would have gladly wrung when I first learned how she'd deceived me. "You already told me that once," I reminded her. "And I was fool enough to listen."

"We have chewed over that already, missy."

"Do you still cling to the hope that if I went away Adam would marry Harriet?"

"Oh, no. That hope was dashed when Harriet told me she would never have an adulterer for a husband. She knows for sure that Adam is one, for she has followed him to town when he leaves here at sunrise and observed him go up to your chamber."

"You must have been scandalized when she told you," I said.

Granny gave one of her sniffs. "'Twould take a heap more than that to scandalize the likes of me. I reckoned it was only a matter of time afore you and my grandson got biblical." She gave me another hard look. "You look a bit green about the gills, Julia."

In truth I did feel both dizzy and nauseated. I hurriedly

went behind the lilac bushes and spit up a stream of yellow bile. When I returned to Granny, she was staring up at the sky.

"Looks to be a storm brewin'. There's a big thunderhead yonder," she remarked.

"Then I'd best bring you inside," I said.

"No need yet. The wind might blow it east of us. We'll just wait and see. Come sit down again and give me yer hand, dearie." Her request for my hand astonished me as much as her calling me dearie, but I did as she asked. "Now where were we?" she said.

"You were telling me to get the blazes out of Plumford."

"No, I said I was *goin'* to tell you that. Afore I saw how things were with you." Granny squeezed my hand as best she could with her stiff, crooked fingers. "Does Adam know yet?"

I shook my head. "I wanted to be completely sure before I told him."

"Well, I am as certain that you are with child," Granny said, "as I am certain that thunderhead is about to burst."

We watched as the roiling storm cloud, shaped like an anvil, rose higher and higher up into the sky until it towered over the countryside a few miles east of us. The head of the cloud was gleaming white in the sun, and its base as black as night, with pulses of light coursing through it. Suddenly, a dazzling bolt of lightning shot forth, quickly followed by another bolt of even more intensity. The air shuddered with the crack and boom of thunder. Then, just as Granny had predicted, rain burst from the massive cloud in heavy, gray sheets.

"I pray no man nor beast got struck by that awful lightning," she said.

The wind shifted, and the thunderhead swiftly moved off like a tall clipper ship tacking away. In less than five minutes the sun was shining down on the unfortunate area that had been so terribly deluged.

ADAM

Thursday, May 18

'Tis no wonder Henry's surname is pronounced the same as the word *thorough*. By following his systematic procedure, our search party managed to cover every foot of the bog in a comprehensive, efficient, and timely manner. Even so, the unstable terrain and the exceptional warmth of the day, not to mention the fearsome thunderstorm, wore all of us out, and I was feeling as logy as a porcupine as I drove Henry toward Tuttle Farm. The last thing I wanted to do was get into a heated discussion, and Henry seemed even more inclined to silent contemplation than usual. But there was a bone of contention between us that needed gnawing at, one I was not about to let go of.

"I don't want Julia put in danger again," I told Henry without preamble.

He had been observing a tanager flit through a stand of beech trees, and he turned to me with a rather startled expression. "Julia was in danger? When?"

"Last night, of course. You put her in harm's way by bringing fugitive slaves to her door."

"I brought an exhausted young couple with a frail babe,

and Julia welcomed them into her home. I see no harm in that, Adam. Only good."

"Did you not consider that we have a cold-blooded killer on the loose? One who is most likely a slave hunter?"

"In fact, that was my primary consideration. Because Julia's house has never been used as a Station before, I was confident no one was watching it. Your concern is unwarranted, Adam. I shall remove the Cooper family from Julia's house and bring them to another safe Station tonight."

"Julia already did so, dammit! So do not tell me my fear for her safety is unwarranted." My agitated tone caused Napoleon, pulling the gig along at a placid trot, to glance a wide-eyed look back at me. In a calmer voice, I proceeded to inform Henry of Constable Beers's arrival at Julia's door and the flight to Acton that ensued.

"All's well that ends well," Henry said in response. "Julia acted with good sense and courage."

"What is courageous in a man is foolhardy in a woman," I countered. "And you know from past exploits how foolhardy Julia can be. That's why you should never have involved her in this Underground Railroad business. Her inclination to take risks is too great."

"Are you saying that she should be denied participation in a cause she believes in because she is a woman, Adam?"

"Because she is the woman I *love*."

My declaration was hardly news to Henry. I'd told him of my intention to marry Julia two years ago, and that I loved her still, even though she was married to another, did not seem to surprise him. "Loving a woman doesn't give you leave to control her actions, my friend," he said in a rather kindly tone. "It's up to every individual to decide how to act, and Julia has made her own decision."

I saw no point in discussing this further with Henry. I do not think he will ever deliberately put Julia in harm's way, but

I also realize it is up to me alone to protect her. If only I were her legal husband! Then, as the acknowledged head of our household, I could make sure she was safe at all times.

When Henry and I arrived at Tuttle Farm I was astounded to see Gran under the chestnut tree, reclining on her parlor sofa no less. I asked Henry if he would be so kind as to barn Napoleon, jumped down from the gig, and hurried to her.

"You should be in your bedchamber, Gran," I said.

"I am better off right here," she retorted.

I placed my palm against her forehead and then reached for her hand and took her pulse. "I allow that being removed outdoors does not seem to have done you any harm. Did you finagle a couple of the farmhands to lug this sofa out here for you?"

"Harriet and Julia did it."

"Julia is here?"

Gran nodded. "Here she comes right now."

I looked over my shoulder and saw Julia walking from the house toward me. She was holding a quilt and proceeded to place it over the one already covering Gran. She then turned to me, eyes filled with apprehension, and inquired about the bog search. When I reported that we had not found the runaway's body, Julia expressed her certainty that the runaway must still be alive. Gran was not so optimistic. She accepts nothing as truth unless proven to her. Except for the existence of heaven and hell, that is.

When Henry joined us he drew Julia aside to hear her firsthand account regarding the Cooper family. He then gave his full attention to Gran.

"You look like a rajah lounging on that sofa, Mrs. Tuttle."

"And what pray is a rajah?" she asked him.

"A royal person in India."

"What do you know of India, Henry?"

"Only what I read in Hindoo mystical writings."

Gran squeezed tight her face to show her disapproval. "Ain't Hindoos heathens?"

"I suspect Hindoos would say the same of Congregationalists."

"You are a heretic, young man!" There was color in Gran's cheeks and a sparkle in her eye. She loved sparring with Henry.

He laughed. "Will you accept a present from a heretic?"

Gran's eyes got brighter still. "You brung me a present?"

"Flora from the bog." Henry reached into the deep pocket of his jacket and withdrew a long, thick stem decorated with small yellow blossoms. No doubt noticing that Gran's arthritic hands would be unable to grasp it, he placed it on the quilt.

"What is it called?" she said.

"Platanthera hyperborea."

"I'll never manage to get my tongue around that."

"Call it a bog orchid then," Henry said. "It's an early bloomer of the species, and when I saw it in the sphagnum I thought of you and plucked it."

Gran wrinkled her nose. "It's got a funny smell."

"To me it smells like snakes," Henry said.

Gran hooted. "Is that why you thought of me?"

"No, it was the delicacy of the blossoms that brought you to mind, Mrs. Tuttle."

Gran sniffed off his remark, but the color in her cheeks deepened. Julia and I exchanged an amused glance. What a charmer Henry could be when he chose to. Which was not all that often.

I fetched two ladder-backs from the kitchen and placed them under the chestnut tree for Henry and me. Before he sat down in his, Henry admired the workmanship, and Gran looked proud as punch.

"My husband made them chairs," she said. "Eli was real handy with a spokeshave."

"Indeed he was," Henry said, running his hand along the rounded legs and stretchers. "And who wove the rush seats?"

"I did," Gran said.

"You did a fine job of it."

Gran was not one to accept compliments concerning herself and quickly changed the subject. "Let's hear more about the bog search."

Henry began to describe the sudden storm we'd endured.

"You could see the thunderhead break from here," Julia said. "We had no idea you were right under it, but Granny prayed no one got struck by lightning. Perhaps her prayer protected you."

"Or perhaps the bog phantom protected us," Henry said.

Gran looked at him with narrowed eyes. I thought she was going to reprimand him for his pantheism as she had in the past. Instead, she asked, "Did she show herself to you?"

"You acknowledge the existence of the bog phantom, Mrs. Tuttle?"

"When I was a girl, most everybody did. And many had seen her. But then she hid herself away, never to appear again. I reckon 'twas because witless boys started tryin' to espy her for sport. Ain't that right, Adam?"

"Maybe the phantom stopped appearing when folks stopped believing in her," I replied.

Gran ignored my comment. "Did she show herself today, Henry?" she asked again. He nodded, and Gran gave out a hoot. "I wager she scared the dickens out of you menfolk."

That said, she relaxed against the pillows. But only for a moment. Her gnarled hands started twitching, and her eyes began darting hither and thither. I knew these to be signs of the anxiety that has plagued her since her illness took root.

"I am all aback in my chores!" she cried. "I have not even put the peas in the garden!"

"Harriet and I sowed the seeds two weeks ago," I told her. "So don't you worry about your peas."

She found a new worry. "The Indian corn must be planted!"

"It's been done, the first field work of the year," I assured her.

"The cows should be put out to pasture, poor cooped creatures!"

"They have been taken out to pasture every day this week," I said. "Nothing is behindhand, and you need not be concerned, Gran."

Since Grandpa's death near a decade ago, Gran has directed the farm work, and of late I have taken on the job of foreman. It is no burden to me, for the farmhands are reliable and hardworking, and Tuttle Farm is thriving. But Gran cannot be made to rest easy.

"Something must be done about them foxes!" she said. "The sly critters must sense they are out of danger now that I got no strength to lift a musket, for they have made themselves to home in the henhouse, helpin' themselves to as many eggs as they please. For two morns in a row, Harriet's come back with an empty basket."

"Are you sure that foxes are the problem?" Henry said. "The hens may just be broody."

"Then off with their heads!" Gran cried. "What good are hens if they ain't layin'?"

"Calm yourself, Gran," I said and patted her hand.

Little good that did. "By the bye, where in the Sam Hill *is* Harriet?" Gran demanded. "I sent her on an errand an age ago. I wager she has stopped in town to chinwag with that gossipy friend of hers, the constable's daughter."

"Don't concern yourself about Harriet," I told Gran. "Or wear yourself out with too much talking."

"I am already all worn out, my dearest boy. And useless to boot," Gran replied.

My heart went out to her, for she looked so very miserable, and I was tempted to give her a measure of laudanum to soothe her nerves. I held off doing so, however. Eventually I will have to dose Gran with the drug to assuage her pain and do not want to prematurely dull her sharp mind.

"If I had half a hope I'd go to heaven," Gran continued, "I would implore God to take me up there to be with Him right now."

Henry leaned forward in his chair and regarded Gran most earnestly. "But you *are* with God right now, Mrs. Tuttle."

"How can I be if I ain't dead yet?"

"All you need do to receive God's inflowing spirit is accept that it is freely yours to have."

Gran shook her head. "If 'twere that easy, what purpose is there to goin' to church?"

Henry smiled at her. "As far as I know, there is none. But I have little patience with preaching. My own convictions come from what I experience, not from what others tell me."

"We all have to listen to someone, young man."

Henry tapped his chest. "I listen to the voice within. And I don't need to go to church to be with God."

"Where do you go then?"

"The woods. The pond. The fields and mountains. God is everywhere in the natural world around us and culminates in the present moment." Henry took both Gran's hands in his. "Stop all this worrying about what should have been done yesterday or what needs to be done tomorrow and simply be right here, right now. Just be still and look around you. Tell me what you see."

Gran turned her gaze toward the apple orchard on the hill. "I see the blowth on the fruit trees, and it is a mighty pretty sight," she said.

Henry nodded. "That is the bloom of the present moment."

Whether Gran grasped his meaning or not, his deep, gentle voice seemed to settle her down. None of us spoke for a while. Then my stomach rumbled. And Gran heard it.

"Faith! You and Henry must be famished after all that tramping in the bog," she said, all in a biver again. "I would fetch you some victuals if only I could. Or ask Harriet to do so, if only she were here."

Julia immediately rose from the sofa. "I reckon it's up to me then."

"I thank you kindly," Gran told her. "Pray go to the smoke-house and hack off a nice hunk of ham. Then go to the root cellar and bring up a small wheel of cheese and a big bottle of cider."

"No ham or cider for me," Henry said.

Gran sighed. "I clean forgot your aversion to meat and fermented beverages, Henry. Now what am I goin' to feed you? I know. Fetch up some apples from the pit for Henry, Julia."

Julia looked bewildered. "What pit?"

Gran gave one of her impatient sniffs. "You sure weren't raised up to be a farmer's wife, were you? Adam, go along with Julia Bell and show her where the apples are stowed."

I was happy to oblige, for I welcome any opportunity to be alone with my love. When we went into the root cellar I pulled Julia to me and gave her a deep kiss. She kissed me back, and we lingered in our subterranean embrace for a few blissful moments, then drew apart and caught our breaths, inhaling the earthy scent of the root vegetables stored in the racks along the stone walls. The walls sloped upward to an arched ceiling, and the dirt floor dipped toward a pit where apples from last fall were stockpiled between layers of straw. I'd left the rough plank door open, and a thin light seeped into the cool darkness of the cellar. Looking about, I saw that the cellar was not as orderly as Gran had trained Harriet to keep it. Carrots and parsnips were strewn about, and a red neckerchief Harriet had carelessly dropped was on the dirt floor. Julia picked it up and put it on a shelf. After tapping the plug in a cider keg with the heel of my hand to stop it from dripping, I looked into the pit. The straw had been cast aside willy-nilly, and the apples were in disarray.

"Ah, well. Harriet is still but a girl," I muttered.

Julia got a basket from a shelf and placed the apples I handed her into it. "They look fresh-picked," she said.

"And taste fresh too. Try one."

She bit into an apple and exclaimed over its sweet juiciness. That inclined me to take a taste myself by licking her sweet, juicy lips, and we started kissing all over again.

When we returned to the chestnut tree with the apples and cheese, neither Gran nor Henry remarked upon our long absence. They were intent upon watching a man on a sorry-looking gray horse coming up the long drive. He was a tall, lean fellow wearing a slouch hat with a brim wide enough to near qualify as some sort of umbrella.

"Do you know who that is, Adam?" Gran said.

"Never saw him before."

When the stranger reached the end of the drive I walked over to him. "How do," he said and touched his ridiculous hat. His clean-shaven face was burnt brown as old leather, yet there was a youthful set to his countenance.

"Good day," I replied and waited for him to announce his business. I spied the barrel of a large-caliber rifle extending out beyond the bedroll behind his saddle, and when Henry left his chair and came to stand beside me, I was glad to have him there.

"My name is Shiloh Prouty," the stranger said in a low and melodious voice that indicated his Southern origins.

I was not inclined to introduce myself back to him until he told me what he wanted. Henry too remained silent. Shiloh Prouty stared back at us with eyes as washed-out blue as his worn, patched overalls. It seemed further communication was at a standstill until we figured out each other's protocols.

Julia came over to us, and Prouty doffed his hat. His hair was the color of wheat and looked to be as stiff and dry. "What brings you to Tuttle Farm, sir?" she asked him right off.

"Well, ma'am, that is a complicated question." His demeanor became more relaxed as he addressed her. "What brung me has nothing to do with this farm in particular. I have been stopping by a number of farms hereabouts. And so far nobody at a one of them has offered me so much as a cool drink of water."

"If it's water you want, help yourself," I said more gruffly than graciously and gestured toward the old stone well a rod from the kitchen door.

Prouty dismounted and went to the well, where he filled a bucket with water and drank from his cupped palm. I expected him to leave after he'd refreshed himself, but instead he approached the sofa and doffed his hat again. "Fine farm you got here, mistress," he told Gran.

"Where you from, mister?" she asked him.

"Virginia."

"Well, I reckon it must seem a mighty small farm compared to them plantations you got down there," she replied. "But we don't use slave labor in these parts of the country. We do the work with our own hands."

"Appears to me you folks up North got a lot of opinions regarding how we do things in the South, but no firsthand knowledge," Prouty replied in a friendly enough drawl. "I got me a farm, not a plantation, and I work it mostly myself, as my pappy did afore me. Raise some cotton and some tobacco and some corn and got a good hundred pigs out below the oaks. It's a fine farm like yours, and I take a good deal of pride in it."

"What you doing away from it during planting season?" Gran said.

He shifted from one foot to the other and twisted the brim

of the hat in his hands. "I fear my words may not please you, but I must speak them. I am looking for my slave who run away from me."

Gran didn't so much as blink. "Well, we don't countenance slave owners 'round here, young feller, so you'd best be on yer way."

Prouty's amiable expression turned grim. "Seems I can't get nowhere with you prejudiced Yankees." He turned toward his sorry horse.

"No, wait," Henry said. "It is never too late to give up our prejudices. Let us hear you out."

I gave Henry a startled look, but in the next instant realized that his intention was to interrogate this Southern stranger, who might very well be Tripp's murderer. So I too urged Prouty to tell us more about his slave.

"I cannot fathom why she run out on me," Prouty said most woefully. "I have always treated Tansy as good as I know how to. Here, I got a picture of her, taken but a few days ago. Maybe you seen her." He pulled from his pocket a small velvet case and opened it to show us a daguerreotype of a hefty young Negro woman with a stern expression. "She looks better in the flesh, 'specially when she's smiling. Tansy's got a real nice smile."

"How long have you been looking for her?" Henry asked him.

"Since she lit out on me two weeks ago."

"And how long have you been looking for her in these parts?"

"I come from Boston just today."

"Why were you in Boston?" Henry said.

"Tansy's got a sister livin' there. She's married to some shipyard worker who bought her freedom. Figured Tansy would run to her, and I was right. I come this close to catching her." He lifted a grubby hand and made a hairsbreadth space between index finger and thumb. "But she got wind of my being in Boston, and someone carted her off to a hiding place here in Plumford. I had to pay dearly for that information, and now I'm asking you direct and plain. Have you seen her?" We all shook our heads. "Have you heard tell of her?" We stared back at him in silence. "I am wasting my breath, ain't I? You would never tell me if you had. You Yankees got no respect for another man's rightful possession." Shaking his head over our perversity, he went to his horse.

"Might I ask you a few more questions before you go, Mr. Prouty?" Henry said.

"No! I am fed up to my back teeth with you asking me questions but telling me nothing in return." He mounted and looked down at us, his long, narrow face more sad than angry. "I ain't leaving Plumford till I find Tansy or hear where next to look for her. Don't care what it cost me in time or money. Not that I got much of either, but I aim to put up at that tavern down in the village for a spell." He turned his horse and headed back down the hill.

"That's the first slave owner I ever seen in the flesh," Gran said. "He don't look as evil as I expected." She sounded disappointed.

"You cannot always perceive the evil lurking within a person," Julia said. "Nevertheless, Mr. Prouty does seem more a lovesick swain than a hidebound slave owner."

"That's not the way I view him," I said. "Prouty has come here to reclaim his property. And he probably shot Tripp trying to do so the other night. He then pursued his slave across the bog, but she managed to escape him. That's why he is looking in this area for her."

"We don't know for a fact that the slave he calls Tansy is the fugitive Tripp was transporting," Julia said.

"Fact or not, it seems more than likely," I said.

"Let us not underrate the value of a fact, Adam," Henry

said. "It will one day flower in a truth. I too suspect Prouty, but we cannot prove anything against him without evidence."

"Tripp was shot with a powerful rifle like the one Prouty is traveling with," I pointed out.

"But the only way we can establish as *fact* that his was the gun that shot Tripp," Henry said, "is if the bullets it fires come out looking like this one." He fished in his deep pocket and then displayed in his palm the nicked bullet we had found in Tripp's coat.

"I hope you are not going to propose we find out by getting Prouty to shoot at us," I joked. I glanced at Gran, hoping I hadn't alarmed her, but she was once again dozing.

"I propose something far more sensible," Henry said. "After poor Tripp's burial service tomorrow, let us go to Boston and establish if Prouty was there when he claimed to be. If he was, he could not have been in Plumford when Tripp was shot."

That didn't sound too sensible to me. "How can we possibly know who might have seen Prouty in Boston?"

"The Vigilant Committee makes it their business to keep watch for men like Prouty. And I know committee members we can talk to."

"I would like to come to Boston with you," Julia said.

Henry shook his head. "In order for your house to remain a safe Station, you can't be seen associating with people on the Vigilant Committee."

"Yes, of course you're right," Julia told Henry. I would be most appreciative if she ever told *me* that.

When Harriet returned from town Gran awoke and made much of offering Henry a cup of tea. He refused, as he always does. Shortly thereafter, Julia took her leave. The late afternoon light had begun to wane, and I carried Gran upstairs to her bed. She urged me, in another fit of fretfulness, not to leave the sofa outside. Harriet came up to read to Gran out of the Bible, which always calmed her down.

When Henry and I brought the sofa back to the parlor, we were impressed that Julia and Harriet had managed to carry out such a big, heavy piece. We returned to our chairs under the chestnut tree to watch high, thin streaks of cloud ease in from the west and reflect the ruddy color of the setting sun. Long-winged nighthawks coursed back and forth above the meadow, catching insects in their choppy flight, and off along the stone wall whippoorwills called each other back and forth.

Henry asked me how far the Tuttle property extended, and I told him it encompassed all the hill, from the meadow down below in the valley to the rocky top.

"I reckon that would be about three hundred acres," he said. His surveyor's eye had estimated correctly. "What are your biggest crops?"

"Corn, rye, and oats," I said. "In my grandfather's day it made economical sense to use most of the land for pasture and field crops, but now I'd like to devote more of it to orchard and experiment with new varieties of apples. Scientific farming, that's the modern way to go, and I've been keeping careful records of seeds, sprouts, transplants, and grafts. My goal is to develop an apple more resistant to blight and less prone to bruising during shipping and storage. Thanks to the railroad, it's possible to ship heavy produce fairly cheaply now, and that means city folk can have fresh, affordable apples. That would be a real boon to them, for I am convinced of the health-inducing qualities of apples. Why, I have seen certain of my patients with digestive and liver disorders improve from a diet of . . ." I glanced at Henry and saw that his eyes were closed. "Well, I guess I have gone on too long about apples."

"Oh, I was listening to you with great interest," he assured me, opening his eyes. "The subject of apples has always fascinated me. I find it remarkable how closely the history of the apple tree is connected with that of man."

Henry then cited where the apple was mentioned by Homer,

Herodotus, and Pliny. Although I too had studied the classics at
Harvard, I had forgotten most of what I'd read. But Henry has
a mind that retains impressions of all he sees and reads.

"Well, now I'm the one who has gone on too long about
apples," he concluded. "Let me only say further that I applaud
your ambition to cure man's ills with the fruit, Adam."

"Not *all* man's ills, of course," I said. "I did not mean to
sound overly optimistic. Indeed, it is most doubtful that my
ambitions concerning Tuttle Farm's future will ever be realized."

"They certainly won't be if you have that attitude," Henry
said. "You must advance confidently in the direction of your
dreams, Adam. If you endeavor to live the life you have imagined, you will meet with unexpected success, I assure you."

"The life I imagine has always included Julia in it," I said.
"Unfortunately, it is impossible for her to get a divorce. Therefore, we intend to head west, where no one will know we
aren't legally married, and we can live openly together. We
often talk of California as a possibility, a dream of ours since
childhood."

Henry and I are not in the habit of discussing such personal matters, and my frankness concerning my intimate relationship with Julia seemed to leave him at a loss for words.

"Have I shocked you into silence, Henry?"

"It is indeed a shock to learn I will be losing two good
friends. When do you plan to depart?"

"In truth, we would have gone already if not for my
grandmother's grave illness. I cannot leave Gran when she
most needs me, and it is only a matter of months, I fear, before
she passes."

"And when she does? What will happen to Tuttle Farm?"

"I have not worked that out as of yet," I admitted. "I would
be loath to sell it. I reckon I can always get someone to manage it for me. How about you, Henry?"

He gave out a sharp laugh. "That would not suit me at all! I came near to purchasing a farm a few years ago, and then realized it was better for me to live free and uncommitted. But I was not born into a farm family as you were, Adam. Farming is in your blood."

"Yes, but Julia is in my heart and soul. I would be willing to give up far more than life on Tuttle Farm for a life with her. Besides, our situation may change." I hesitated, then went ahead and expressed what was topmost in my mind. "If Julia became a widow, we could marry and stay right here in Plumford. I cannot help but wish for the passing of an elderly man who made his fortune trading in human lives."

Henry studied me a long moment, his clear, luminous eyes like lenses on a microscope. "Be careful what you wish for, my friend," he said.

With that, he bid me Good Evening and headed back to Concord, leaving me alone in the gathering dusk, smelling the fresh, growing grass.

JULIA

Friday, May 19

It is said that the full force of sexual desire is seldom if ever known to a virtuous woman. Well then, I can hardly claim to be virtuous. My desire for Adam has caused me to swerve so far from the straight path of rectitude that there is no going back. Nor do I even want to. I knew full well what course I was taking the first time Adam and I made love in December. And I have continued to willingly and wantonly have intimate relations with him nearly every morning since. We have done our best to be careful, following methods prescribed in Knowlton's *Fruits of Philosophy* most diligently, but we have eschewed the most reliable method of all—abstinence. Therefore, I should be fully prepared to accept the repercussions that inevitably follow illicit unions such as ours. But what woman ever is?

I was on the verge of telling Adam of my condition when he rose from my bed this morning. But I said nothing at all as I watched him move about the room getting dressed, my very own animated Greek sculpture, as well-proportioned and muscular as those at the Louvre. Whenever I have asked Adam to pose for me he has refused, claiming he is far too busy to remain immobile for any length of time. Far too modest, I think.

Before going down to his office, he lingered at my bedside as is his wont, stroking my hand and playing with my fingers, and I was about to tell him again. But again I held back. I needed a little more time to become accustomed to this dramatic change in my life. And I wanted to come up with a plan to deal with it.

I remained in bed after Adam left me, contemplating what to do. I studied the cracks in the ceiling, as if there were answers in the pattern they made. Such a notion as that would not seem ridiculous to my friend Mawuli. According to him, messages can be read in all sorts of fissures—in timber, rocks, pottery, or wheresoever they appear. Of course Mawuli found it amusing to hoax me with tales as tall as he was, and I'll never know which of his claims, if any, were true. My sole regret in leaving France is that I shall never see his dear old face again. At first sight I had found Mawuli quite ferocious-looking, but once I became used to his scarred visage I saw in it deep intelligence, compassion, and humor. Indeed, Mawuli was the only person I felt comfortable with in Cannes during my miserable marriage to Pelletier. My husband claimed that Mawuli was just his manservant, but I observed that he also served as Pelletier's physician of sorts, mixing up strange concoctions for him when he was ailing. It was apparent to me that Pelletier held the African in the highest regard, for my husband was always at his best behavior when Mawuli was present. Never did Pelletier so much as raise his voice to me, much less his hand, when Mawuli was there to witness. Even so, I sensed Mawuli was fully aware of Pelletier's many cruelties toward me. I think that is why Mawuli always did his best to entertain me with his fantastical stories and claims. Such as being able to read messages in fissures.

The only message I could read in the ceiling cracks this morning was that it was time to hire a plasterer. But I have no money to pay one at present. A good portion of what I re-

ceived from the sale of my diamond ring went to purchase my
passage home, and the small amount I have left is quickly di-
minishing. Portrait commissions have been few and far between, but I still maintain the hope that I will someday support
myself with my paints and brushes.

Therefore, my immediate plan was to get myself out of bed
and into my studio. And a good thing I was dressed and at
work before nine, for who should come calling but Mr. and
Mrs. Ruggles. The burly taverner apologized for their early
visit, but of course I did not mind in the least. I smelt a com-
mission and sure enough, as soon as I'd ushered them into my
studio, Mr. Ruggles proposed that I paint his wife's likeness. As
I regarded the plump little woman, she made a great show of
modesty, shaking her head and covering her face with her
hands, but I could tell she was delighted with the prospect. So
I quoted as high a price as I dared for an oil portrait, and Mr.
Ruggles readily agreed to it. And because he had not quibbled,
I readily agreed myself when he asked if I could paint Mrs.
Ruggles in their private quarters at the tavern so that she
would be close at hand when needed downstairs.

"Roos will be more calm at home, too," Mrs. Ruggles put in.

"Roos?" said I.

"My parrot," Mrs. Ruggles said. "I want her in the painting."

"Will that cost extra?" Mr. Ruggles said.

I had half a mind to charge more. I am no Audubon, after
all. But I rather like Mr. and Mrs. Ruggles and told them I
would include the bird gratis. They, in turn, told me I could
take meals at the Sun Tavern gratis whilst I worked there. It
was a happy arrangement all around, and we shook hands on
it. Mrs. Ruggles's hand was rough and chapped from housework, yet decorated with an assortment of flashy rings. She
smelled of lye soap and flowery perfume. I told her I would
come to the tavern at her convenience, and she suggested tomorrow afternoon.

After Mr. and Mrs. Ruggles left I got right to work stretching and preparing the sizeable canvas they had requested for the portrait. I would not be painting upon it until I did preliminary sketches, but the primer needed time to dry.

No sooner had I completed this task than it was time to attend Ezra Tripp's burial service. Adam and I walked together up the post road to what townsfolk call the "Newcomer Cemetery," established when our ancestral graveyard behind the Meetinghouse ran out of space. I was surprised to see a good number of people already gathered around the open grave, for the Tripps had kept to themselves since moving to Plumford and made few acquaintances here. It turned out that except for Constable Beers, Justice Phyfe, and a woman who was Mrs. Tripp's neighbor, the mourners were from Concord. Henry was there, along with Mrs. Thoreau, her two daughters, Lidian Emerson, and five or six men I did not recognize. I surmise they had come to honor Tripp for his work in the Underground Railroad, although there was no direct mention of that.

Henry did make a short speech, however, concerning our right and duty to resist our government when its laws, like those supporting the enslavement of a sixth of the country's population, are unquestionably evil. He went on to say that the majority of men are without moral judgment, serving the government like machines with their bodies as soldiers and jailers and constables. He looked right at Beers when he stated this. And then he looked at Justice Phyfe and added that most politicians and officeholders, serving the government with their heads, rarely make any moral distinctions and are as likely to serve the devil as God.

Justice Phyfe lost no time rebuking Henry, declaring that he had come to Tripp's burial out of sympathy for the murdered man and his family, not to be insulted by a rabble-rousing abolitionist from another town. He then offered his condolences to

Mrs. Tripp, patted her young son Billy's head, returned his high glossy hat to his own equine head, and marched out of the cemetery like a haughty racehorse. Beers followed in his wake like the ass he is.

Apparently the Tripps did not belong to any congregation, for no minister was present to give a benediction. Instead, Mrs. Thoreau led us in the hymn "Amazing Grace." The gravediggers moved in after that and began shoveling soil into the grave pit. The dull thump of the clods hitting the coffin lid was a most depressing sound after the uplifting notes of the song we'd just sung. Henry went to Mrs. Tripp and told her that a collection had been taken up in Concord to pay for her husband's burial and a mourners' repast at the Sun Tavern. She seemed much relieved to hear it.

When our group arrived at the Sun, the men went directly to the taproom, and Mrs. Ruggles ushered us women, along with little Billy, into the ladies' parlor. Festoons of fresh balsam fir, smelling of strawberries, hung from the rafters, and delftware pots of ferns and ivies were displayed on the mantelpiece and polished tabletops. The windows were graced with stiffly starched curtains. Observing our appreciative glances, Mrs. Ruggles beamed.

"No tobacco or nasty spitboxes allowed in here!" she declared proudly. "That goes for dogs too." But apparently it did not go for parrots. When one flew into the parlor, making us gasp, Mrs. Ruggles clapped her hands in delight. "Here is my Roos come to be greeting you ladies," she said.

The parrot, no doubt the very creature I'd agreed to paint, made dreadful screeching sounds as it swooped around our heads, and I for one was thankful I had not yet removed my bonnet. Mrs. Ruggles was greatly amused by Roos's performance, and so was Billy. He had been solemn and silent during the burial service, but now he hooted with laughter.

"Come to Mama, Roos," Mrs. Ruggles said and patted her

upper arm. The bird did as bid, sinking its talons into Mrs. Ruggles's sloping shoulder. "Please to be sitted," she told us, gesturing to a large round table covered with a spotless white cloth and set with pretty, rose-patterned crockery. "I bring to you refreshments."

She returned shortly thereafter (sans Roos I was happy to see), carrying a tole tray laden with glass tumblers, a painted jug containing cold lemonade, and a heaping plate of what she called Dutch pancakes but looked like French crêpes to me. She offered to bring us a decanter of spiced wine too, or perhaps a plate of meats, but cautioned that it would cost extra. I would not have minded a dram of wine splashed in my lemonade, but since none of the others spoke up, neither did I.

After Mrs. Ruggles left us, we all remained silent for a moment or two, and simply regarded Mrs. Tripp with sympathy. She did not seem inclined to eat or drink anything, so neither did we. Billy, however, dug right into a portion of pancakes and slurped up two tumblers of lemonade. When Mrs. Thoreau congratulated him on his fine appetite, he declared that his big brother Jared could eat twice as much as he and twice as fast. He then proceeded to tell us that Jared had set off for Ohio.

"He left two weeks ago, so I expect he's already there," Mrs. Tripp said, speaking up for the first time. She pressed her napkin to Billy's mouth. "Don't talk with your mouth full, honey."

Billy wrinkled his snub nose and twisted away from his mother. But it seemed he was done talking and went back to eating. For a child under four feet tall, he truly had an amazing appetite.

"Food can be a great comfort during times of loss," Mrs. Thoreau said. "Poor dear boy, to lose his father so suddenly."

"He weren't my father!" Billy shouted, ejecting pancake bits as he spoke.

Once again Mrs. Tripp pressed her napkin to his mouth,

more firmly this time. "I told you to mind your manners, son. And since you can't, you must leave the table. Go wait for me on the Green." Billy seemed more than happy to comply and ran out of the room without a fare-thee-well to any of us. Mrs. Tripp looked about the table sheepishly. "I am sorry for my boy's rude behavior, but he is only ten."

"I should like to meet a boy who *wasn't* rude at that age," Mrs. Thoreau said, and we all smiled and relaxed.

The conversation lagged, however, for none of us really knew Mrs. Tripp or her husband. Usually Lidian Emerson can find apt things to say to anyone in any situation, but today she was uncharacteristically quiet. Neither of the Thoreau sisters are great talkers, nor am I much good at chitchat, and Mrs. Tripp's neighbor seemed content to remain attentively mute. So it was left to Mrs. Thoreau to fill in the gaps of silence. Fortunately, Henry's mother has a real gift for gab and a most sociable nature. And she deliberately kept to general topics of the blandest, most uncontroversial nature. For instance, knitting.

"Your shawl has a very interesting leaf pattern, Mrs. Tripp," she commented. "I have never seen one such as that before."

Mrs. Tripp managed a smile. "Why, thank you kindly for noticing it, Mrs. Thoreau. I concocted the pattern myself."

She adjusted the dapple-gray shawl about her narrow shoulders and proceeded to describe the intricacies of knitting such a garment. As she went on about purling stitches together and skipping and slipping them, I own I had to clamp my teeth together to stifle a yawn. It occurred to me that Mrs. Tripp was as naturally loquacious as Mrs. Thoreau, and her long, solemn silence had been brought about by circumstances rather than inclination.

"It is a most difficult pattern to execute," she blithely continued, "and I made sure to try it out on a smaller article first. I knitted myself a neckerchief in the same leaf design, and I must say it came out quite well. But Mr. Tripp did not approve of the color. He told me I was far too old to be sporting a neckerchief of such a bright red. So I gave it away to a young woman who was embarking on a long journey and had need for a warm scarf. And just as well that I did, for I'll be wearing widow's weeds from now on. I only wish I had kept those I wore to mourn my first husband. Now I'll have to buy a new crape hat and a weeping veil and dye all my clothes black. Even this shawl."

Dyeing her lovely shawl black seemed to be the last straw that Mrs. Tripp could bear, for she began to weep most plangently. We all did our best to comfort her but to no avail. She left with her neighbor soon thereafter, intent on fetching Billy and going home.

"Well, now we can talk more freely," Sophia Thoreau said as soon as they were gone.

Her sister, Helen, nodded. "Best not to bring up the Underground Railroad in front of people who may be unsympathetic."

"Yes, Mrs. Tripp seems most unsympathetic," I said.

"I was referring to Mrs. Tripp's *neighbor*," Helen said. "We don't know where she stands in regard to abolition. But we have been informed by people we trust that Mrs. Tripp is a fervent abolitionist. She and her first husband were most active in the UGRR back in Ohio, and when she removed here with her second husband, she convinced him to become active in it too."

"I am amazed to hear it," I said. "Upon first meeting Mrs. Tripp, I got the impression that she was completely against Mr. Tripp's activities as a Railroad Conductor."

"Perhaps that was the impression she wished to give you because you were a stranger to her. My daughters and I were also most circumspect with you upon first meeting, if you recall," Mrs. Thoreau said. "It goes against my nature to be so reticent, yet the nature of what we do demands it. But now that I can speak freely, Julia dear, I wish to express my admiration of your resolute actions the other night. Henry told me how you prevented Mr. Cooper from being arrested and conducted him and his family to Acton. You did well!" She reached across the table and gave my hand a hearty squeeze.

Mrs. Ruggles returned to the parlor then, to inquire if we were in need of anything more to eat or drink. We said we were not, and she made a joke about Roos eating more than we did. She began clearing the table, making it plain that she did not wish us to linger, and we left her to her task.

The stage to Concord was waiting in front of the tavern, and I shook hands with Mrs. Thoreau and her two daughters in parting. When I then took Lidian Emerson's long, cool hand, I held onto it and inquired softly if she was ailing.

"Oh, I am well enough," she told me. "Considering." I gave her a questioning look, and she pulled me aside as the Thoreau ladies boarded the stage. "I am leaving for Plymouth later today with my children. It will be best for all concerned."

"I do not understand, Lidian."

"Nor do I," she murmured in a low voice. "I am very confused. When I married Mr. Emerson I vowed to devote my every waking hour to him. And I have done so for thirteen years. But over these last nine months, I fear another man has begun to replace my husband in my children's affections and in my very own heart."

Had she not seen this coming when she asked Henry to leave his beloved cabin on Walden Pond and move into the Emerson home whilst her husband traveled abroad? Perhaps not, I thought, regarding her pale, virtuous countenance. If ever there were a saint in human form, it was Lidian Emerson. But human she was, and so was Henry.

"I have no wise counsel to offer you," I told her, "for it seems I am incapable of behaving wisely myself when it comes to matters of the heart."

Mrs. Emerson nodded. "I confess you have always seemed to me too impetuous, Julia. But now I better understand how strong emotions, even when they are misplaced, can sweep one into the most impulsive and wayward of actions. My only recourse is to flee from the temptation. I shall not return to Concord until my husband comes back in August."

"Poor Henry," I said, for I knew how much he cared for Lidian and her three children.

"Henry will be fine," Lidian said most firmly. "He is the most self-reliant man alive." With that she hurried to the waiting stagecoach.

ADAM

Friday, May 19

After Ezra Tripp's burial we men separated from the ladies and settled at a table in the Sun taproom. No longer concerned about offending female sensibilities, the other men felt free to ask Henry and me to divulge the gory details of Tripp's ruthless murder. Although they were all active in the Cause, and two were Conductors in the Railroad, we deflected their questions and revealed nothing to them. We have always made it our policy whilst investigating murder to tell others as little as possible.

Conversation turned to more agreeable topics and everyone relaxed, leaning back in their chairs or forward on their elbows. The Sun may well be one of the most comfortable spots on earth, cool in the summer and toasty in the winter, and smelling most pleasantly of pipes and cigars, leather and whale oil, strong beer and stray dogs. Fortunately Edda Ruggles, despite all her cleaning, has not managed to eradicate these familiar taproom odors. Instead, thanks to her, delicious aromas emanating from the Sun's kitchen now mingle with them.

As Mrs. Ruggles bustled around us, slamming down platters of sausage and pancakes, there came from behind the nearby bar a loud grunt. We turned to see a heavy keg of ale rise into view, held up on Ruggles's thick shoulder by his burly arm. His bald, gleaming head then appeared as he reached the last of the stairs from the storeroom below. He carefully let the keg slip down off his shoulder onto the shelf behind the bar, changed the storage bung for a spigot plug, turned the keg on its side, poured himself a frothy draft, downed it in one long, delicious gulp, and turned to face us. He was sweating profusely.

"Lugging up kegs will be the death of me yet," he cheerfully announced.

Mrs. Ruggles released an exasperated sigh. "I tell him to have built to go up and down a *Speiseaufzug.*"

"She means a dumbwaiter," Ruggles said, "like they have in those fancy Boston hotels. But who could I find around here to build one for me? I've been warned by other taverners that if such a contraption is installed improperly, it is sure to get stuck and sit idle thereafter."

"They're right," Henry said. "The pulleys and guides will likely become tangled, jamming the platform. Furthermore, the heavy frame must move within the shaft with measured exactitude, else it will either wedge tight or pull itself apart."

Ruggles raised his shaggy eyebrows as he listened to Henry. "Sounds like you know what you're talking about."

"Henry usually does," I said. "Among other things, he is both a mechanic and a carpenter."

"Is that so?" Ruggles regarded Henry with an interest he'd never shown him hitherto. The few times Henry had come into the Sun before today had been to fetch me away from it, and he has never bought so much as a small beer from Ruggles. "You ever built a dumbwaiter before, young feller?"

"No," Henry said. "But I've built far more complicated contraptions for our family pencil manufactory."

Ruggles beckoned him over to the bar. "Will you be so kind as to take a look at my storeroom space?"

Henry left the table, went behind the bar, peered down the hatch, and then stomped down the stairs. We all waited with interest until he came up again.

"Well?" Ruggles said. "Could you install a dumbwaiter down there?"

"Easily," Henry said.

Ruggles slapped his palm on the bar. "Do so then! I will feed and house you whilst you work and pay you a fair price."

I expected Henry to refuse the offer outright, for he does not like to encumber himself with worldly obligations beyond his family's business. He greatly values his free hours and prefers to spend them in writing or contemplation when he is not spending them with Lidian Emerson and her children. He has been settled at the Emerson house since September last, and I much doubted he would want to remove himself to the Sun Tavern for even a brief stay. So it rather surprised me when he told Ruggles he would think on it.

I gave him a quizzical look when he returned to the table, but his own interest was taken up by a big-hatted man coming into the taproom. It was none other than Shiloh Prouty. His boots were muddy and his pants dotted with burrs, so he must have been scouring the countryside after his slave Tansy. He looked bushed as he took out from his pocket the daguerreotype of her and began to walk from table to table, showing the picture and asking if anyone had seen her. He glanced toward our table and wisely chose not to approach it.

Ruggles watched Prouty a moment and shook his head. "I'm letting him sleep in the barn with his horse, for he cannot afford a room."

"You should not allow a slave hunter to stay anywhere on your premises," I said.

"So Edda tells me," Ruggles said. "But I cannot help but

take pity on the poor hangdog. What a dark cloud he has over his head."

"That is just his over-large hat." I had no sympathy whatsoever for Prouty. And I was eager to get to Boston to find proof that would make a liar of him and place him in Plumford the night of Tripp's murder. So clearly could I envision Prouty shooting Tripp in the chest with his rifle and then chasing after his slave through the bog that I might as well have been there to witness it.

Before Henry and I left for Boston, however, I wanted to see to my patient Jerome Haven, and I had brought my bag along with me to the Sun for that express purpose. I left the taproom and went up to the Quaker's chamber, where I found him sitting up in bed, tossing playing cards across the room toward his upturned black felt hat on the floor. He was grasping a bottle of brandy in his other hand.

"Helps pass the time and deal with the pain," he said when he saw my stunned look.

"How can you claim to be a Quaker?" I said.

Haven bowed his head. "I do not claim to be a *good* one. May the Lord forgive me, for I cannot help myself. I suffer from dipsomania."

When I'd practiced in Boston I'd treated a few patients with this uncontrollable craving for drink, and I took pity on Haven. The only cure I knew for dipsomania was total abstinence, but I did not think this a good time for my poor patient to suffer through alcohol withdrawal given his leg injury. Therefore I only cautioned him to not drink so much that he would poison himself.

"Oh, I am rationing myself most carefully," he assured me. "I have a very limited amount of cash with me, and once that runs out, the innkeeper's wife will not bring me any more brandy. She has made that clear enough."

I considered asking him to settle his bill with me before

spending all his money on booze but could not bring myself to ask for payment at that particular moment. I checked his wound, which was still draining, and changed the dressing.

"You must stay off that leg," I advised him.

To make sure he did, at least for the moment, I began to gather up the cards on the floor that he had tossed to his hat. As I was doing so Henry came to the room to ask how long I would be. He was anxious to get to Boston. I introduced him to Haven, Henry wished him a speedy recovery, and off we went to the Concord station. I had just enough time to stable Napoleon before the Boston train pulled into the depot.

Henry and I boarded a car and settled in seats by an open window. The warm spring air washed past us as the train sped down the track, and white puffs of smoke from the belching smokestack blew downwind and away from us. We reached Boston in an hour, a trip that used to take three hours by coach no more than four years ago. People used to say of the railroad that nobody could live for a minute agoing at such speed. But now we have all grown accustomed to traveling so fast and only wish to go faster still.

From the Causeway Street terminal in Boston it was but a ten-minute walk to Beacon Hill's North Slope, where several thousand free Negroes have formed a close-knit community. As we walked through this neighborhood I observed that we were being regarded with suspicion by the other pedestrians, who were for the most part Negroes.

"They think we may be slave catchers," Henry told me. "Such men have come right into houses and businesses here and snatched out escaped slaves. They've even taken away free Negroes to sell in the South. The Vigilant Committee was formed by local residents to safeguard the neighborhood, and a constant watch is kept."

Henry suggested that we separate in order to make the most efficient use of our time. He would go to a Brattle Street clothes shop owned by his friend John P. Coburn, who was a leading Negro abolitionist, and I would go to a barbershop on Howard Street. The owner, John Smith, made his business a place where runaway slaves could find safe refuge and be moved along the Underground Railroad. We agreed to meet at the corner of Joy and Cambridge Streets in an hour.

As I walked along Joy Street I glanced across the street and was taken by the familiar appearance of a robust Negress treading the cobblestones with a bold, determined step. She was none other than Tansy, the young woman in the daguerreotype that Prouty had showed us! Pleased to have come across her so easily, I hastened toward her. She saw my approach and hurried away down to Cambridge Street with me not far behind.

I realized I had frightened her but had no course but to follow. On Cambridge Street I near lost her in the press of shoppers, workmen, boys hawking news sheets, and pigs darting about for scraps. To make matters worse, the first parasols of spring were out to shield the ladies against the warm sun, and the bobbing domes blocked my vision.

I increased my pace and Tansy, looking back, saw me coming closer. She darted across Cambridge, dodging fearlessly between handcarts, wagons, gigs, and horsemen. I followed as best I could and glimpsed her disappearing into a dry goods store. It did not take me but a moment to reach and enter the store. The black man behind the counter scowled at me as I approached him. Before I could say a word he ordered me to get out in a commanding tone.

I was on the point of explaining myself when I felt a powerful whack against the back of my neck. I staggered, fell onto a stack of flour sacks, and looked up to see Tansy standing over me, a broom raised to strike again. I rolled away from the blow, and the handle thudded on a soft sack instead, splitting it open. Tansy threw down the broom and ran out the door as I struggled to my feet. The moment I righted myself the shopkeeper leapt over the counter and gripped me by the lapels of my frock coat. I managed to free myself, snatch up my flour-dusted hat, and stumble out of the store just in time to see Tansy run back up Cambridge.

I admit that my hackles were now up, and I rushed after Tansy, determined to catch her and explain myself. She turned and ran into the barbershop on Howard Street, the very place I had been headed before I'd spotted her. When I entered after her I was grabbed by a pair of massive black hands and thrown with such violence to the floor the wind was knocked clear from my sails. As I gasped and tried to speak, a rag was stuffed into my mouth, and I was roughly raised up. A deep voice muttered in my ears that I deserved to die like the rabid dog I was. My arms were held so tight behind my back I felt they were near to being dislocated from my shoulders.

"Easy with him, Cato," another man cautioned. "We won't get much out of a feller with his bones all broken."

"He come chasing after my wife, Mr. Smith!" this Cato brute said in his own defense, easing slightly his vise grip.

"Rose, tell us what happened," the middle-aged black man addressed as Mr. Smith said evenly. He wore a white apron tied around his waist, and above his black waistcoat and starched shirt, his face radiated both intelligence and wariness.

The woman he called Rose (and who I believed to be Tansy) cast both fearful and angry looks at me. Her dark brown face was damp from her exertions to stay out of my clutches.

"I saw him staring at me too close," she said. "So I started walking away, and sure enough he came snuffling after me like a bloodhound. Faster I went, faster he did too. I couldn't lose him. So I came running here."

"Nobody with a scrap of sense is going to try and just haul a Negro from this neighborhood in broad daylight anymore,"

Mr. Smith said. "That's why I can't figure out what this one was up to." He pointed a long straight razor at me that still bore flecks of shaving cream on its gleaming edge. His deep-set eyes held more curiosity than hate as he observed me, although there was no respect in his regard either. "Could be he's just dumb as a bag of hair."

I cared not for Smith's observation nor the unjust rough treatment from Cato. I could only manage to breathe in short, wheezing gasps around the gag that near choked me.

"Set him down in the chair, Cato," Smith said, and I was summarily dumped down in the leather seat like a sack of potatoes with the three of them looking down at me.

"There ain't nothing more low-down than trying to kidnap a free Negro to sell to a slave trader," Cato said to me, his voice quivering with emotion. "And my wife is free as any white woman."

"My husband bought me my freedom last year," Rose/Tansy added. She extracted a lace-trimmed handkerchief from her sleeve and reached up to gently wipe shaving cream off one side of Cato's glowering face.

"Must have caulked the sides of fifty cargo and whaling hulls down in the shipyards to earn enough to buy Rose from her owner," Cato said to me. "And now you come along to try and steal her away!" I shook my head in the negative and made protesting sounds through my gag to no avail. Cato turned to Smith. "Let me deal with this bastard. When I'm through with him he won't be trying to steal our black women no more."

"Best we have the Vigilant Committee decide what to do with him when we meet this evening," Smith said. "Meanwhile, we will make sure our slave catcher don't get away." He walked to a box in the corner of the shop and pulled out shackles that he dangled in front of me. "I got these from another slave catcher before he could use them on one of us. We will now give you a taste of your own medicine and see how you like it. Chain him up, Cato. We will lay him in the space below my chair for the time being."

As Cato locked the heavy iron shackles round my wrists and ankles there came over me a revolting sense of helplessness that near made me ill. I struggled with every muscle of my body and yelled out against my gag to no avail. Smith then took from the box a metal plate of perhaps four inches round with several lengths of light chain attached.

"You keep to hollering," he said, "and I will lock this plate round your head to shut you up. It goes tight against your mouth and nose so if you ain't careful you'll drown in your own drool. You understand? Yes, I see the fear in your eyes. It is not a pretty prospect, is it? But I will do it to you if need be. It's been done to thousands of us. So why should I spare you?"

I stared with disbelief and revulsion at this medieval apparatus of torture. To be so shackled and then have that device tightened against one's face! I could see that instrument alone might drive a man mad. I made not another sound, and Smith put down the plate. But then he bound tight my arms and legs with rope.

Cato slid the heavy barber's chair to one side and lifted out several wide planks. I stared down into a space small as a child's coffin, and there I was stuffed, forced to lie curled up on my side like a fetus in the womb. The floor boards were replaced not six inches over my head, and I heard the chair being slid back over me. I could see a bit of light out of the edge of one eye.

I heard Smith and Cato and Rose talking in low, muffled tones, and then there was silence. I know not how long I lay there until I was suddenly roused out of my troubled, dazed condition by a familiar voice. It was Henry's voice! He greeted Smith most cordially and was greeted the same way in return.

"It is very good to see you again, Mr. Thoreau," Smith said. "What brings you here today?"

"I am looking for Dr. Walker," Henry replied. "He didn't show up where we had arranged to meet, and I hoped to find him still here."

I struggled against my bonds with all my might and moaned and groaned loud as I could through my gag. I became quickly exhausted as I could barely breathe. I heard the voices over me continue without pause.

"*Here?*" Smith said. "I do not understand. I have never heard of this Dr. Walker."

"He didn't come here to ask you questions concerning a fugitive?"

"No. What concern is this fugitive to you?"

"Dr. Walker and I wish to find her and help her." Henry said. A brief pause. "Who is that young woman standing over there?"

I heard the tread of heavy boots cross the room. "Why you asking about my wife, mister?"

"She looks familiar to me."

"The hell she does! Why all this interest in my wife today by white men?"

"Cato, stop talking," Smith said. "Rose, would you please come here?" I heard lighter footsteps. "This is Mrs. Davis, Mr. Thoreau."

"And I am *Mister* Davis," Cato said. "Me and my missus are both free, and we got papers to prove it. That's all you or any white man need know about us, so best you get the hell out of here."

"No need for such rudeness, Cato," Smith said. "Mr. Thoreau and his family work on the Underground Railroad."

"I hear tell there are plenty of spies on the Railroad," Cato said.

"Well, I am not one of them," Henry said. "I am here out of concern for Mrs. Davis's twin sister."

"She ain't got a sister!" Cato shouted.

"Hush up now, dear," Rose/Tansy told him. "Let's hear Mr. Thoreau out."

"Your sister's name is Tansy," Henry continued, "and she is fleeing from a man called Shiloh Prouty. He is presently in Plumford looking for her."

In the long silence that followed I made another effort to be heard through my gag. The sound I produced was most feeble, but it has been said that Henry can hear as with an ear trumpet.

"Whoever is under your floorboards, Mr. Smith," Henry continued calmly, "seems to be protesting his interment, so I do not think you are hiding a runaway slave."

"Just the opposite of one," Smith replied.

"Ain't none of your damn business who's under there," Cato said.

"Indeed it is not," Henry easily agreed. "Unless, that is, he is a tallish, youngish fellow with brownish hair and bluish eyes and . . . if I recall correctly, a cravat of a greenish color. If this matches the description of the poor fellow you have stowed down there, then it is very much my business. For I have just described my friend Dr. Adam Walker, and I will not leave here without him."

Another long pause. Perhaps they were trying to stare Henry down, which cannot be done. "Show him our prisoner, Cato," Smith finally said. "Members of the Vigilant Committee trust Mr. Thoreau, and we should trust him, too."

The barber's chair was slid aside, the boards pulled up, and I saw Henry's face appear above me. He put his hand down on my shoulder. "Well, Adam, 'tis no wonder you did not meet me on time. I see that you got all tied up."

If that was meant for humor it got not a chuckle out of me. I was hoisted out of that coffin-space, unbound, sat down in the barber's chair, and dusted clean, all the time receiving many sincere words of apology from the three Negroes.

"Oh, Dr. Walker is fine. He's had far rougher treatment than you gave him and managed to survive it," Henry cavalierly assured them. He turned to Rose. "I would like you to tell us about your twin sister, Mrs. Davis. The more we know, the more we can help her."

"Help her? Has she met with a mishap on her journey to Canada?"

"I can better answer that if you tell me how she came to be on that journey."

Rose nodded and proceeded to tell us her and Tansy's history. They had been raised up together in Portsmouth, Virginia, in the small but comfortable home of their kindly owner, Miss Prouty. The elderly spinster treated them almost like daughters, even taught them how to read, write, and cipher although it was against state law to do so. And they always did their best by her too. When Miss Prouty fell on hard times, Rose and Tansy took in laundry and mending to keep a roof over their dear mistress's head. And when Miss Prouty needed expensive medical treatment they hired themselves out to make sails and ships' colors at the Gosport navy yard to pay for it. It was there that Rose met Cato, a slave shipwright who eventually managed to earn enough money to purchase his freedom. When he left Virginia for higher wages up North, he promised Rose he would one day marry her.

Miss Prouty made her own promise. To thank her beloved twins for all their care, she told them she would give them their freedom in her will. But she did not. Instead she bequeathed Rose to her brother and Tansy to her nephew Shiloh. They were the only property of any value Miss Prouty owned. Cato managed to make enough money at a Boston shipyard to buy Rose from Miss Prouty's brother, and a year or so later, he and Rose earned enough together to buy Tansy from Shiloh Prouty.

"But he refused to sell her," Rose told us. "Not for all the money in the world, he told us."

"When Cato informed me of this impasse, I interceded," Mr. Smith said. "I felt justified in suggesting that if Tansy's freedom could not be bought fair and square, she would just have to take it. By way of the Underground Railroad, she made her way to Boston. She arrived here Monday last."

"How we wept for joy when we were reunited," Rose said.

"Just wouldn't stop bawling, them two," Cato added, tearing up himself at the memory.

"But Prouty was hot on her trail, and came to Boston soon after she did," Rose said. "The Vigilant Committee was quick to warn us that he was prowling round the neighborhood, and we sent Tansy off. So when Prouty finally managed to find out where we live, I let him come right in and look around our rooms as much as he wanted to."

"When did Prouty call on you?" Henry asked her.

"That's a mighty polite way of putting it. He came banging on our door in the small hours of Wednesday morn."

"Are you sure?" I said, unwilling to accept that Prouty had still been in Boston when Tripp was shot.

"Yes, I am sure of it," Rose told me irritably. It seemed she still held some resentment for the way I had unintentionally frightened her. "The sun had not come near to rising yet. Even so, he was too late. Tansy was long gone."

"She left here with Rusty on Tuesday," Smith put in. "When he got wind of her predicament, he offered to drive her to a safe Station in Plumford."

"Rusty who?" I said.

"Rusty the picture taker," Smith replied.

"He must have a last name," I pressed.

"Does John the Baptist need a last name? Or Joseph of Nazareth?"

"I believe Rusty is the alias of an Underground Railroad Conductor," Henry said. "I've never met him, but I've heard many a story regarding him."

"All true!" Smith said. "Rusty is a hero to us colored folk for sure. No one knows his real name, and he is called Rusty for his red hair and face full of red freckles. I was most proud to meet him and put Tansy in his care. He drove her to a Station in Plumford, where another Conductor would take her farther north from there."

"I heard of him even afore I come north," Rose said. "Rusty used to travel all through the Southland in that wagon of his, taking pictures of the plantation gentry in the day and then driving their slaves north to freedom in the night. Then he got found out and had to run for his life, but he is still active here in the North."

"Rusty can outfox hounds," Smith said, "and he can swim faster than men can row a boat. Once he held his breath for ten minutes underwater whilst them slave catchers paddled back and forth right above his head, looking for him. They would have strung him up if they'd caught him."

"They came near to getting him more than once," Cato added. "But that never stopped Rusty from doing what he thought was right. He was born brave."

"He was born musical too," Rose added. "It's said he can play the guitar better than an angel can play the harp."

"We asked him to play a tune afore he left with Tansy," Cato said, "but he wouldn't take the time for it. He said getting Tansy to safety was more important."

"He made time to take Tansy's likeness for me, though, bless his good heart," Rose said. "Then Prouty went and stole the picture from me when he come."

"He has been showing the picture around Plumford," I said. "I saw it myself. That's why I mistook you for her."

Rose gave me yet another withering look and turned to

Henry. "Now that we have told you how Tansy came to be in Plumford, you must tell us what has befallen her since."

Henry did so in his straightforward way, holding back nothing. And as Rose listened, her big eyes became glossy with tears. "How can you be sure Tansy did not drown in that bog?" she asked him.

"We searched it most exhaustively," Henry reassured her. "We think your sister may still be hiding in the area, but if she is, Prouty will eventually find her. The man seems most resolute to get back his property."

"Tansy is far more than that to him," Rose said. "And I pity her for it. It is a black woman's curse to be loved by her white owner. What good can come of it?" Tears spilled from Rose's eyes and ran down her full, smooth cheeks.

"Tansy is going to make out just fine, honey," Cato told her. "She's smart just like you and strong just like you." He pulled Rose against his broad chest and wrapped his mighty arms around her. After experiencing his death-like grip, I was astounded by his gentleness.

Henry drew Smith and me aside. "I have just learned from Mr. Coburn that another Conductor on the Railroad has been murdered," he told us. "His name was Ned Vogel, and he was a dedicated abolitionist who conveyed many runaways to freedom. He published a newspaper in the town of Waltham, and he was killed at his place of business in the early hours of Wednesday last."

"The very same day Tripp was killed," I said. "Surely that is more than a coincidence."

"Far more," Henry said. "A letter was slipped under Mr. Coburn's door earlier today. It declared that Underground Railroad Conductors will continue to be assassinated until they cease such activity."

My heart tightened. "Then Julia is in danger."

"I will send no runaways her way until we put an end to this danger, I assure you," Henry promised me.

"A warning must be dispatched along every line counseling extreme caution," Smith said.

"Yes, by all means," Henry said. "But we cannot allow ourselves to be intimidated, through fear, into submission."

"Was Vogel shot down like Tripp?" I asked Henry.

"The letter gave no details. We must go to Waltham to find out more. I volunteered your assistance along with my own in investigating this matter for Mr. Coburn, Adam. I hope you do not mind."

"Of course not! This assassin must be run to ground before he kills again."

We left straightaway and caught the next train to Waltham, just up the Fitchburg line from Boston. As soon as we'd settled in our seats Henry took a folded piece of paper from his jacket pocket.

"Here is the missive Mr. Coburn received. I asked if I might have it to analyze." He handed it to me. "There is something I noticed right off and would like your opinion on it, Doctor. Observe the very small brown smudge in the left-hand bottom corner."

I opened the letter and held it up to the car window. "Oh, yes. I see it."

"Is it blood?"

"It could be." I sniffed the stain. "It smells like chaulmoogra."

"Chaulmoogra," Henry repeated. He liked the sound of Indian words. "What is that?"

"A very foul-tasting, foul-smelling oil used to treat Leprosy and various skin conditions," I said. "Some doctors even use it to treat Consumption."

"Do you see any other physical evidence?" Henry said.

When I shook my head he urged me to look more carefully at the letter's bottom fold.

"There's a slight green tinge running along it," I said, finally managing to discern it. "As if from a light dusting of green powder."

"Yes," Henry said. "What could that be, do you think?"

"Pollen?" I suggested.

"Perhaps, for there is certainly enough of that in the air of late. But can you think of anything of a more medical nature?"

"Tobacco leaves in powder form," I said, "are sometimes used to relieve the catarrh."

"Hence the letter writer might be a consumptive, a leper, or a sufferer of phlegm," Henry remarked sardonically.

"More likely a doctor dosing patients with such oils and powders," I said.

"What think you of the penmanship?"

"Quite grandiose," I said, observing the bold strokes and curlicues.

"The sentiments expressed are also grandiose." Henry's tone was scornful. "Go ahead and read the letter."

I read it three times over with great care, and here it is to the best of my recollection:

I have been sent to destroy the spider's web of wrongdoers who flaunt justice by aiding escaped slaves to flee from their Rightful Owners.

At the behest of certain Propertied & Honorable Gentlemen of the South I am come to derail the Underground Railroad. I possess a list of the Conductors of this illegitimate network. May what I did to Vogel serve as a warning for all the others. I will continue to eradicate these Outlaws, until enough are slain for the survivors to see their certain fate at my hands and cease their illegal activities.

See the light of reason, quit any and all assistance to escaped slaves, and your lives will be spared.

The Hand of Justice

"So we are up against an assassin hired by a band of slave owners," I said to Henry, handing back the letter, which I found repulsive to hold.

"Worse yet, he sounds as if he believes his mission to be a messianic one," Henry said. "There is nothing more relentless than self-righteous egotism."

When we arrived in Waltham we were directed to Vogel's newspaper office at the edge of town. No one was operating the press on the first floor, and we went upstairs to the office. The door to it was locked. We looked through the glass panel, and a stoop-shouldered old man wearing thick glasses looked back at us from across the room. He made no move to come forward, and Henry shouted out who we were and why we had come. He finally walked over to the door and unlocked it. He introduced himself as Mr. Vogel's chief assistant, Tom Baker.

"You must understand my caution," Mr. Baker said in a thin, strained voice. "Before Ned was murdered this door was open to one and all. But now I am afraid the man who killed him may return. Yet I feel it is my duty to get out this issue of the *Gazette* in honor of its esteemed editor and publisher, and I came here directly after his burial today. May poor Ned rest in peace." His voice choked, and he turned away to collect himself.

We looked around the office. An open window let in a breeze but did not dispel the heavy scent of printer's ink. There were cases of type, composing sticks, cutters, type saws, bodkins, tweezers, forms of type, and stacks of proof sheets scattered on benches along one wall, and against the other wall was a large desk.

Mr. Baker turned back to us. "I shall never forget the sight of him there." He pointed toward the desk. "Every detail is pressed into my mind like molten type metal into a mold."

"Were you the one to find his body?" Henry said.

"I was right downstairs when he was murdered!"

"Then you heard the gun go off," I said, assuming Vogel had been shot like Tripp.

Mr. Baker shook his head and continued to recount what had happened in his own methodical fashion. "As I was saying, I was working the press downstairs and caught a glimpse of someone going by the open door and up the stairs around midnight. That is not unusual. We work quite late to get out the paper, and people bring stories and advertisements at any hour of the day or night. I thought maybe that was the case, and decided to go upstairs to see if Ned wanted any additions to the page I was setting up to print. As I entered the office I saw a man jumping out the window. I hurried to the window and watched him tumble down the slope and disappear into the trees. You can see for yourself how steep it is in back."

Henry and I went to the window. The slope below plunged into the woods and was indeed very steep. The drop from the window to the ground was a good twenty feet.

"Did you notice anything particular about the man that would help identify him?" Henry asked Baker.

"Well, he was slender. Can't say how tall he was. He was dressed in dark clothes."

"Did you see his face?"

"No. His slouch hat was jammed on his head most securely, for it didn't fall off even as he rolled head over heels down the slope. He appeared very nimble."

"Would you say he was a young man?" Henry said.

"Sure as heck wasn't an old one like me," Baker said irritably. "Are you going to keep interrupting or let me get on with it? I already told all this to the constable and then to the Coroner's Jury, and it ain't easy on me to be telling it again. So I'd just as soon get it done with."

"Pray go on," Henry said.

"I turned back to the room and looked toward Ned's desk.

He was slumped forward in his chair, his head down on the desk like he was taking a nap. He often did that. He'd just lay his head down, take himself forty winks, and then be bright as a button again. I went over to him and . . . oh, dear, oh, dear, oh, dear." Baker pulled out a checkered handkerchief from his trousers pocket and blew his nose.

Henry and I went over to the desk, and Baker joined us. He smoothed his palm across the polished surface of mahogany veneer. "Cleaned up good, didn't it?" he said. "But I couldn't get the bloodstains out of the floor."

I looked down and saw a dark, irregular stain at least a yard in circumference on the pine boards. "There must have been a great deal of blood," I said.

"Oh, my, yes!" Baker said. "It was sliding off the edge of the desk and dripping down onto the floor. I thought at first Ned had gotten punched in the nose and had a real bad nosebleed. 'Put your head back, Ned!' I yelled at him. But he didn't budge. I figured maybe he was unconscious, so I placed my hands against his ears and pulled his head back for him. Oh, dear, oh, dear, oh, dear." Out came the handkerchief again.

Neither Henry nor I said anything. We just waited this time.

Baker cleared his throat. "When I pulled back Ned's head I found myself looking into his slit-open throat. I could see down to the base of his skull! I screamed and stepped back, letting go of his head, and it flopped backward and dangled over the back of the chair. It was still attached to his body, but just hanging there by his neck bone. His eyes were wide open. Dead eyes staring at me upside down. I kept on screaming all the way to the constable's house."

"Was a weapon found?"

"No," Baker said. "The constable and his boys combed for it everywhere. Not just the office, but beneath the window and down into the woods. They found nothing."

"What did the neck cut look like?" I asked Baker.

"It looked horrible!"

"I am sure it did. But was the cut jagged or clean?"

"As clean as when my wife slices cheese with a wire," Baker said.

"What conclusion did the Coroner's Jury reach?" Henry asked him.

"That Ned was murdered, of course. Death by near decapitation."

"Was any speculation made concerning the type of murder weapon used?"

"They concluded it was a very sharp knife indeed."

Henry turned to me. "Could a length of wire wrapped around the neck and clinched from behind slice clean through it?"

"If sufficient force is brought to bear, it could be done in short order," I said.

Mr. Baker gave us the name of the coroner, who was also a doctor, and we went to interview him at his office. Dr. Hamilton was in the process of dry cupping a patient and had us wait outside on the porch as he performed what I myself consider a useless procedure. When Dr. Hamilton joined us on the porch, he gave us less than five minutes of his free time. He described in professional detail how the tissue, muscle, nerves, arteries, and veins of the neck had been cleanly severed, but he thought Henry's hypothesis that Mr. Vogel had been garroted with a wire ridiculous. His own hypothesis was that the killer had used a scalpel.

Once again Henry and I took the rail cars, this time back to Concord. We discussed what we had heard and concluded that if Vogel had been murdered near midnight, the assassin would have had ample time to get himself to Plumford and shoot Tripp a few hours before dawn.

"Unfortunately, we have no suspect now that Prouty's alibi has been confirmed," I said.

As our train clattered along we both got lost in our own contemplations concerning what we had heard. We were both pretty down.

"Tell me more about that Quaker imposter," Henry finally said.

"You think Haven is not what he claims to be?"

"Since when does a Quaker drink liquor and amuse himself with gambling cards?"

"Haven readily admitted to me that he could not follow the tenets of his faith because he has an unmanageable weakness for drink," I said.

"Is Haven his first or last name?"

"His last. He never actually introduced himself to me, but according to Sam Ruggles, the name he signed in the registry book was Jerome Haven."

"Do you know when he arrived at the tavern?"

"Before dawn Wednesday morning."

"How was he dressed?"

"In simple Quaker attire, a black coat and trousers, along with the traditional Wideawake Hat."

"It is easy enough to steal a hat from a Quaker," Henry said.

"Haven may indeed be trying to deceive with such a disguise," I allowed. "Beneath his somber outer attire he was wearing red stockings. He surely didn't steal those from a Quaker."

"Vogel's killer was also dressed all in black and wearing a wide-brimmed hat," Henry said. "Now tell me about Haven's leg injury."

I described the wound and how Haven claimed he had acquired it.

"Would it not be more likely to sustain such an injury jumping from a second-story window and tumbling into the woods than by falling off a horse?" Henry said.

"Far more likely," I said.

"Did Haven give a reason for traveling in the night?"

"He told Ruggles he was on his way to a Quaker community in Amesbury."

"I wager no one at that community has ever heard of Jerome Haven," Henry said. "I'll write a letter of inquiry to the pastor as soon as I get settled at the Sun tonight."

"You intend to stay at the tavern?"

"I intend to keep a close eye on this Haven, and the best way to do that is to accept Ruggles's request to construct a dumbwaiter for him." Henry smiled at me. "Why do you look so surprised, my friend? I could possibly sit out the sturdiest frequenter of the barroom, if my business called me thither."

"No doubt you could," I said. "But I am sure you will be missed in Concord."

Henry's smile disappeared. "Lidian left Concord with her children today to stay with friends in Plymouth, so I will not be missed at all."

JULIA

When I parted with Lidian and the Thoreau ladies after our repast at the Sun, I went to my studio and tried my hand at drawing Edda Ruggles's parrot. I could not concentrate. My thoughts kept going back to the red neckerchief I'd seen in Granny Tuttle's root cellar yesterday. I'd assumed Harriet had dropped it. But if it were the neckerchief Mrs. Tripp had knitted, it would most likely have been dropped by the runaway slave. Hoping it remained on the cellar shelf where I'd left it, I set off for Tuttle Farm.

All the way there I kept my eyes peeled for signs of the runaway. If she were hiding in the vicinity of the farm, that would explain the disarray in the root cellar and the stolen eggs from Granny's henhouse. I decided not to apprise Granny or Harriet of my suspicions, however. Why concern them unnecessarily if I were wrong? For this reason I took a roundabout route to reach the root cellar so as not to be seen from the farmhouse.

When I threw open the cellar door, I must admit my heart picked up a beat in anticipation of finding the runaway inside. But of course she was not there. It had been naïve for me to think she might be. Most probably she foraged for food at night, when there were no field hands about and no expectation of being discovered by the women of the house coming into the cellar for provisions. I did find the neckerchief, however. It was just where I'd left it. I brought it out into the daylight and examined it. Same leaf pattern as Mrs. Tripp's shawl!

I asked myself where I would hide if I were a frightened fugitive slave lost in a strange land. No answer came. I went back inside the dark cellar to breathe slowly and calmly and quietly await a message from my intuition. 'Twas a trick Henry had taught me. Eventually the image of a hut with gray-weathered shingles and a lichen-spotted roof sprang into my mind. The Tuttle sugarhouse! It offered protection from the elements and had a cot with a cornhusk mattress for use during the long nights spent there boiling syrup when the sap was running. The last of the syrup had been bottled a good two months ago, so no one had reason to visit the hut now. In truth, Adam and I had reason to visit it one blissful afternoon a week or so ago, and that's why I recalled the hut's amenities.

It was located in the middle of the sugar bush on the north hill, and to reach it I had to cross a pasture that was being plowed by one of Granny's farmhands. I slowed down my pace and gave him a wave as I ambled over the furrows, as if I had nothing better to do with my time. I had forgotten to take a parasol to shield myself from the sun's rays, and it was a great relief to leave the open field and get under the shady canopy of the maple trees. The sugar bush was as quiet and cool as a cathedral. Adam once brought me here when we were children to show me a giant maple that his grandfather Tuttle had just felled. Embedded near its core were arrowheads shot several hundred years ago from an Indian bow. How I did marvel at that! And even more marvelous to me was the box Adam made for me from the bird's eye timber of that tree. When

Papa and I relocated to France the box went missing, and I wept for days over the loss.

Nearing the sugarhouse, I approached with caution, for I did not want to frighten the runaway I supposed was hiding within. I slowly pushed open the door, and as it squealed on its hinges I heard scurrying movements.

"I come as a friend," I said and walked farther inside. "I brought the red neckerchief you left in the root cellar."

A young woman of solid build stood up from where she was hiding behind a woodpile and took a few steps toward me. I recognized her to be the slave Tansy from Prouty's daguerreotype. She took the neckerchief and pressed it to her face. "I'm mighty glad to have it back. Lady who gave it to me said it would protect me from harm. And it has! I didn't get shot, and I didn't drown. Now I just need to figure out how to get to a safer place."

"I will help you," I said.

"You wouldn't be so quick to offer if you knew what happened to the last person who tried to help me, ma'am."

"I do know. The man who was conducting you to Carlisle was gunned down. He died instantaneously."

Tansy began to cry. "It happened so quick he didn't even have time to make peace with his Maker."

"Did you see who the shooter was?"

"No. I was lying under a blanket in the back of the wagon when I heard the gun go off. I jumped out and ran, never once looking back. I ran all night until I found this shack."

"Could the shooter have been the man who claims ownership of you?"

Tansy shook her head vehemently. "He would never shoot a man in cold blood."

"Who else could have been after you?"

"A vicious slave hunter is my guess."

"Thank God you got away, Tansy," I said.

She wiped the tears from her eyes and narrowed them at me. "How do you know my real name? I've used a different one on the Railroad."

"Shiloh Prouty spoke your name when he showed me a daguerreotype of you."

Tansy's eyes now widened. "Prouty is hereabouts? I thought I'd lost him for good back in Boston."

"He managed to track you to Plumford and is asking after you everywhere. Looking for you everywhere too. And sooner or later he will find you here if you stay. I found you easily enough, didn't I?"

"Why were *you* looking for me?"

I explained that my house was a Station on the Railroad and that I had helped fugitives before. "Come home with me, Tansy. I can help get you back on the track to Canada soon enough."

She stared at me intensely, sizing me up, as she considered my offer. "Where is this house of yours?" she finally asked me. "How far?"

"Not far at all. Right in town."

"How we going to parade ourselves through town without Prouty or some slave hunter grabbing me?"

"We'll wait here until dark," I said.

Tansy nodded and gestured to the cot. "Why don't you set yourself down, ma'am?"

"Very well. And please call me Julia."

"Is that what they call you on the Railroad?"

"No. But since I know your real name, you might as well know mine."

Tansy pulled a bench from the wall and sat across from me. "I never called a white woman by her first name afore." She did not sound as if she liked the idea.

"I would be pleased if you did me the honor," I told her.

She did not say if she would or she wouldn't. "How's he look?" she asked.

"Who?"

"Shiloh Prouty. Must be thin as a railbird without me around to feed him. The man can't cook a lick. Don't know how he survived afore he got me."

"He looked most gaunt," I told her.

"What about Belle?"

"Who's Belle?"

"His quarter horse. Didn't he make a point of introducing her to you? Why, Shiloh Prouty thinks more of his fine bay mare than he ever did of a woman."

"He was riding a gray nag just as skinny as he was," I told Tansy.

"What happened to Belle, I wonder." She rose from the bench and paced the small room awhile. She sat down again and regarded me. "You married?"

"Yes, I am legally bound to a man."

"You talk like you are his slave, not his wife."

"Sometimes there is little difference between the two."

"But there is all the difference in the world!" Tansy said. "Shiloh Prouty owns me like he owns an animal. He claims he *treats* me like a wife, but that is not the same as being one. A wife cannot be sold off on the auction block."

"No, but her husband owns her just the same. A married woman has no legal rights of her own."

"Then don't you need your husband's permission to take me in?"

"I don't live with him anymore. I left him back in France, and I will never return to him."

Tansy slowly smiled at me. Her teeth were as fine as any I have ever seen, as even and white as piano keys. "So we are both runaways."

I saw that she had decided to give me her complete trust.

And because of that I would have to be completely honest with her. "You should know that my husband used to be a slave trader."

Her eyes once again became wary. "That's like telling me you are Satan's wife."

"Do not damn me for it! I didn't know what manner of man Jacques Pelletier was when I married him. And learning the truth was the reason I left him."

"Most likely the reason you take in runaways, too."

Her insight impressed me. And the longer Tansy and I talked as we waited for nightfall, the more impressed I became. She was intelligent and well-read, or leastways as well-read as I was, and we shared a taste for the tales of Edgar Allan Poe and the novels of Charles Dickens. She was also far better versed in the Bible than I was and could rattle off lines from Shakespeare's plays like a thespian. It saddened me to learn that the woman who had given Tansy and her sister the precious gift of literacy had not seen fit to give them their freedom.

We set off from the sugarhouse as soon as it was dark enough. Rather than take the public road to town, I led the way down to the river, and we took the overgrown fishermen's walk that paralleled the water. It was slow going. I kept imagining footsteps behind us and turning to peer into the leafy gloom. Eventually, we came upon an old rowboat half-full of leaves and rain water that someone must have pulled up on shore a while ago and had no further use for. The oars were still in the locks!

"We're rowing the rest of the way to town," I said. "It will be safer on the river. No one can come on us unawares."

Tansy nodded and with a heave flipped the boat over to clear it of water, righted it, and shoved it into the river.

"I'll do the rowing," I said.

Tansy gave me a dubious look. "You got the strength and know-how?"

"Of course I do. Just because I'm a white female doesn't mean I'm a weak imbecile." Apparently it did to Tansy, for she did not look convinced. "And I know this river like the back of my hand," I added.

Without further protest, Tansy went and sat behind me. I took up the oars, and we set off. The full moon cast a strong light on the water, so I had no trouble rowing us to the center of the river, safely away from the shores, and keeping us there. Adam and I had often rowed and fished along the Assabet when we were children. Being a city girl, I'd lacked such skills when first I came to Plumford, but Adam had been happy to teach them to me. Despite being a most rambunctious boy, he'd had a great deal of patience with me in those days. And has so little patience with me now! I knew he would be most displeased with me when he learned that I had taken in the very runaway who might have been the cause of Mr. Tripp's death. But if Tripp had been shot by a slave hunter in order to get the reward for Tansy's capture, that was hardly the poor girl's fault.

The Assabet hereabouts flows quickly and smoothly, and as the boat glided us toward town I was enjoying the row until we saw torches moving on the water ahead.

"Men out looking for me?" Tansy said.

"Most likely men looking to spear fish," I said. "They put a pitch-pine torch in a basket out over the bow, and when fish rise to the light they spear them, or try to. Mostly millworkers and farm boys out just having fun."

"What are they going to think when they see two women on the water at night?" Tansy said.

"Maybe you should lie down so they can't see you."

"It might seem even stranger to them to see a lone woman out rowing," Tansy said. She threw the neckerchief over her head and tied it under her chin. "They can't see my color unless they get close, so let me row and you sit back here and do the talking. We are just two friends coming back late to town."

I nodded at the good sense of what she said, and we changed places. I saw right away she could row with more power than I could muster and handled the oars with a practiced ease. We came round a curve and saw two rowboats in a quiet pool where the river spread out and flowed slower. There were two men in each boat, one rowing but turned to face forward in order to better steer and watch his partner standing up in the bow with a spear. The pitch-pine torches crackled and sparked and blazed out over the water, and the light cast huge shadows of the men against the dark trees along the banks.

Each boat was patrolling the water along the opposite bank. Tansy kept our boat out in the middle and began to row hard to drive between the fishing boats and be away downstream as quick as we could.

One of the rowers saw us and stopped rowing. "Hey, ladies," he shouted in a drunken voice. "What you doing out so late? What's the hurry? Come on over. We got pigs' feet and bacon to chew on and something to wet your whistle."

"We are gettin' mighty lonely out here!" a man from the other boat shouted as he turned and began to row across the river, intending to cut us off. "Lookin' for a little adventure, are you, my girls? Why, that's what we'll give you for sure. Now, come on over here."

"No, thank you," I said in as strong and severe a tone as I could muster. Tansy rowed harder. I could feel the boat surge forward with each pull of the two oars by her strong arms. "We are just headed back to town and are late getting back to our families."

"They can wait," a man holding a spear said as his boat came toward us. The boat came on so fast that in but a moment the caged fire at the bow of their boat came driving toward the middle of our boat. It was clear the men intended to stop us and did not care a whit for our safety.

As the rowboat neared us Tansy jerked an oar from the lock and speared the wide end of the oar into the flaming pitch pine, showering blazing embers onto the chest and waist of the man balancing behind it, ready to grab at us. I saw his eyes go wide as he looked down at his shirt that went instantly ablaze. He flailed at his chest, cursed, and then dove into the water. Tansy pushed the bow of their boat away, slid the oar back into the lock, and then she pulled us away from the now shouting men. I felt a wave of relief, but then turned to see the boat from the opposite shore sliding across the current toward us. When it came alongside, the rower held up his oar and reached forward to grab our gunwale. "You think we gonna take that kind of treatment from mere women?" he said.

As his oar came at me, I quickly grabbed hold of it, stood up, and with a great heave of my legs, flipped their narrow boat right over, dousing their fire and rolling both men underwater. Tansy rowed hard, and we got clear of both boats and away. Curses were shouted after us, but we were not pursued. Once we were clear round the next bend Tansy stopped to catch her breath.

"Appears they lost the appetite for our company," she said.

A laugh of relief burst out of me. "I cannot imagine why!"

Tansy grinned. "I don't know how we could have done that better."

"I think it helped that they were liquored up to their noses," I said.

"You think they saw I was a Negro?"

"No, too much happened too fast, and I don't think they'll want to talk about how they attacked two women and got beaten by them."

As we neared town I took the oars again, for I knew just

where to pull the boat over before we got too close to the mill and the dam. I led Tansy up through the woods to the back of my house and inside. As we went we crouched and crept along in silence, and I was certain that no one caught sight of us.

Once inside the house, we hugged each other, and then, because we are "mere" women, we shed a few tears of relief.

ADAM

Saturday, May 20

Julia, once again, was not awaiting me in her bed this morning. But at least this time she was at home rather than traipsing the countryside with fugitives. When I came through the passageway that connected my office to the kitchen, I found her at the stove. That in itself was an unusual sight, for if my darling knows how to cook, she has certainly kept it from me. Yet there she was watching several eggs boil in a pot of water, and I suppose you could call that cooking. To my great disappointment, she was fully dressed.

She gave me a quick kiss on the cheek in greeting. "I am preparing breakfast for someone quite special."

"It's not that I don't appreciate the gesture," I told her, "but I'd much prefer us to be in bed together right now."

"You think I would not?" she replied archly. "I'm not cooking up these eggs for *you*, Adam. I have a guest whom I brought here under cover of night."

"Good Lord, Julia, you're not hiding another runaway?"

She nodded and removed the pot from the stove.

"I will not allow it!" I said. As soon as the words were out of my mouth, I regretted them. "Pray listen to me, my love.

Henry and I learned in Boston yesterday that another Railroad Conductor was murdered, this time in Waltham." I did not spare her the grisly particulars concerning poor Mr. Vogel's near decapitation, for I wanted her to appreciate the danger she was in. "A letter declaring that more Conductor assassinations would take place was sent to a leader in the Negro community. And Henry believes the assassin may be staying at the Sun Tavern, posing as a Quaker. So whoever it is you are hiding must leave immediately, or you may well meet a fate equally violent."

"No one knows the runaway is here except you, Adam. And I do not intend to conduct her anywhere. I want her to stay put."

"Where exactly have you put her?"

"She's in the attic. Not the most comfortable hiding place, but far more secure than the Tuttle Farm sugarhouse, is it not? That's where I found Tansy yesterday." Julia smiled at my astonishment. "Yes, the fugitive slave everyone has been looking for was hiding out at your family farm. Would you like to meet her?"

Still at a loss for words, I nodded. Julia led me up the two flights of stairs to the attic and knocked on the door. "Tansy, I have brought my friend Adam, the doctor I told you about. May we come in?"

Permission was granted, and we entered. Light came from two small gable windows, and I saw that all the attic clutter had been pushed to the perimeters. There was a mattress covered with sheets and blankets in the center space, and beside it stood a young black woman wearing a dark dress and a bright red neckerchief. When Julia introduced me to Tansy, she shook my hand firmly and met my eye directly. I liked her right off and decided there and then to move into my office for as long as she was under Julia's roof. I would bring a shotgun from the farm and do my utmost to protect them both.

"I have just been looking out the window," Tansy said, "and I saw—"

"Oh, do not look out the window!" Julia interrupted. "Someone may glimpse your dear face."

"My dark face, you mean. But don't you worry. I was careful. I saw the top of a closed wagon down on the Green and was wondering what it was doing there."

"Oh, that's just Rusty's wagon," Julia said. "He's one of those newfangled daguerreotypists."

Tansy clapped her hands together. "I hoped as much!"

"Now is not the best time for you to have your picture taken, Tansy," Julia admonished gently.

"Lordy, don't you think I know that? Rusty drove me here from Boston last Tuesday, and I'm hoping he can drive me someplace else now."

"Rusty is an Underground Railroad Conductor?" Julia said in disbelief.

"Apparently he is a legendary one in the Negro community," I told her.

"Will you go talk to Rusty, Doc Adam?" Tansy asked me. "Maybe I could leave with him tonight. He's got a secret compartment under the wagon to hide runaways."

I thought this an excellent plan and went directly to the Green. There was not a sign of life coming from the red wagon so early in the morn, and I surmised the daguerreotypist must still be asleep inside. That did not stop me from pounding on the rear door, however. A moment or two passed before Rusty opened it, wearing but his undervest and unbuttoned trousers. I was glad Julia had not insisted upon accompanying me.

"How do," he said as he buttoned himself up. "I do not open for business until nine, sir."

"My business is rather urgent," I told him. "You see, I am Dr. Walker and—"

"A doctor?" Rusty ran a hand through his disheveled mass

of red hair. "Well, in that case, I'll take your likeness right now, despite the weak morning light. A doctor's time is precious, after all. Who knows when you'll be called upon to save someone's life?"

"You have saved lives yourself, I hear," I said.

He gave me a closer look. "Now where would you hear such a whopper as that?"

"In Boston yesterday from the barber Mr. Smith."

"Come inside, Doctor."

I entered the wagon and sat down in the plush chair he indicated. He took a seat beside his camera apparatus and stared at me for a long moment. His lighthearted demeanor had been replaced by a crafty wariness. "What do you want?" he said coolly.

"I would like you to help a young black woman. You transported her from Boston to Plumford just a few days ago, but the Conductor you left her with was killed whilst taking her to Carlisle."

Rusty nodded. "Everyone in town has been talking about it."

"Did you know Mr. Tripp well?"

"No, I dealt with his wife, not him. She welcomed the fugitive I brought to her very warmly. I heard tell the poor girl might have drowned in a bog after Tripp got shot. I'm glad to hear from you that she didn't."

"She survived that ordeal, but now she must deal with the man who claims ownership of her. His name is Shiloh Prouty, and he's tracked her down here. She hopes you might take her away tonight."

"Where is she?"

"Hiding out in the house adjacent to my office."

"And where is this Prouty?"

"At present he's staying in the Sun Tavern barn."

"So close! It would be best for the fugitive to keep safely

hidden until her owner leaves the area. When he does so, I will oblige her, but no sooner."

"She will be disappointed to hear that," I said. I certainly was.

"There are others in need of my assistance right now," Rusty said.

"Yes, of course. I'm sure your services are in great demand. But has anyone yet communicated to you what happened in Waltham?"

When Rusty shook his head I told him the details of Vogel's execution and of the letter Mr. Coburn had received from the assassin. As Rusty listened he looked concerned but not frightened. I could plainly see that such a man as Rusty would not easily be dissuaded from his purpose.

"Henry Thoreau and I are investigating the murders of both Conductors," I went on to inform him. "We have had success in such investigations before."

"Is Mr. Thoreau a lawman?"

"Hardly. Indeed, he thinks little of breaking laws he does not feel are just."

"He sounds like a man I would like to meet," Rusty said.

"That can be easily arranged. He's presently staying at the Sun Tavern across the Green."

"Is he? Perhaps I should get a room there myself. Living in such cramped quarters as these can become tiresome after a spell."

"Breathing in the fumes from the chemicals you use day and night cannot be healthful," I said, for the wagon interior reeked of them. "But you must take care if you go stay at the Sun. It is entirely possible that one of the guests is the very assassin I told you of."

"No! What's his name?"

I hesitated, not wishing to disparage Haven, who might well be innocent despite all the circumstantial evidence against him.

"Never mind," Rusty said. "It's enough to know I should keep my guard up. Besides, an inn filled with people is surely a safer place for me to be at night than all alone in my wagon where I'm as vulnerable as a little ol' lamb."

"You look to be more a wily red fox than a lamb."

"Do I?" The smile he gave me did indeed look vulpine.

I noticed a guitar leaning beside my chair and picked it up. "I play a git box myself on occasion," I said. "I'm not very good at it, but I hear you are."

"You sure did hear an earful about me," Rusty said.

"You are spoken of with high regard by Mr. Smith and his friends." I strummed the guitar. "Appears you have a string missing."

"Haven't gotten round to replacing it." Rusty took the guitar from my hands. "I been neglecting my sweetheart something terrible." He rested the instrument on his lap and held it as one would a woman rather than a guitar, patting the curved rosewood body. He then turned his attention back to me. "Well, I reckon we both got a busy day ahead of us and should get on with it, Doctor."

Thus dismissed, I stood and made my way to the door. "You won't forget about Tansy?"

"Tansy?"

"The runaway being hounded by her owner," I reminded him.

"Oh, right. I never ask their names, you know. That way, no one can make me give them up. But I haven't forgotten her plight, I assure you, and I'll get her moving north again in due time." I sensed he did not share my sense of urgency.

When I left the daguerreotype wagon I crossed paths with Constable Beers on the Green. We crossed swords, too.

"I want a word with you," he said, blocking my way.

"You need only ask politely," I said, not much liking his commanding tone and belligerent stance.

"I'll ask any way I please," he said. "Who the hell gave you and Thoreau the authority to organize a search party to look for that slave girl?"

"You sure weren't about to do anything about finding her, Constable."

"And it turns out I was right. Ferreting about Phantom Bog for the wench was a big waste of time for all involved."

"If you think we proved you right, you have no grudge," I said.

"Oh, I got a mighty big grudge against the both of you. You have no call to keep interfering in my business."

"No call? The summer before last an innocent man almost got lynched thanks to your incompetence," I reminded him. "Last winter you allowed a vampyre hunter to terrorize our town. And now you are not making the slightest effort to discover who murdered Ezra Tripp. If you won't perform your constable duties, Mr. Thoreau and I will continue to interfere. And you can stick that big grudge of yours up the terminal part of your large intestine."

I took a step forward. Beers placed his hand against my shoulder to halt me from taking another. "I am warning you, Walker, that I am keeping a sharp eye on not only Thoreau and you, but also that light-heeled woman you keep such close company with."

"If you are referring to Mrs. Pelletier, you had better show more respect. And that's a warning to *you,* Beers."

A leer slid across Beers's fat, sweaty face. But he must have seen unleashed fury in my eyes, for he stepped aside to let me pass. Apparently he did not want our confrontation to become physical, and it was just as well that he backed off. The good people of Plumford would have found it disturbing to witness the town doctor giving the town constable a trouncing. I must admit, however, I felt more disappointment than relief when it did not come about.

I continued on my way to the Sun to talk to Henry. He would want to know that Julia was harboring our missing fugitive. And he would also be surprised to learn that the legendary hero Rusty, so admired by Mr. Smith and his associates, was right here in Plumford.

JULIA

Adam returned to the house with Henry, who told me he was staying at the Sun to keep his eye on a guest he suspects to be the Conductor assassin. He was eager to question Tansy about what she saw the night Tripp was murdered, but when he did she told him nothing more than she had already told me. And although Henry was most sympathetic when Tansy expressed how anxious she was to continue her journey to Canada, he agreed with Rusty that she should stay well hidden whilst Prouty was so close by.

Later in the day, when I went to the Sun to sketch Mrs. Ruggles, I found Henry and Rusty sitting together on the porch, which affords a fine view of the Green. I greeted Rusty warmly, for my opinion of him had greatly improved after hearing Tansy's recounting of his brave deeds as an Underground Railroad Conductor. Indeed, I sorely regretted my initial prejudice against him just because he was a Southerner. He looked slightly different to me, but I could not pinpoint how. Perhaps it was only that I now viewed him differently. He told me he had decided to stay at the Sun for the rest of his time in

Plumford. Business was so brisk, he said, that he could well afford it.

As Henry and Rusty chatted with me they kept glancing in the direction of another man seated at the opposite end of the long porch. He was wearing a Quaker hat, and his leg was propped up on a bench, so I knew that he must be Jerome Haven, the murder suspect. Frankly, he did not look much like a killer to me, but I am not the best judge of character. I had married Jacques Pelletier, after all.

The three of us did not talk long. Henry went back to his carpentry work, Rusty went back to his daguerreotype wagon, and I went to find Mrs. Ruggles. Her husband sent me up to their private suite on the second floor of the rambling old inn, where she awaited me arrayed in layers of lace and ruffles. She need not have bothered to dress up, for it was her countenance, not her clothes, that I would be concentrating upon, but I could see that she enjoyed having the opportunity to display her best finery. The sitting room proved to be most commodious and bright, well suited for my work. The only drawback was that Mrs. Ruggles's parrot Roos considered it her territory and cawed at me most vociferously as she flapped over my head.

"Roos get used to you one time soon," Mrs. Ruggles assured me.

"And I hope I get used to Roos," I replied.

"You have no liking for birds?"

Not this particular one, thought I. Although Roos was a beauty, with velvety feathers of bright red and vivid violet, her black hooked beak looked sharp and cruel, her claws looked menacing, and her beady jet eyes, rimmed in blue, looked merciless.

"I have no familiarity with parrots," I told Mrs. Ruggles. "How did you come by one so extraordinary?"

"My brother bringed her to me back from Indonesia. I

have her with me always since a girl." She looked up at the bird and said something in Dutch. The parrot immediately perched on her shoulder. "Very smart, my Roos."

"Does she know English?"

"Only little. Mr. Ruggles teaches her words, and one day Roos speaks English more good than me."

"You are a very gorgeous creature, Roos," I told the bird.

"Merci," she replied.

"Oh, she speaks French too!"

"No, no, how could she?" Mrs. Ruggles said. "Roos and me never been to France."

"But *merci* means thank you in French."

Mrs. Ruggles laughed. "Roos hears the English word *mercy* from my husband. Mr. Ruggles cries out *mercy, mercy me!* when he . . . you know, reaches height of pleasure with me."

That was more information than I cared to know about the Ruggleses' personal life, and I hoped the image now filling my mind of the parrot watching them with beady-eyed intensity as they made love would soon fade.

I inquired as to which chair Mrs. Ruggles favored, and she pointed to a rocker. I dragged it to a window and posed Mrs. Ruggles in it so that the angle of the light gave her flat, broad face more definition. I then sat myself down across from her, opened my sketch pad, and brought out my pencils and charcoals.

"No paint?" Mrs. Ruggles said, sounding most disappointed.

"Not yet. I make a number of preparatory drawings before settling on a pose to paint on canvas. Composition is the key to a successful portrait."

"Composition," she repeated.

I could tell she no more understood the word than Roos did and went on to explain the Aristotelian concept that portraits should not only resemble the sitter but also be harmoniously arranged. Even a pose that seemed spontaneous involved the most contrived components of design, viewing angle, and harmony of hues.

Mrs. Ruggles found my explanation of little interest. "Just don't make me ugly," she said.

My goal, of course, was just the opposite—to depict her as precisely as I could, yet at the same time flatter her. That was what her husband was paying me to do, but I also had my own artistic needs to satisfy. I always try to capture the essential being of my subject, which goes well beyond outward appearance. It is this portrayal of human dignity that draws me to portraiture, along with the pleasure of revealing the unique personality of the sitter. The viewer takes all this for granted, for such elements register with a glance, but to convey them upon a flat piece of canvas requires intuition as well as technical skill. A rapport with the subject is essential.

Therefore, my first order of business was to put Mrs. Ruggles at ease, and I encouraged her to tell me about herself, which has proven to be the most satisfactory topic of conversation for most of my subjects. Mrs. Ruggles, however, was not very forthcoming, perhaps because she felt awkward speaking English. All I learned about her was that she had come here from Rotterdam only six months ago to work at a relative's brewery in Boston, and there she had met Sam Ruggles. She much preferred talking about him than herself, and she could not say enough about his fine character, looks, and humor. Her stiff posture relaxed, her countenance became animated, her pale eyes lit up, and she became quite pretty. She was obviously very happy to be the innkeeper's wife and helpmeet.

Roos became quite talkative too. Although I did not understand a word the bird was saying, I rather enjoyed listening to her chatter, for she had an unexpectedly pleasant voice, rather like a little girl's.

By the end of our first hour together Mrs. Ruggles, her

parrot, and I were all much more relaxed with each other. I had already sketched Mrs. Ruggles from both a profile and a three-quarters view and was drawing her full face when the sound of a stagecoach stopping in front of the Sun caused her to fidget in her chair.

"Horses need watering, and travelers do too," she said. "I go down and see if Mr. Ruggles needs help. Lady passengers could be wanting tea."

"Pray give me but a moment or two more," I said, for I was almost finished with the drawing and did not wish to leave it undone.

She agreed, but the peaceful mood had been broken, and her expression was no longer serene. So I did not really mind when Mr. Ruggles interrupted the session shortly thereafter.

"We got us a real important guest coming here tomorrow, Edda," he said. "Rooms need to be readied for him."

Mrs. Ruggles shot up from her seat, ready to oblige. "Who is he?"

"Don't know his name or nothing about him."

"Then how do you know he's so important, Sam?"

"From the appearance of the valet he sent ahead to prepare us for his arrival, that's how," Mr. Ruggles said. "Dressed to the nines, he is. Very tall and black and fine-looking but for all the scars on his face."

"Oh, I want to see him!"

"You'll have to wait till he comes back, Edda. He asked me where he could find the town doctor, and I directed him to Dr. Walker's office."

I stood up slowly on trembling legs, my heart thudding. I could barely breathe, yet I managed to say good-bye to Sam and Edda Ruggles and make my way home, where I knew the man just described awaited with dreaded news.

ADAM

Saturday, May 20

When I stopped by the farm to look in on Gran this after-noon I informed her I would be spending my nights at the Walker house for a short while.

"There is a good reason for it," I said, "but I cannot tell you what it is just yet. The fewer people who know the better."

"I already know anyways," Gran said.

"How did you find out?"

"How do you think? From Julia."

I'd assumed Julia had not told anyone but me about finding Tansy on Tuttle Farm. "Who else knows?"

"No one. Not even Harriet," Gran assured me. "But you ain't gonna be able to keep it a secret for much longer, my boy. Folks ain't blind, you know."

I nodded. "The sooner she leaves here, the better. I will be much relieved to see the last of her."

Gran looked much taken aback. "Does Julia know how you feel?"

"Oh, I have made it clear to her that I didn't want this to happen."

"But it has! And now you must do the right thing and go with her."

"There's no need for me to do that, Gran. She'll be taken care of by others once she leaves Plumford."

"Oh, Adam, I cannot believe what I am hearin' from you! How can you bear to part with Julia when she is carryin' yer child?"

I stared at Gran. She stared back at me. Harriet was out in the garden, and the only sound in the farmhouse was the ticking of the tall clock at the bottom of the stairs.

"Julia is with child?" I finally said.

"Ain't she who we been talkin' about?"

"I was talking about a fugitive slave Julia has taken in."

"Oh," Gran said. She closed her eyes. "I must sleep now."

"Don't leave me hanging, Gran. Did Julia tell you she was pregnant?"

Gran kept her eyes and mouth shut tight. Not about to badger a sick old woman who might have only been relating a fantasy of her own making, I assured Gran all would be well, kissed her cheek, and departed. Needless to say, I was eager to get back to town and talk to Julia.

She was not at home, and I recalled that she had an appointment to sketch Edda Ruggles at the Sun. I went to my office and did my best to concentrate on squaring my patient accounts, never an easy matter of dollars and cents. Notes and coins are in short supply in the country, and I am often paid in cords of wood, or farm produce, or services such as horse shoeing or gig repair. Since my wants are simple, my needs have been sufficiently met up to now, but it would be a struggle to make ends meet if I had a family to support. But I would have Tuttle Farm one day, and a good number of country doctors supplement their incomes with farming. It would suit me fine to do so too. Indeed, I would relish it.

Of course, there was always the possibility of earning a far more lucrative living with my scalpel. Six months ago Dr. Oliver Wendell Holmes had offered me a staff position at Massachusetts General Hospital, which would give me use of its splendid operating theater. At the time Plumford had been in the throes of a Consumption epidemic, and I could not abandon my suffering patients, so I'd turned him down. But now that the scourge has passed and there is general good health in the community, I am tempted to accept his offer. Yet even in Boston, Julia and I could not live openly as man and wife, for far too many people there know our personal histories. Julia would be shunned by society as an adulteress, and our children would be considered bastards. No, the only solution, as I'd confided to Henry, is to remove west and start life anew.

The absolute futility of contemplating the future, however, was proven to me in the next moment when there came a knock on my office door, and I opened it to a Negro of extraordinary height. He was dressed as a cultured European gentleman, in fine dark wool, starched linen, and black silk, but the raised scars upon his countenance, running from his high cheekbones to his jaw, the edges of his full mouth to his ears, and across his broad forehead from temple to temple, made clear that he had come from another culture entirely.

"Mr. Mawuli!" I said, for he could be none other than the man Julia had described to me as Jacques Pelletier's ostensible valet and personal healer.

He bowed and removed his high-crowned beaver hat. His shaved head gleamed like polished black ebony. "You need not address me as mister. I prefer just Mawuli." His deep voice carried a melodic but heavy accent that had never before reached my ears. "I inquired at the tavern where to find you, Dr. Walker. I did not wish to ask for Madame Pelletier, knowing that would have aroused far too much curiosity."

"What do you want?" I demanded.

"If you know who I am you must know who sent me."

"Julia's husband." It pained me to say it.

"Yes, I have come at his bidding."

"He remains in France?" I asked, for hope springs eternal.

Mawuli shook his head. "He is presently in Boston, but he will arrive in Plumford tomorrow."

"Julia will not wish to receive him. Go back to Boston and tell him not to come here."

Mawuli gave me a long, steady look. His eyes contained a limitless depth of darkness. "I do not take orders from you. Only from Monsieur Pelletier. And he has ordered me to speak directly to his wife."

I realized I was being churlish to no purpose. "You may wait for her in my office. She should be returning home shortly."

He stepped inside, his head near reaching the ceiling, and immediately went over to the anatomical skeleton I have hanging in one corner of the room. He tenderly cupped the skull with his palm, then picked up a bony hand and gently shook it.

"I knew this man," he told me. "His name was Elinam, and many years ago we were chained together on the long march to a slave ship headed for Martinique."

Although Mawuli's tone and expression were somber, I was sure he was hoaxing me. "Amazing that you can recognize your friend in such a reduced state," I said wryly.

"The bones of the dead speak to those who know how to listen." Mawuli regarded the skeleton a moment and pointed to where the left arm had been broken and the bone partially healed, and then to an indentation on the right parietal bone of the skull. "I witnessed those very injuries inflicted upon Elinam."

"Quite a coincidence that he should turn up here," I said. My tone was still sardonic, but I was impressed that Mawuli could have spotted those hairline fractures so quickly.

"There are no coincidences nor accidents, Dr. Walker," he

replied. "Nothing happens by chance, for there is a purpose to everything. And that purpose is determined by the Spirits, not us."

"I prefer to think we shape our own destinies," I said.

Mawuli shook his head. "What opportunity had Elinam to shape his? He was a young man when I knew him, and I was already an old one. Yet here I am in the flesh, well into my seventies, and all that is left of Elinam is this."

He gave the skeleton a light push, and it swung on the string from which it was hanging. His attention was then drawn to my medicine cabinet, and he had the audacity to try opening the door.

"I keep it locked," I said. "Drugs such as laudanum and calomel can be dangerous in the wrong hands."

"It is the same with Vodun medicine," Mawuli said. "Extremely dangerous in the wrong hands." He continued to look about. "Your office does not appear to be very well stocked, Doctor. Where are the crocodile heads? The monkey paws? The cobra skins?"

"Now I am sure you are jesting with me, Mawuli."

"Are you? Well, it so happens I kept such supplies on hand when I practiced the healing arts in Africa, and I assure you my patients took me most seriously."

"That I am willing to believe," I said. "Patients are eager to accept any cure a trusted doctor proffers, no matter how outlandish it is. The elder Dr. Walker used to keep a big jar of leeches here in the office. He would apply them to his patients to suck out bad blood."

"How savage," Mawuli said dryly.

"I reckon it's how you look at things," I allowed.

Mawuli stroked his cheek. "And do you look upon me as a savage because of the scars on my face, Dr. Walker?"

"They do fascinate me," I readily admitted. "I am aware, as

a surgeon, of the intense pain that must have been incurred in the process of inflicting such brutal cuts, given the concentration of nerves in facial tissue. Then some sort of irritating substance was rubbed into the open cuts to cause the healing tissue to harden and stand out, was it not?"

"I rubbed ash into the wounds to inflame them," Mawuli said, "after slashing my face with a sharpened stone."

"You performed the operation upon yourself?"

"Of course. If the wounds had not been self-inflicted, how could they attest to my courage? It was how a boy of my tribe proved he had become a man."

"Did all the men in your tribe have such scars?"

"No. Only the most respected ones."

Before I could ask him more questions, Julia flung open the office door. She looked at me with a stricken expression and then turned to Mawuli.

"It's good to see you again, my friend," she told him in a shaky voice. "But I fear you have not come all the way from France alone."

Mawuli nodded. "Monsieur Pelletier is in Boston and will be arriving here by private coach tomorrow."

"Surely he cannot expect a reconciliation. I am astounded that he has traveled all the way from France to meet with me."

"He has come to these shores on other business too, Madame."

"Good. Then his voyage here will not be wasted. What sort of business?"

"He would not tell me."

"Well, it matters not to me," Julia said and hooked her arm in mine. "My life is with Adam."

Mawuli said nothing to that. He turned and picked up his hat from my desk. "I have delivered the message that brought me here, and now I bid you and Dr. Walker adieu. You must want to talk in private now."

"Pray stay, Mawuli," Julia said. "Your counsel would be welcomed."

"How can I possibly counsel you? My loyalty lies with my employer, does it not?"

Julia tilted back her head and regarded Mawuli's countenance closely. "I can never tell when you are being serious or cynical."

"One can be both," Mawuli said.

"Still, I cannot conceive how you can be loyal to a man like Pelletier."

"I think you would understand better if you knew how we came together."

"But you always refused to tell me," Julia said. "Nor did you ever tell me that he was a slave trader."

"It was not up to me to divulge Monsieur's past to you, Madame. And when you finally did learn the truth about him, you left so quickly I had little opportunity to tell you my own story."

"Tell us now," Julia urged.

"No, now I must go make sure Monsieur's rooms are prepared properly. I am still in his employ, after all. And unlike you, Madame, I will most likely remain at his side till death do us part." The shadow of a smile touched Mawuli's lips, and with a bow, he was gone.

Left alone with Julia, I took her into my arms and held her tightly. When we at last drew apart she looked up at me with a bleak expression on her wan face.

"Everything will be all right," I assured her. "What harm can Pelletier do us?"

"We will find out soon enough, I fear."

"There's no need to fear him, Julia. You're with me now, and the two of us can face anything together." I lifted her chin and smiled. "Or are there three of us now?"

She managed a smile too. "You have discerned my secret. Leave it to a doctor."

"Or a blabbing grandmother," I said. "The old dear cannot keep a secret."

"Hah! She kept the secret of your parentage long enough, Adam. If she had told us we weren't related, I would never have sailed off and met Pelletier, much less married him."

"Let's forget all about that."

"How can we? He's *coming* tomorrow!"

"And tomorrow we'll deal with him, Julia. But right now let's just be thankful for this new blessing in our lives."

"A mixed blessing," Julia said. "This is hardly the best time for me to be pregnant."

"We'll make it the best time," I said. "We're young and healthy and strong-minded, and we can overcome any obstacle that gets in the way of our happiness."

"You're right," she said. "We should be celebrating, not worrying about the future."

"How do you suggest we celebrate?"

She gave me a look I fully understood. "Throw the latch on the door, Adam."

I did as she requested, swept her off her feet, and carried her to the cot in the office. We then confirmed to each other, in the most intimate fashion, that we are truly and forever husband and wife, no matter what circumstance, the law, or society dictates. And we would welcome a child with gratitude and open hearts.

A short time later, when Julia went to the attic to visit with Tansy, I went off to the Sun to question Mawuli. My plan was to stop Pelletier from coming to Plumford tomorrow. No good could result from it, only unnecessary distress for Julia. I was sure I could convince Pelletier that Julia belonged with me rather than him. No matter what the damn law said, he had married her under false pretenses, and therefore the marriage itself was false. That's the way I saw it. That's the way Julia saw it. And I was confident I could get Pelletier to see reason too. But in order to do so, I needed to learn from Mawuli where in Boston he was staying.

I located Mawuli easily enough. He was sitting on the Sun porch with none other than Henry. They were sharing a pitcher of lemonade and looked for all the world like old friends.

"Come join us, Adam," Henry said. "I would like you to meet a most interesting individual."

"We have already met," I said.

"Is that so?" Henry turned to Mawuli. "When I mentioned Dr. Walker to you, why did you not tell me that you knew him?"

"Because I am the soul of discretion," he replied.

"And I appreciate your discretion, Mawuli," I said. "But you may speak freely in front of Henry Thoreau. He is a good friend of mine and Julia's, and we have taken him into our confidence." I pulled up a chair and lowered my voice. "Mawuli is Jacques Pelletier's envoy," I informed Henry. "Pelletier himself will be arriving tomorrow unless I discourage him from doing so."

"How do you propose to do that?" Mawuli said.

"By explaining to him how futile coming here would be. I shall take the cars to Boston as soon as you tell me where I can find him."

Mawuli shook his great dome of a head. "Your plan will not work for two reasons, Doctor. You cannot persuade a man like Monsieur Pelletier. And I will not tell you where in Boston he is." When I started to protest, he rose from his chair. "Rather than argue with you, I will leave."

"Pray wait," Henry said. "If Dr. Walker accepts that it will be useless to press you further on this matter, will you stay and talk to us awhile?"

"It would be my pleasure to do so," Mawuli replied most graciously. He looked to me, and I nodded my assent. It would do me no good to drive him off, after all.

Mawuli resumed his seat, and it took Henry but a few inquiries to get him to tell us more about himself. I here set down, as best I can, Mawuli's story:

If you are to understand me you must know, despite the clothes I wear and the manners I have learned to suit your society, I am a creature of the jungle. I have spent most of my life in the rainforest of Africa. In my head and heart and bones and blood are the heat and damp and dark of days and nights lived amongst creatures thrashing between birth and death far from any outside civilization.

I am of the Ewe tribe and came into the world as the son of a healer, one we called an inyanga, *who practiced Vodun, what you call voodoo. It was my good fortune to live in a part of Togo far from the sea, out of reach of the raiders who seized people to sell to the white men of Europe, who took them away by ship. For the first fifty blessed years of my life I never laid eyes on a white man.*

For as long as I can remember I wanted to follow my father's path. But he would not begin to teach me his arts until I knew the ways of the jungle. When I was old enough to survive on my own he sent me off to live deep in the rainforest, where I spent half a year watching and listening to every living creature. I returned to the village, and my father sent me away again. This time, he said, I was to not only observe but to become every living creature in the jungle. I sat with gorillas in the bamboo, slept high in the fig trees with the sloths, walked with the elephants, swam with the river otters, stalked with the leopards, and followed the enormous claw prints of the mokele-mbembe, *a being with a body bigger than an elephant's but with a small head on a neck long as a tree trunk. No white man and few of my own kind have ever seen this river creature, and some say it does not exist, but I saw it and smelled it.*

After a year I returned to my village, and my father judged me ready to become a healer like him. He taught me songs, chants, and spells and the use of roots, herbs, animal skins and bones to make good or bad medicine. When my father died, I took his place as the village inyanga. I became such a powerful healer that people came from villages near and far to receive my treatments. I turned no one away. I practiced my arts day and night. I did not take a wife or have children, for my tribe was my family. I did not want any other life.

But I got another life.

Treachery brought me low. I was so loved and respected by the Ewe people that the tribal chief came to believe I was a threat to his power. One night I was attacked and knocked senseless, and the next morning I found myself being walked in a slave caravan to the coast. A long line of us, perhaps two hundred men and women, were bound together and beaten and lashed to make us walk toward a life worse than death. The slavery business is most wasteful. So many die before they reach the coast to be sold. Many more die going across the sea. And then a great many die as slaves in the sugarcane and cotton and rice fields. So there is no end to the wanting of more and more men and women to feed the jaws of slavery.

I chanted and sang to relieve the suffering of those around me as we walked. The white slave drivers would taunt me as I chanted, but when one of them fell ill with a fever and white medicine failed to cure him, he asked for me. I was allowed to go into the jungle and find the herbs I needed, and I cured him. He rapidly recovered, so the caravan could go on. Why did I help him, you may wonder. Because I am a healer. As the scorpion stings and the leopard bites, I heal. I can do great harm as well, but that is very much against my nature.

By the time we reached the fort on the coast, I believed the man whose life I had saved had forgotten me altogether. But he had not. At the fort, buying slaves for his ship, was Pelletier, and, like so many Europeans, he fell ill from the rotten water and the spoiled meat. Thinking he could gain advantage with Pelletier, the slave driver brought me to him and swore I could cure him. But Pelletier, ill as he was, laughed in the man's face and sent me back to huddle with the rest.

Yet he bought me. Why? Perhaps he saw something in me. Or perhaps, because I was too old to work long in the fields in the sun, he got me very cheaply. Whatever his reason, he bought me, and that saved him as well as me.

Pelletier was both owner and captain of his slave ship. The French then and for long afterward transported and sold more men and women into slavery than any other nation. He captained what was called a tight-packed ship, which was the most cruel and wasteful way to carry slaves. It meant shackled slaves were packed together hip to hip in the hold and never moved the entire voyage. Many died from living in their own filth or from lack of food and water. Pelletier believed this cruelty was cheaper for him than taking the trouble to feed us or even give us water but once a day. He also feared that if we were unshackled to exercise, we would revolt and kill him and the crew. To avoid that danger we sat in one place and suffered. Those who died amongst us were left for days in the suffocating heat before they were unshackled and thrown overboard. Many tried to take their own lives rather than live in that misery. Those of the highest value, such as the strongest young men and most attractive girls, were force-fed by pouring porridge down their throats, like the French stuff a goose, so they would not die.

Then one day I was unchained and hauled up onto the deck and washed with sea water and taken to the captain's cabin. Pelletier was far more ill than when last I saw him at the fort. A fever was burning his body up like a fire smoldering in charcoal. He had been given every medicine on board, and nothing had worked. In his fear of death and desperation he remembered me and demanded that I be brought to him. He stared at me a long time, and then I was made to understand through an interpreter that if I cured him he would give me my freedom.

What was there to lose? I had no plants or animal parts, so I gathered up some seaweed, and took bits of the eyes, beak, and suckers from a caught octopus as well as the edge of the tail and juice from the stomach of a great shark. The ship always had schools of sharks trailing after it, waiting for the sick, dying, or dead of my kind to be tossed overboard. I also took a drop of my own blood, the quill of a feather from an albatross that had died and fallen on deck, and a chip of wood from the topmost tip of the mainmast. You may wonder why I collected these particular items, but I can only answer that my Spirits told me to. When I put them all together in a cooking vessel, they glowed with a light that perhaps only I could see. I boiled the mixture down and added a dram of brandy to it. I brought it to Pelletier.

His eyes widened with fear when he saw me, for I had painted myself with whitewash and red from some iron in the stones in the ballast. I started in with my song that would make all that I had shredded and sliced and ground and thrown whole into my pot into a healing potion of great power. Pelletier drank the liquid, gagging with each swallow. That he managed to keep it down proved to me that he very much wanted to live. I chanted by his side for a day and a night, and at the next dawn his fever lifted. I was glad of it, for he had ordered that if he died, I was to die with him.

Pelletier recovered good strength in a matter of days. I never returned below decks. As he drank my potions and listened to my chanting, he became convinced of my powers. He thereafter looked at me with gratitude and I know a touch of fear, which has helped me all these years since. I told him I could keep him alive and healthy for as many years as he wished if he would give up the slave trade. He agreed. It was only later that I learned the French Government had outlawed the trade and so it was not so great a sacrifice for him and he was already a rich man. That was his last voyage as a slaver.

He told me I would be treated well, better than any Negro, free or slave, could expect to be treated, and he has been true to his word for twenty years now. I had the best of tutors to learn French and English so as to be of use to him in many ways. I have even been allowed to retain a small portion of the profits Pelletier makes in business enterprises my Spirits advise me to have him invest in. In truth, my Spirits never advise in such matters. What care They about worldly profits and *losses? I have managed to give Pelletier good advice by listening to my own good sense. Using his money to make some for myself has been a great incentive for me to stay at his side. Health and profits have been Pelletier's incentives to keep me there.*

There have been times over the years, however, when Pelletier has been foolish enough to doubt my usefulness to him. He then becomes quite ill. And I then cure him once again, and his faith in me is restored. He has of late fallen prey to a stomach ailment for which I am most carefully treating him.

And now that he had told us all that he cared to, Mawuli gave us no opportunity to question him further, but left us rather abruptly and went for a stroll in the Green. I watched him amble down the shady path, paying no notice to the townspeople who stared after him.

"Well, he certainly has an original view of the world," I remarked to Henry.

"He is a man sprung from Nature," Henry said, "and his intimate knowledge of it has revealed to him truths and insights beyond most people's comprehension. I do not doubt he has great power to affect those to whom he ministers."

"His power comes from ignorance and superstition," I said.

Henry smiled. "Ever the skeptic, Doctor."

"Ever the man of science," I replied. "I know from experience that if a patient believes in the efficacy of some particular treatment or pill or device, it can have a positive result. Why, just last month an elderly patient of mine who is suffering from the Consumption demonstrated this to me. When I placed my new ivory stethoscope, an instrument she had never before seen, to her chest to listen to her heartbeat, she declared that she felt a weight lifted from her lungs and asked why I had never given her this special treatment before. Her breathing actually eased, and her heartbeat dropped. But of course the effect was only temporary."

"Even so," Henry said, "your example proves that our reality is a manifestation of our minds. Mawuli believes in his powers, and his perception is his reality. Hence, his power is real."

"Do you think he truly saved Pelletier's life with his mumbo jumbo?"

"I think his mumbo jumbo, as you call it, comes from deep within his being," Henry said. "Mawuli's intense study of Nature gave him a far better understanding of the laws that govern life than the study of musty books filled with secondhand knowledge gives us."

"Such as the books I studied at Medical School?"

"I don't mean to disparage your education, Adam. But my own experience at Harvard left much to be desired. There are far better ways to learn than by rote."

"To be sure, hands-on experience is the best education for a doctor," I said. "And I do not hold with treatments such as purgatives and blood-letting that those musty old medical books you refer to advocate. Medicine should move forward, not backward into the past. I predict great advancements will be made in the near future. It is beginning already. The use of ether in surgeries, for example. How I wished I'd had ether to administer to that poor Quaker when I cleaned and stitched up his wound."

"That *quack* Quaker, you mean," Henry said. "I posted a letter to the Friends' pastor in Amesbury, but I need not wait for confirmation from him that Jerome Haven is not who he claims to be. I merely had to look at a clock. Come, I will show you."

We went into the tavern entrance hall. There stood a tall teacher's desk that held a guest registry book, a candle in a pewter holder, a steel dip pen, an inkstand, and a wooden mantel clock.

"Read the clock face," Henry urged me.

I did so with a glance and then checked my pocket watch. "It is correct," I pronounced.

"Not the time," Henry said impatiently. "Read the writing on the dial."

I looked at the area surrounded by the twelve Roman numerals. Therein the clockmaker's name and place of business was written in script: *Chauncey Jerome New Haven Conn.*

Henry opened the book to Wednesday, May 17th and pointed to the one signature on the page: *Jerome Haven.* "Obviously an alias the Quaker imposter concocted by looking at the clock."

"It does seem suspicious," I said. "Did you compare this signature to the assassin's handwriting in the letter?"

"Yes, of course," Henry said. "They are not at all similar. But that doesn't mean they were not written by the same hand. The penmanship could have been deliberately disguised either here in the registry or in the letter."

"Or someone else could have written the letter for Haven," I suggested, "if indeed he is the assassin."

"The more I observe him, the more I suspect him," Henry said. "He doesn't come downstairs too often, and when he does he acts both nervous and restless. Whenever a stagecoach pulls up and passengers come in for refreshments, he slinks away. He went up to his chamber a few hours ago and has not left it since, but I cannot keep continuous watch. I have to look like I'm working once in a while."

"How's the job progressing?"

"As slowly as possible," Henry said. "Building a dumbwaiter is a relatively easy project, but I want it to last for as long as Haven stays at the Sun. And when he leaves here, I intend to follow him. How much longer do you think it will take for his leg to mend well enough for him to travel?"

"That depends."

Henry smiled. "You sound just like a doctor, Adam."

"Well, the human body is a complicated organism. In fact, I think I'll go check on Haven now. My main concern is infection setting in."

I went up to Haven's chamber and found him sound asleep, or more likely passed out. His breath stank of rum with every snore he respired and the telltale empty bottle lay on its side by the bed. I attempted to awaken him, and, when that proved impossible, I examined his wound without his damn permission. It was healing quite well. As I was reapplying the dressing the door creaked open, and Edda Ruggles peeked in. She saw me and quickly withdrew. When I left the room she was not in the hall.

I stopped by the taproom to ascertain what Sam Ruggles knew about Jacques Pelletier. Henry banged away in the storeroom below us whilst we chatted.

"So who is this important guest you are expecting tomorrow?" I asked Ruggles in an offhand manner.

"Edda and I call him the Mysterious Stranger, for his valet will not even tell us his name. All we know about him is that he is most particular about his food. Our Mysterious Stranger will eat nothing but beefsteak! He believes it the secret to longevity or some such nonsense. And it must be cooked *bleu*. I had no notion what that meant, but Edda did. In plain speak, he wants his steak very rare. And hark this, Adam. He must eat this near raw beefsteak four times a day. Morning, midday, late afternoon and midnight. Served with very strong coffee for the first two meals, and with claret for the last two. You think that sounds like a healthful diet, Doctor?"

"I have never heard the likes of it."

"Our Mysterious Stranger must be a foreigner," Ruggles said. "Of course every American man worth his salt likes a beefsteak now and then. But every meal, every day? Not for me. I say variety is the spice of life. Not in all things however.

Certainly not in women." He raised his index finger. "One woman is enough variety for me if her name be Edda Ruggles!"

I was spared another discourse from Sam on his wife's many fine attributes when Shiloh Prouty came in, looking hangdog as usual. He was carrying a stack of handbills and placed one down on the bar. Depicted above the printed words was a silhouette drawing of a marching woman carrying a basket, the symbol of a female runaway.

"Will you kindly post this on the tavern's notice board, sir?" he said.

Ruggles glanced at the handbill without touching it and shook his head. "I don't post such notices, Mr. Prouty. And I doubt any other place of business in this town will either."

"I hope you are wrong about that," Prouty said, "for it has cost me the last coins in my pocket to get them printed."

"Then how you going to pay the reward money you promise here?" Ruggles stabbed his finger at the handbill.

"I got that amount put in safekeeping. I won't use it for nothing but to get Tansy back."

"Not even to pay for your supper?"

"I reckon I won't be eating supper no more," Prouty replied and slumped off with his bundle of handbills.

Ruggles shook his head as he watched Prouty depart. "He's sleeping for free in the barn, and now he can't even pay for his vittles."

"Since he can't pay his way, you should send him on his way, Sam," I said. "If Prouty hangs around here he might succeed in finding his slave. You wouldn't want that to happen, would you?"

"Of course not. And to my way of thinking, the longer Prouty sticks it out here, the less likely he is to find her."

"How do you figure that?"

"Well, no one has seen hide nor hair of her, have they?" Ruggles said. "My guess is she must be well on her way to

Canada by now. So if Prouty is under the delusion that she is close by, let him remain so."

"I still say good riddance to him, Sam."

"I just don't have the heart to kick him out of the barn," Ruggles said. "That poor son of a Southerner looks like he's been kicked around enough in life."

I considered telling Ruggles there and then where Tansy was and how Prouty's persistent presence around town was keeping her in hiding. But along with his good heart and generous spirit, Sam Ruggles had a big mouth, and I wasn't sure I could trust him to keep it shut concerning Tansy. He just gabbed with too many people day and night. Besides, even if he didn't let something slip to a customer, he most likely would tell his wife where Tansy was hiding. And there was something about Edda Ruggles I didn't trust.

When Ruggles went to the other end of the bar to serve a customer I slipped the handbill into my pocket. I brought it to the house to show Julia. It enraged her beyond measure.

JULIA

Tansy was sitting Indian-style on the makeshift bed reading the Bible she'd requested when I fetched up her breakfast this morning. She stood up in the cramped attic space, stretched her strong, solid body, and groaned. "My limbs are crying for locomotion," she told me.

"Yes, I'm sure it must be very tiresome for you to be cooped up here day in and day out," I said. "And I'm afraid you'll have to keep even more still when my hired girl comes to do housework tomorrow. Molly has no reason to go up to the attic, but she will be in and out of the rooms right below you. She comes on Wednesday and Friday too."

Tansy groaned again. "If I'm still stuck up here by Friday I am sure my poor joints will be ossified. I have half a mind to take a stroll out back when it gets dark."

"I don't think that would be prudent, Tansy. Especially now."

She looked at me sharply. "Why especially now?"

I took the handbill from my pocket. I'd been reluctant to upset her with it but realized that she needed to be aware of the danger she was in. "Prouty has had a stack of these printed up, and he's aiming to post them all over the area."

Tansy took the handbill and read aloud from it. "*Absconded from my farm in Virginia, young Negro woman named Tansy . . .*" She gave out a short laugh. "Since when does Prouty know a fancy word like *absconded?*"

"It means to have departed secretly."

"I know what it means, Julia. I just didn't think Prouty did. His aunt gave my sister and me a far better education than his pappy ever gave him. Poor boy had to leave off schooling to work the farm. Prouty isn't stupid. Just ignorant. There is a difference, you know." She continued to read. "*About five feet seven inches in height, well made, skin smooth and without scars, dark bay in color . . .*" Tansy rolled her eyes. "Leave it to Prouty to describe me as the color of his horse." She read on. "*Talks very proper, knows her letters and sums, very smart.*" She smiled. "Leastways he allows me a brain." She went back to reading. "*Should Tansy return on her own I will forgive her.*" She nodded. "I believe he would. He has a real forgiving nature."

"What is there to forgive, Tansy?" I said. "You have done nothing wrong by taking what is rightfully yours—your own freedom."

"But how can Prouty understand that?" Tansy said. "He was born a Southern white man, and he believes what he was taught to believe. Even so, he has a good heart. And he never so much as hurt a hair on my head."

"Well, now he has put a bounty on your head. Read the last part, Tansy."

"*One hundred and fifty dollar reward will be paid for her delivery to me unharmed.*" Tansy dropped the handbill. "Good Lord, that dang fool has gone plumb crazy."

"Crazy like a fox," I said. "Such a large sum as that will even tempt more than a few Northerners to start hunting for you."

"But there is no way Prouty could have so much money unless he . . ." Tansy put her hands to her cheeks and shook her head. "I can't believe he would sell his horse Belle. He *loves* that horse."

The Meetinghouse steeple clock began ringing the hour, and neither of us spoke over the sound as it reverberated through the attic. Ten o'clock. Pelletier was scheduled to arrive in two hours.

"Are you all right, Julia?" Tansy said when the ringing stopped. "You sure don't look it."

I had not told Tansy of my husband's impending visit, for I felt she had enough concerns without adding mine to them. In truth, I disliked talking about Pelletier to anyone, even Adam. Especially Adam! And Adam has never pressed me to learn more about him. We both have preferred to forget that my husband exists, or leastways pretend that he doesn't. But soon Adam will be meeting him in the flesh. I should have known such a day was inevitable. The only way it could have been avoided is if Adam and I had removed ourselves across the continent, which had been our intention before Granny fell so ill.

I assured Tansy that I was fine although a now familiar wave of nausea swept over me. I hurriedly left the attic to avail myself of my chamber pot. Whilst on my knees I prayed that all would be well, and then I rinsed my mouth, washed my face, put on my bonnet, and went off to the Meetinghouse.

Attending Sunday service at the Meetinghouse has been my custom since returning to Plumford. I find the sermons are far less bleak than the ones I'd been forced to endure when I was a girl. The past minister used to expound on the depravity of man and the wrath of God, but the current one preaches about a God who is understanding of human foibles and forgiving of our transgressions. Today, however, I found little comfort in the good minister's preaching. My mind was too troubled to attend to his words, and even as the congregation sang uplifting hymns I heard the Voice of Doom in my ear, chanting *Pelletier is coming* over and over again.

When morning service was over, I paused on the Meeting-house steps to exchange pleasantries with Molly Munger and her parents. I considered telling Molly to forego her house-keeping duties until further notice but could not come up with a plausible explanation as to why. In the end I decided it would only arouse suspicions. Prouty had made it well known about town that he believed his slave to be hiding in the area and asking Molly to stay away from my house would be tanta-mount to admitting that I was hiding the fugitive there. Better to let Molly come as usual. If she heard movement in the attic, I would take her into my confidence. She is a kindhearted girl, and I believe she would welcome the chance to help me har-bor a runaway slave. At the same time, Molly is young and gar-rulous, traits that are not conducive to keeping a secret. It was a worrisome situation indeed. Mr. and Mrs. Munger, mean-while, expressed to me, not for the first time, how happy they were that I had taken Molly on as my housekeeper. Once again I told them that the pleasure was all mine and bid the Munger family Good Day.

As I walked back to the house through the Green, I no-ticed that a number of townspeople were waiting in line by Rusty's wagon to have their likenesses taken. That in itself was not noteworthy, for they had been doing so all week. How-ever, today was the Sabbath, the day when all manner of busi-ness or work was prohibited. Yet rather than object to the daguerreotype operation being open, there stood two of the town Selectmen and their families in line with the others. Our eminent First Selectman and Justice of the Peace Elijah Phyfe wasn't there, but even he must have decided to turn a blind eye to this blatant violation of a blue law, for blind he'd have to be not to notice what was going on right in front of his big house overlooking the Green. Of course, town officials have ignored the breaking of an even more significant blue law for gener-ations. Al-though it is forbidden to consume or sell alcoholic beverages on the Sabbath, the Sun Tavern does so with impunity during the hours between the forenoon and the afternoon church services. Over the years so many men have gone from Meetinghouse to tavern and back again that a direct path has been worn across the Green. Custom, it seems, always trumps law.

I returned to the house to find Adam waiting in the parlor. He had gone to Tuttle Farm to care for Granny this morning, and I'd feared that he would be delayed there. I smiled at him with relief. His open and honest countenance had a determined set to it, and he exuded a confidence that always reassured me, even back when we were children. We had faced many a challenge and danger together, Adam and I, and had always managed to triumph. Surely we could face down Jacques Pelletier.

ADAM

Sunday, May 21

Although I could well understand Julia's anxiety over her husband's impending visit this afternoon, I myself welcomed it. I wanted things settled between us man to man, once and for all, the sooner the better. I even suggested to Julia that she wait in her chamber and let me deal with Pelletier alone, but she would not hear of it. So we both waited upon his arrival together in the parlor.

Julia was restless and would not stop pacing until I took her in my arms and stroked her back to help calm her. Just as she relaxed against me, comforted by my optimistic assurances, I heard someone shouting my name on the Green. I flung open the front door and identified myself to a panic-stricken young fellow in rough workman's clothes. He implored me to come help his friend who was having so much difficulty breathing that he was near to dying. I gave Julia a parting kiss, fetched my bag, and hurried off with the youth to a boarding-house down by the carding mill.

There I found an Irish millworker lying on the floor of his room desperately gasping for breath and holding his chest. I quickly checked his mouth and throat for obstructions and saw none. I then stripped off his shirt. There was considerable swelling on his left side behind his ribs, and I concluded that his trouble was empyema, a fluid build-up in the wall of the chest outside the lung that had become large enough to press on the lung and cause it to collapse.

"I must make a small puncture in your chest," I told him and took out my scalpel.

His eyes widened in fear, and he shook his head.

"It is the only way to save your life, son."

I felt with my finger for the space between the ribs above the greatest swelling—between the fifth and sixth rib on the left side—and with great care stabbed him in a shallow fashion so as to penetrate the pleural wall, but not into the lung beneath. I was rewarded with a spout of fluid that soaked my hands but instantly brought relief to the fellow, as I knew it would. I turned him onto his left side to allow the watery discharge to further drain. Once that pressure was removed, his lung, after fits and starts and much coughing, began to take in and expel air again. His eyes, a moment before wide with panic and the fear of death, filled with tears of relief. He gripped my arm tight and said something, I would guess in Gaelic, to thank me. I stayed an hour to allow time for the pleural cavity to drain as much as possible through the puncture. Then, after giving him a dose of laudanum, I wiped the perforation clean and sewed him up with catgut and left a slit with a bit of linen dipped in honey protruding from the wound to allow further drainage if necessary. Told him I would be back to remove the linen in a day. Washed my hands at the pump behind the boardinghouse and ran back to be with Julia. I hoped I had not missed Pelletier's visit entirely.

JULIA

Sunday, May 21

After Adam was called away to help a patient, I continued my restless pacing in front of the parlor window as I awaited Jacques Pelletier. I glimpsed a private coach roll down the road on its way to the Sun Tavern, and a short time later I saw Jacques coming up the road on foot, no doubt directed to my house by Mawuli. It had been half a year since I'd laid eyes on my husband and the nearer he got, the more aged he looked. I discerned a slight hesitation in his stride, and he was using his silver-tipped cane more as a support than a fashion accessory now. He held his other hand in his waistcoat, a gesture he thought made him look dignified but that also gave him comfort when his stomach pained him. There was pain in his expression now, and I began to feel sorry for him until he glanced toward the window and I saw the fierceness of his gaze. I drew back as if he had pointed a firearm at me. When I opened the door to the sharp rap of his cane, I greeted him aloofly, but with supreme politeness, in keeping with his own manner toward me. His lips twisted into a semblance of a smile.

"My beloved spouse!" he said. He caught my hand and brought it to his lips. I tugged it from his grasp. His eyes flickered with malevolence, but his smile stayed in place. "How I have missed you, my darling." As always, he spoke to me in English, for he cannot bear to hear my slight American accent when I speak French.

I did not challenge his lie that he had missed me. But neither did I respond with a lie of my own. "We are quite alone," I told him. "We can be completely honest with each other."

"You have always overrated honesty, Julia. You seem to be under the delusion that it is one of the cardinal virtues."

I let his glibness roll over me and brought him to the parlor. He glanced around the room with an amused expression upon his haughty countenance. I suppose to him the dark mahogany claw-and-ball furniture, paneled walls painted dull ochre, and thin, faded Turkey carpet looked absurdly dowdy compared to the elegant gilded décor of his chateau in Cannes. "So this is the grand estate you inherited and left me for," he said.

"I didn't leave you for a *house,* Jacques."

"No, of course not. You left me for a principle." He made it sound like a taunt.

"Pray be seated," I said.

He carefully placed his extremely tall hat upon the sofa and flipped out the tails of his coat before he sat down. He was dressed as tastefully as always, in an old-fashioned manner. The edges of his stand-up collar touched his sunken, clean-shaven cheeks, and the diamond in his stick pin winked at me from the folds of his carefully tied cravat. Jacques has a great affection for diamonds. And during the brief time he'd also had affection for me, he'd bestowed upon me a large diamond ring.

I sat across from him, at the edge of my chair, hands folded in my lap. I offered no refreshments. We both knew this was not a social call.

"I have always admired your good posture, Julia," he told me, "if not your good intentions. Indeed, your goodness became most tedious to me, as did your prudishness."

My heart rose on a small wave of hope. "If you find me so tedious, you must not wish for me to come back with you."

"It has been my experience that all wives are tedious, my dear. It is in the very nature of the beast."

Jacques had been widowed twice, without issue from either marriage. How sad he had looked when he'd told me this soon after we'd become acquainted onboard ship. He never mentioned that he had found his wives tedious. Or beastly. Indeed, he'd referred to them as heavenly angels keeping watch over him from above. And so I'd shared with him my own belief that my mother, whom I'd lost as a child, kept watch over me too. Monsieur Pelletier and I soon fell into the habit of strolling the deck together during the three-week voyage from Boston to France, and as my trust in him grew, I divulged more and more about myself. Eventually I even told him all about Adam and the curse of our close blood relation. How sympathetic Monsieur Pelletier was. How he admired me for leaving the young man I so loved so that he would be free to find love with another. Indeed, the old gentleman called me a saintly young woman, comparing me to Joan of Arc for my selfless action. He went so far as to inquire if I too was a virgin like St. Joan, and I saw no reason not to admit to my grandfatherly friend that I was. When he then proposed marriage to me, I tried not to show my astonishment, but refused him as kindly as I could. He graciously accepted my refusal, and upon landing we parted cordially.

I never thought I would see Monsieur Pelletier again, but a week later he found me at my father's studio in Paris. My father had been hauled off to debtor's prison, not for the first time. But this time he had contracted cholera in prison, and I feared he might not survive the ordeal. Monsieur Pelletier saved Papa's life by paying off his debts to free him and then finding him proper medical treatment. I felt forever beholden to Monsieur Pelletier, and when he proposed marriage again I accepted. I reasoned that since I would never love any man but Adam, I might as well marry this lonely old gent who only wanted my devoted companionship and had my best interests at heart. I had misjudged Jacques Pelletier completely.

He now regarded me with his cold, clever eyes. I saw not a glimmer of affection in them. "Why aren't you wearing the ring I gave you, Julia?"

"I sold it," I told him forthrightly. Well, I was not completely forthright. In truth I had given the diamond ring to Mawuli to sell.

Jacques laughed. "How disappointed you must have been when you learned it was merely paste."

Paste? But Mawuli had fetched a great deal of money for that ring, enough to pay for my passage back to America and then some. I said nothing, and a brief silence followed, whilst Jacques furtively stroked his stomach beneath his brocade waistcoat, never taking his scornful eyes off me.

"Is it not the custom here for married women to wear indoor caps, Julia?" he finally asked.

"Most do," I allowed.

"But you do not. Are you trying to pass yourself off as still a maiden?"

"No, of course not. I just don't care to wear a cap."

"So do people here address you as Madame Pelletier?"

"Mrs. Pelletier actually."

"Do you claim to be a widow?"

"No, Jacques. I have told no lies. Townspeople know I left a husband alive and well in France."

"What else do they know about me?"

"Nothing. I have made it a point never to talk about my husband."

"Well, now your husband has come to claim you like the lost piece of baggage that you are. I would have come sooner, but one thing after another prevented me from doing so. Initially it was my health. I fell very ill the day you ran off. And then the Monarchy was overthrown, and France was in chaos for months. Fortunately, I had made investments elsewhere. Even so, these have been extremely difficult months for me, times when a man needs his wife by his side. And where were you instead? Hiding from me in this little hamlet."

"I was not hiding, Jacques. You knew exactly where I was. I wrote to you, and so did my lawyer."

"Your lawyer is an imbecile. He has little grasp of French law. You are married to me in the eyes of the government and the church both, and such a marriage is indissoluble."

"But you broke every vow!"

He gave me a weary look. "A man's mistresses are his own concern, not his wife's. And perhaps, if you had been more compliant in bed, I would not have needed to go elsewhere to satisfy my desires, *ma femme.*"

"Your desires were disgusting."

Jacques shrugged. "I am getting on in years and need novel stimulations. Your duty as my wife was simply to obey my wishes. Instead, you bolted like a frightened filly."

"I fulfilled my duty as best as I could and would have remained your wife despite my aversion to certain acts you requested." I was grateful Adam was not present to hear this conversation. "But I could not stay with a man who has slave blood on his hands."

Jacques raised his wrinkled, blue-veined hands and turned them over. "No blood, my dear. It was long washed away. I gave up the trade nearly twenty years ago."

"But you did not give up the fortune you made from it."

"Of course not. We have been over all this once already, so do not be tiresome, Julia."

Six months ago I'd attended a soiree in Cannes and overheard talk that Jacques Pelletier had been a slaver. When I'd reported this to him, he'd given me one of his insufferable shrugs and replied that he saw no reason to deny it, since I'd most likely be hearing such rumors again. He went on to tell me the truth of his past. He'd been born into a Nantes seafaring family and had made a successful career for himself in the navy, becoming a frigate captain when he was only twenty-six. He'd left the navy, however, to captain a slave ship, for that was far more lucrative. Soon he'd made enough money to build his own ship, and for many years thereafter he'd transported captured Africans to the French colonies of Martinique and Guadeloupe. On his last such voyage, right before the French government finally made slave trade a punishable crime in 1830, he'd purchased Mawuli in the African slave market, and in theory Jacques still owned him. Jacques had related all this to me in a nonchalant tone, and as he'd watched my horror grow, his mouth had twisted in a sardonic smile. *I own you too, dear wife,* he'd concluded. I left him a few days later, as soon as I'd secured enough money to pay for my passage home.

"What you find tiresome, I find loathsome," I said to him now. "Before we married, you told me you had made your fortune in textiles, not human lives. And because you lied, I consider our marriage null and void."

"What you consider matters not, Julia. I am and always will be your husband in the eyes of the law. So you had best accept me for who I am. I cannot change the past."

"Change your heart then!" I cried. "Have you no regrets whatsoever?"

"Indeed I do, my dear one." He leaned toward me and spoke quietly. "I regret that as the end of my life draws nearer, I have no progeny to carry on my name." He looked at me as he had when first we'd met twenty months ago, with a tenderness that softened the hard angles of his face. "My deepest desire is to beget a child with you, Julia."

So this was his latest use for me! "You never expressed such a desire to me before, Jacques," I said. "Indeed, your sexual desires had nothing to do with conception."

"I wanted to enjoy you as I did my mistresses before you took on the role of mother. I hoped that would make you more . . . malleable. Instead, you became defiant."

"And I shall continue to defy you."

"No, Julia." All tenderness in his expression dissolved. "Because you are my lawful wedded wife, you are the only woman on the face of the earth who can produce for me a legitimate child. Therefore, you will return to France with me or else."

"Or else what?"

"I could have you kidnapped."

"You aren't serious."

"Of course I am. I will use any means possible to get what I want. But why make me go to extremes? Go pack your bags like a good little wife, for you will be leaving Plumford with me tomorrow morning. I have booked passage on a ship that sails in three days."

"Threaten and bully me all you will, Jacques, but I will not do your bidding. You will be leaving here empty-handed tomorrow, but perhaps you will have better success in the business you're conducting in Boston."

The look he threw me was knife-sharp. "Why do you assume I have business in Boston?"

If Mawuli had been indiscreet in mentioning it, I did not want to get him in trouble. "I know you well enough to assume you had more than one purpose in mind when you came to America," I replied. "The purpose you wish me to serve, however, is no longer yours to control."

He rose from his seat and yanked me up from mine. I had forgotten how unexpectedly he could move when provoked.

Or how strong he was, despite his age. "I will rape you here and now to get you with child."

He twisted my wrists in the vise of his grip, and I held back a gasp of pain, knowing that would only encourage him to hurt me further. "I *am* with child, Jacques."

He released me. "Who is the father?"

"Adam Walker."

Jacques sneered. "So you and your cousin are not so virtuous after all. You finally gave in to your lust despite the possible consequences. That child you are carrying will most likely be born a monster, will it not?"

"It would have been likely if Adam and I were blood related. But in fact we are not. I learned this when I came back here in December." I dared place my hand on my husband's arm. "Jacques, you know I have always loved Adam. I was completely honest with you before we wed."

He shrugged off my touch. "An unfaithful wife is not honest!"

"How could I remain faithful to a man as deceitful as you? Please go, Jacques. You have nothing to gain here."

"You are right. Everything here is mine already." He waved his hand around. "This house? By law, I own it, not you. And I can sell it right from under you. As my wife, your property belongs to me. Indeed, *you* are my property." He looked at me with disdain. "The child in your belly? By law, I own it too. The laws are the same here as they are in France regarding a husband's rights. And the day you bear that child, I will demand custody of it. I will take it to France, and you will never see it again. If it pleases me, I will make it my heir. If it does not please me . . ." He gave one of his odious shrugs. "Then perhaps it will not live very long."

Blood drained from my face, and my knees buckled. Wavering, I grabbed onto the back of a chair, but I did not allow myself to faint. I stood my ground.

"I am not alone and at your mercy as I was in France, Jacques. I have Adam to support me here. Together we will defeat you."

"Not in court you won't. Both here and in France, every law is on the side of the husband. *Au revoir, ma femme.* You need not see me out."

He picked up his hat and cane and departed. I could not move. I could barely breathe. Adam found me standing in the parlor, immobile as a statue.

ADAM

Sunday, May 21

Julia was in such despair over Pelletier's visit that she could barely tell me what had transpired. I coaxed it out of her as I rubbed her ice-cold hands. The more she divulged, the angrier I became, but I maintained a calm demeanor for her sake. She was upset enough as it was.

"Pelletier will never carry out his threats," I told her. "He's bluffing."

"You don't know him, Adam. He's vindictive enough to take possession of our child just for spite. Or even kill it!"

"No man in his right mind can be that cruel."

"He was cruel enough to enslave thousands of people for profit, wasn't he? And he feels not the slightest remorse over it."

"I will make him see reason."

"I'm afraid that will do more harm than good," Julia said.

"It never hurts to try and reason with someone."

"Just don't let him goad you into doing something you'll regret."

I headed for the Sun, confident that I could persuade Pelletier that it would benefit him as much as me to find a loophole in French law that would nullify his misbegotten marriage to Julia, setting them both free. At the same time, I felt the inclination to thrash the old fool for frightening Julia with his vile threats. But that would only give me temporary satisfaction and accomplish nothing. So I tamped down my anger once more and managed to put a passably pleasant expression on my face as I greeted the ladies sitting on the Sun porch sipping tea and nibbling sandwiches, Molly Munger and her mother amongst them.

I proceeded into the taproom. Ruggles, pouring out mugs of beer, greeted me heartily. Henry too was behind the bar with a measure rule in hand. I gave him a nod, but did not pause to speak with him. The room was crowded with "nooners" quaffing drinks to fortify them for the afternoon service back at the Meetinghouse whilst the womenfolk and children took their luncheon on the porch. At such a busy time at the Sun you'd have thought Mrs. Ruggles would have been scurrying about taking customer orders and then giving her own orders to the waitstaff. Instead, she was standing as still as I'd ever seen her, listening intently to a man sitting at a far corner table. After a moment she shook her head vehemently and exited the taproom in a huff. The man she had so abruptly left smiled after her. I concluded from his European top hat and arrogant bearing that he was none other than Jacques Pelletier.

As I approached the table he watched me with a reptilian stare. He did not look as old as I'd expected him to, but he did look quite ill. A plate containing an untouched piece of steak had been pushed aside.

"I have been expecting you, sir," he said when I was near enough to hear the low intonation of his voice.

"Then you know who I am?"

"Who else but the young, virile Dr. Adam Walker? Before we married, my dear wife, with whom I believe you are well acquainted, described you to me as exceedingly handsome. Of course, Madame Pelletier does have a tendency to exaggerate. In truth, I do not find you handsome at all."

If this was Pelletier's way of trying to get under my skin, I would have no problem keeping my temper with him. "May I join you?"

He waved toward a chair with such a majestic flourish I don't believe the Sun King could have done it better. Indeed, Pelletier seemed to think of himself as the king of the Sun Tavern, observing one and all from the great height of his superiority. I reckoned that he'd just hurt Edda Ruggles's feelings by telling her the food he'd been served was unpalatable.

I sat across from him and leaned forward to communicate confidentially. "You expressed intentions most evil to Julia a short time ago, Mr. Pelletier."

"I merely told her what my rights were," he mildly replied.

"I am willing to believe you spoke in the heat of passion and would never carry out such threats," I said magnanimously. "Indeed, I believe that you and I can reach an understanding that would result in a happy future for all concerned."

"You seem to hold many lofty beliefs, Dr. Walker. Please continue. I am all ears." He actually cupped a hand to his ear to demonstrate his willingness to listen.

I was beginning to think that perhaps Julia had exaggerated this man's implacability as much as she'd exaggerated my good looks. "Let us go to your room where we may speak in private," I suggested.

"Very well," he said. He reached for his cane and used it to help himself rise to his feet, at the same time pressing his palm to his abdomen.

"Primrose oil soothes stomach disorders," I could not help but prescribe.

He waved away my suggestion. "My valet knows best how to treat me for stomach ailments. This latest bout began in

Boston, despite my caution to avoid foul American cooking by eating nothing but beefsteak. And the beefsteak I've just been served here has proven to be inedible. The little Dutch strumpet who cooked it insists it is *bleu,* but any fool can plainly see it is almost *bien cuit.*"

He slowly made his way across the taproom, and I shortened my own pace to accommodate him. But he suddenly stopped as we came to the crowded bar. He turned and raised his cane at me in a threatening manner. I thought he was going to strike me with it, but instead he whacked it against the side of the bar. The resounding crack it made, loud as a gunshot, got everyone's attention. Conversations stopped.

"No reason to talk privately, Dr. Walker!" he shouted at me. "Let all who care to listen know you for the man you are. You have made a whore of my wife and a cuckold of me and you are a disgrace to your profession."

Overcome with indignation and humiliation, I was at a loss for words.

Alas, Pelletier was not. He turned away from me with a look of disgust and addressed the tavern patrons. "Do not trust that man with your wives and daughters." He pointed his cane at me. "Beneath his doctor's cloak of dignity crouches a carnal beast. He seduced my dear wife Julia, and they have had illicit relations ever since she came back to Plumford. She told me so herself less than an hour ago! Sick old man that I am, I nearly dropped dead from the shock of it. The two of them would have danced upon my grave if I had."

"Stop these lies!" I finally yelled.

"Lies? If you deny that you have fornicated with your cousin Julia Bell Pelletier, then whose bastard is she carrying in her belly now?"

I glanced about me and saw some of the women from the porch gathered in the open taproom doorway, eyes wide as they stared at me and my accuser. The men stared too. Many were longtime friends, such as the butcher Ira Munger and the fellows at his table, all members of the town-ball team I played with. Present too was a man who considered me his enemy, namely Constable Beers. His broad smirk made it clear he was enjoying Pelletier's performance.

Henry alone stepped forward to stand beside me. "You know Adam Walker to be a good man," he loudly proclaimed. "So why do you listen to a man you know not at all? I will tell you about Jacques Pelletier. He captained a slave ship and profited as a slave merchant. Therefore nothing he says can be trusted."

"I have spoken the truth," Pelletier replied, not to Henry, but to his audience. "And I have never broken the law. Unlike Dr. Walker here." This time he made so bold as to actually prod my arm with his cane. "Is not adultery illegal?"

"It is a crime!" Beers shouted from his table near the bar. "A crime subject to imprisonment in this good and godly state of Massachusetts. Why, I have half a mind to arrest Walker here and now."

That did not go over as well as Beers must have expected it to, for his threat was met with a chorus of boos. Not that such a reaction from my fellow townsmen made me feel any better. The most sacrosanct part of my being, my love for Julia, had been besmirched and displayed like dirty laundry by Pelletier. I have never hated a man more.

Henry looked at me and said in a low voice, "Stay calm, my friend. Say nothing more and walk out of here with your head high."

Such good advice. I was about to follow it, too. But then Pelletier spoke again.

"My wife should be arrested too!" he cried out. "The shameless bitch is as guilty of the crime as he is." Again Pelletier touched his cane to my person, prodding my chest with it this time.

The last time! I roared like a baited bear and yanked his cane from him. I took it in both my hands and swung it back like a bat. "I should kill you!" I bellowed.

If I had struck Pelletier with his cane, I am sure I would have struck him dead. But before I could act upon my murderous impulse, Henry grabbed hold of the cane from behind. I struggled to wrest it from his grip for only a moment, and then I let go of it, along with my homicidal rage.

"Best you leave now, Adam," Henry said in a low tone.

Now I listened to him and strode out of the taproom looking neither left nor right. In the hall Mawuli stepped forward from the shadows of the stair landing. From such a position he would have heard everything whilst remaining completely out of sight. "No need to kill the old man," he told me as I passed, apparently concerned over Pelletier's welfare.

JULIA

Monday, May 22

Molly didn't come to work this morning. Her mother came to call instead. I invited Mrs. Munger into the parlor and pointed out how good the Turkey carpet looked, thanks to Molly's application of her magical ox bile potion.

"Your daughter is a most diligent housekeeper," I said. "She'll make some man a fine wife someday."

"That is the very reason Molly cannot work for you anymore," Mrs. Munger replied.

"Molly is going to be married? How lovely! I didn't even know she had a suitor."

"You miscomprehend me," Mrs. Munger said. "That Molly does *not* have a suitor is the reason she cannot remain in your employ. She needs to keep her good name if she ever hopes to change it. Do you get my meaning?"

I did indeed, for Adam had recounted to me Pelletier's vile accusations at the tavern yesterday. It had pained him greatly to repeat them to me, and for me to hear them, but at least I knew what Mrs. Munger, and no doubt the whole town, was talking about now.

"What you are trying to tell me, Mrs. Munger," I said in a

level tone, "is that to protect her own reputation, your daughter must stay away from my house of ill repute."

"I would never call your house that," she protested, looking down at the rug. "But others will."

"Then you are right to keep Molly away from here."

She looked back at me, relieved. "I told Molly you would understand. You and Doc Adam always wanted what was best for her."

"And we still do."

"Ira and I wish you both the best too." Mrs. Munger placed her hand on my arm. "We will never forget that you and the doctor helped get Molly through a real bad time. You're the only ones who know about her troubles back then. And now you have your own troubles. Is it true that you are with child now, Julia?"

"I am. And I consider it a godsend rather than a trouble."

"To be sure. But some folks in town might not see it that way." There was sincere concern in Mrs. Munger's eyes. "Anyway, next time Ira butchers a calf, I'll have him bring you the liver. Best thing a woman who is eating for two can consume."

The very thought of it near made me gag. But I understood this was meant as a gesture of goodwill and thanked her kindly.

I went to Adam's office and found him standing before his open medicine cabinet. "I doubt many patients will be coming to the office today," he said, "so I thought this a good time to take inventory of my supplies."

"Can I help?"

"Would you write down the items I need to order?"

I took up a pencil and paper from his desk, happy to oblige him.

"Let's see," he said. "It seems I'm running low on monkey paws. And I'm clean out of cobra skins. As for crocodile heads, nary a one."

I laughed. "Have you become a witch doctor, Adam?"

"Apparently Mawuli was one back in Africa. He told me about such cures. Was he being facetious, I wonder?"

"I have always wondered that about Mawuli," I said.

"Did he ever speak to you of his past?"

"Whenever I asked him about it, he would tell me outlandish stories instead."

"Maybe they were true."

"Impossible!" I said. "The powers Mawuli claimed to me that he had were not based in medical science, I assure you."

"I suppose everything he says must be taken with a grain of salt," Adam said.

"For certain. I would not go so far as to call Mawuli devious, but I cannot call him forthright either. After all, he deliberately kept the fact that my husband was a slave trader from me. But to Mawuli's credit, he did help me get away from Pelletier."

"If only you had gotten away from him forever," Adam said bleakly. "If only we'd left Plumford and gone where Pelletier could never find you."

"Our list of 'if onlys' is indeed a long one," I said in just as forlorn a tone. "If only your grandmother had told us the truth, if only I hadn't married Pelletier, if only I hadn't come back and—"

"I thank God you came back, Julia!"

"But is it not ironic," I said, "that I fled Plumford to prevent you from ruining your life by marrying me, and now that I've returned I have ruined your life because you *cannot* marry me?"

"You have ruined nothing, for I have no life without you," Adam replied, taking me into his arms. "We are soul mates, Julia. Whatever else happens to us in this life, that will always remain true. And neither of us must utter the useless phrase *if only* again. Promise?"

I promised him with a kiss. The world fell away from us for

a moment, and we existed within ourselves alone. But even soul mates have to eat, so I forced myself to withdraw from the comfort of Adam's arms and go off to Daggett's Market.

The usual loiterers were there, smoking their pipes and listening to Mr. Daggett read aloud from the Boston newspaper that is delivered by the mail coach three times a week. They paid me no mind whatsoever, so enthralled were they with the account of a thief who had managed to scale the side of the Tremont Hotel to its uppermost fourth floor and enter, through an unlocked window, the suite of a leading lady of the Boston stage and abscond with her jewelry. The steeplejack climbing skills of the thief suggested that he was none other than the infamous burglar known as Jack Steeple in New York City, where he has succeeded in similar hotel thefts.

I stood at the counter as I listened, waiting for Mr. Daggett's wife to acknowledge me. She did not. Although there were no other customers in need of her attention, apparently the potatoes were, for she spent a great deal of time rearranging them in the bin. And then she walked right past me to the other side of the store and gave the same amount of attention to the doodads and thingamajigs displayed in a glass case on the other counter. I joined her there and said Good Day. She did not so much as look up at me. So that's the way it was to be for me, I realized. I had become invisible to the good people of Plumford.

Edda Ruggles came bustling in with a basket hanging from her plump arm, and I expected her to snub me too. Instead she greeted me as usual, and when Mrs. Daggett offered to assist her, she suggested that I be waited on first. In fact, she insisted upon it. And so it was thanks to Mrs. Ruggles that I was able to purchase what I needed from Mrs. Daggett. And as I crossed the Green she caught up and fell into stride with me.

Because she was a newcomer in town, and a foreigner to boot, I thought I'd better set her straight. "Perhaps you do not realize that I am being shunned, Mrs. Ruggles."

"Oh, I know all about shunning," she said.

"Yet you dare be seen talking to me? Even after the vile things Pelletier said about me?"

"Worse has been said about m . . . many women," Mrs. Ruggles said. "How come you married such a bad man?"

"He tricked me into thinking he was a good man."

Mrs. Ruggles gave me a pitying look. "Not the first time that happened to a young woman."

How understanding she was! It was good to know I had at least one friend left in town. "Your kindness is much appreciated, Mrs. Ruggles." We stopped at my front gate. "Would you care to come in for a cup of tea?"

She shook her head. "That Frenchman would not be here but for you," she said. "Make him go away before something bad happens."

"If I could, I would," I said.

"Maybe *you* should go away."

"But that's exactly what Pelletier wants me to do! He wants me to leave here in shame!" I said.

Mrs. Ruggles's expression hardened. "If you go away, so will he. And there won't be no more trouble."

I realized Mrs. Ruggles had no intention of being a friend to me after all. She just wanted to make sure there were no more nasty scenes at the tavern.

"There won't be any more trouble at the Sun," I assured her. "Dr. Walker realizes that he fell right into Pelletier's trap by seeking him out in a public place, and he will never do so again."

"Go away," Mrs. Ruggles said again. "The doctor too. This is good advice I am giving to you. Listen to it!" She turned her back to me and marched off to the Sun.

ADAM

Monday, May 22

Only one patient came to the office today, and not until late afternoon. He was a small farm boy brought into town by his father. The lad had been hitting two hammers together for no reason other than he liked the sound, and a shard had broken off from one of the heads and imbedded itself into the corner of his right eye. It was delicate work to tease out the steel splinter with my smallest forceps. The shard lay quite close to the rectus muscle controlling eye movement, and, to make matters worse, it was jagged. But with patience I was able to work it free and out. It took only four tiny stitches of my finest catgut to close the wound, and I expect a full recovery. I felt mighty good when I sent father and son on their way.

But the good feeling left me less than five minutes later, for I went back to turning over and over in my mind that Julia and I could no longer remain in Plumford. Henry bounded into my office and interrupted my morose ruminations.

"I have something of great interest to relate to you and Julia," he declared. His large clear eyes were shining bright.

We went down the passageway and into the house and

found Julia in her studio. She invited us to sit down at a large table strewn with sketch pads and artist paraphernalia.

"First off," Henry said, "I think you would like to know that I just witnessed Pelletier being shat upon in the Sun taproom."

"Figuratively or literally?" I said.

"Quite literally. The culprit was Mrs. Ruggles's parrot Roos."

"I am beginning to like that bird," Julia said.

"Well, Pelletier most assuredly does not," Henry said. "He was at his usual table at the back examining a sheaf of papers when Roos took a notion to fly off her perch near the bar and alight on his head. Startled, Pelletier stood up with such violence that he tipped over the table and sent all his papers flying in every direction. Roos too was startled by his sudden movement and fluttered overhead, squawking madly. Pelletier swatted at her most viciously and would have surely killed her if his flailing hands had made contact, but Roos managed to elude him. Before she flew off she also managed to decorate Pelletier's forehead and the front of his coat with a long and thick streak of white, viscous guano flecked with nuts and seeds."

Julia and I laughed most unsympathetically at her husband, no credit to us, but most understandable, I think.

"Pelletier was livid with anger and disgust at his condition," Henry went on, "and Ruggles hurried over to him with a wet cloth to remove the offending ordure from flesh and fabric. As Ruggles attended to Pelletier's person I made myself useful by scooping up the papers strewn about the floor. Of course I had no interest in being of service to Pelletier. My interest was in the papers themselves. I feared they might be legal documents that could be injurious to the two of you."

"And were they?" I said.

"No. They were drawings."

"Of lewd carnal acts?" Julia said.

Henry looked surprised. "Actually, they were technical drawings of a large ship," he said. "One of them depicted the craft in profile, as if one side had been cut away to reveal the innards of the vessel. I committed it to memory before Pelletier even noticed me studying it. When I gathered up all the drawings and handed them back to him he did not even bother to acknowledge my helpfulness. I believe Pelletier thinks I am some sort of menial at the Sun, so of course he discounts me entirely."

"Can you tell us more about this ship?" I asked him.

"I can show you." Henry took a pencil from the box on the table. "May I?" he asked Julia.

"Of course. That's the box of Thoreau pencils you gave me after all." She opened a sketchbook and set it before Henry.

"I have a most accurate recall of visual images," he said as he started to draw. "It has been most useful in my studies of flora and fauna. Unfortunately, I lack your artistic talent, Julia. But I shall do my best to duplicate exactly the ship drawing I studied."

As Henry drew he began to speak of a subject entirely different from the ship, and it seemed to me his hand and eye operated separately from his power of speech.

"Last night," he said, "I was roused from sleep by a strange sound seeping through the wall from the next room, which is occupied by Mawuli. The sound began low like a growl and then went high like a keening wail and faded away and came back again, over and over."

Julia caught her breath. "I too once heard such a sound emanate from the room Mawuli occupied in Cannes. I even knocked on his door and asked if he were ill. The sound stopped, and he told me to go away."

"My impulse to go to his aid was the same as yours," Henry continued. "I rose and crept out into the hall and stood before Mawuli's door to listen, wondering if he were sick or mad. He must not have seated his door bolt properly, for when I gently pushed I heard the bolt slide away, and the door eased open. Now, I know it was surely not my business to peer into another man's room. I would have stopped if the strange sound had not risen to a new intensity, not in volume but in energy so the very air vibrated as from a bass drum.

"I pushed the door open and saw a naked black man seated cross-legged on the floor, facing me. I could not at first even recognize him as Mawuli, as his face was painted with thick white circles around the eyes and red and white bands across the forehead and cheeks. The effect was rather terrifying. His eyes were wide as he stared unseeing or perhaps seeing into another world entirely. He chanted with such intensity that he seemed to be calling up Spirits from that world, and I sensed a dark malevolence around him. I suddenly realized I was spying on a man in a deep state of consciousness that it was not my affair to know, and so I went back to my room. His chanting came to an end perhaps fifteen minutes later."

"I am glad I was spared such a sight of him as that!" Julia said. "And I have never sensed such a malevolence around Mawuli. Indeed, I have always felt safe around him. Pelletier is the one who exudes evil."

Henry nodded. "Evil such as this?"

He showed us his drawing. It was a fair rendition of the innards of a lean and beautiful sailing ship with three very tall masts and a sharp narrow bow raked far forward for speed.

"It looks to be a clipper ship," I said.

"The fastest ship there is," Henry said. He pointed to long, narrow compartments, stacked one atop the other, from the bilge right up to the deck. Then he pointed to a large cargo space without compartments, lined around its perimeters with a bold, thick pencil line. "This area was lined thus in the drawing I saw, which indicates heavy caulking. Hence, I believe this area is a leak-proof tank large enough to hold ten or fifteen thousand gallons of water. There is only one reason a ship built for speed would have such a large water tank as that." He pointed back to the tightly spaced compartments. "To keep the cargo stored in this other area alive."

"Human cargo," I said.

Julia looked appalled. "This is a depiction of a slave ship! Is it the one Pelletier owned twenty years ago?"

"I fear," Henry said, "it is a depiction of a new ship. Here is what was printed beneath the drawing." He picked up the pencil again and quickly wrote: *Designed for J. Pelletier, to be launched May 26, 1848.*

"But it's now illegal to transport slaves across the Atlantic," Julia said. "The waters along the African coast are patrolled by American and English navy squadrons to prevent it."

"A clipper ship can outrun any naval patrol ship," Henry said. "Especially a Boston clipper. They set new records every month."

"And that's why Pelletier had his ship built here," I said.

"He can't have openly commissioned it as a slave ship, though," Henry said. "The building or outfitting of ships for that purpose has been illegal in America for decades."

"Prove that Pelletier has broken the law," Julia said, "and he will be arrested or deported." She looked at me with hope in her eyes. "We would be free of him!"

I was willing to risk my very life to be free of Pelletier. I turned to Henry. "We must act now. The ship is near ready to sail."

"I have a plan in mind already," he replied in his calm, steadfast way. "We will begin by asking Cato Davis to help us. As a caulker he knows the docks."

Off we raced to the Concord station once again and managed to catch the last train heading for Boston that day. We located Cato and Rose in the North Slope. They were both overjoyed to learn that Tansy was safe. Cato most willingly agreed to help us. He found a rowboat and just after sunset he rowed Henry and me across the harbor toward the East Boston shipyards. He weighed his oars as we approached the long line of wharves, where we could see the hulls of ships being laid or in various stages of completion.

"Let's wait here for the cover of night," he said. "If what you say is afoot, that clipper is sure to be guarded."

Henry asked him how the building of a ship designed to transport slaves could be kept secret with so many men working on it.

"Shipbuilding ain't no different from any other enterprise," Cato replied. "A few men see the whole of it; most just see the parts. My part is caulking the hull inside a ship afore work gets started on laying out decks and such. Those caulking the outside hull never see the inside. There's bound to be some that know more about what's going on, but they can be paid off easy enough. Men need the work and don't mind looking the other way if it profits them."

Several ships eased out into the harbor, letting the outgoing tide slowly drift them out toward the sea. The sailors of one fat-bowed whaler waved to us and hollered they were headed to the South Pacific after sperm whales.

"They most likely be gone two, maybe three years," Cato said, shaking his head. "I couldn't do it. No sir. That's way too long away from my Rose for me. Sometimes they don't come back at all. You heard about that whale that stove in a whaler and sank her? Near all the men were lost, and the rest drifted about till they went near crazy. No, no, I'll caulk ships but not sail off in them. Call me a landlubber if you care to, and I will not take offense. No sir."

When it became dark enough to suit Cato, he rowed the boat closer to the wharves. "There are more than a few clippers being built out here," he said.

"The one we want is ready to sail," Henry said. "There cannot be so very many of those."

We drifted by sloops, barks, brigs, cutters, ketches, and schooners. Then the first clipper hull came into view, the bow narrow and raked far out over the water.

"That one is being built for the China trade," Cato said. "I got a friend working on it, and I know that she ain't ready to sail."

We passed three more clippers in various stages of construction. Henry told Cato to stop near the dark hull of another. "Why is the shore end of this ship's wharf blocked off?" he asked Cato.

"Beats me. It's not under repair, and that's the only reason to block a wharf."

"Another reason would be to keep people off it," Henry said. "And it looks to me as if this ship is ready to sail."

"It sure is," Cato said. "The rigging's set, and every sail's furled and ready."

The ship was as fine a sailing vessel as I ever set my eyes on, sharp-lined, with three uncommonly high masts supporting wide yardarms that could each carry enough sail to catch all the wind in the sky. As we eased closer I could smell fresh pine tar and varnish and new hemp rope.

"Avast, there!" a man bellowed at us from the deck of the ship. He was no more than fifty feet away and pointed a musket at us. "Be off with you, or I'll put a hole in the head of each of you."

"Sorry, sorry," Cato called. "Wrong ship. Got two gentlemen here looking for a brig that's sailing on with this tide."

"A brig! You blind as well as thick as pitch? We got three masts here, not two." With that he leveled the gun and fired a shot that whistled just over our heads. "Away with you."

Cato put his back to the oars and had us around the bow soon enough.

"That must be the one we're looking for," he said. "No reason to be so tetchy unless you got something to hide."

"We must get aboard to find hard evidence this clipper is a slaver," Henry said.

"Don't include me," Cato said. "If I got caught sneaking on board, I'd get banned from the shipyard."

"No need to risk your livelihood," Henry said. "Just row close in so Adam and I can get aboard."

"That I will do," Cato said. "But best to wait for clouds to block out the moonlight. Then we got a chance of not being seen if I come in right under the bow from dead ahead of the ship. The lookout can't see to forward so easy with that high bowsprit."

When clouds rolled in and covered the moon Cato sprang into action, silently and quickly rowing right under the bowsprit. "I'll wait for you here," he said in a low voice. "Eyes on deck can't look this far over the side to see me. You take care now. Don't get yourselves shot through like Swiss cheese."

Cato boosted Henry and then me up onto the long and slippery bowsprit. We crawled onto the deck and saw it was deserted but for the man with the musket. He stood at the stern facing away. We quickly made our way to the main mast and crouched behind it.

I began to have doubts of the sanity of our venture and re-minded myself that I was there for Julia, to free her from Pel-letier, one way or another. I crawled on hands and knees and slid over the edge of a hatch, held onto its edge, let myself down my full length whilst holding on, then dropped down perhaps two feet onto the deck below. I heard no running feet or alarmed voices. Henry soon followed, and there we stood below decks in near pitch dark. Now what?

We stepped away from the hatch when we heard a heavy tread approaching overhead as the armed watchman walked from aft to fore along the starboard side.

On cat feet we began to venture into the bowels of the ship. It seemed clear of men. On the first level below decks we found carpenters' tools and heavy boxes spaced down along the length of the hull but nothing else. A narrow set of stairs led down to the next level. We had prepared ourselves for the darkness, and I scratched and lit the first locofoco match, which flared so brightly it blinded us for an instant.

And then we saw all too clearly the evidence we sought. Bolted into the sides of the ship and at regular intervals in the floor away from the sides hung and lay sets of hand and ankle manacles, each ready to hold a slave for the voyage from Africa to Brazil, the Indies, or our own shores. The sight chilled me to the marrow.

And there were more horrors to discover. We forced open a box that contained branding irons with the initials *JP* at one end. And in another box we found six-foot-long plaited leather whips that tapered to a cruel knotted end that could no doubt tear flesh and draw blood at every lash.

I could not see Henry's expression in the dark, but his voice was so filled with fury when he spoke I hardly recognized it. Even so, what he said was levelheaded and practical. "I will take away a pair of branding irons, and you take a whip, Adam. We need to have some physical evidence to show the Boston police."

"Let's be gone then," I said, as yet another locofoco burned out and filled the atmosphere with the smell of sizzling phosphorus. I imagined how stifling the air in here would become when the hold was packed with the bodies of men and women stacked close as cordwood. Many would surely die in the suffocating tropical heat. We could not let that happen.

We found a set of stairs at midship and emerged out onto the deck, where I breathed in welcome draughts of clean air but could not keep myself from coughing lightly.

"Who goes there?" the guard shouted from the bow. "I seen you. Stop, the both of you, or I will shoot you dead where you stand." He rushed toward us.

"We cannot surrender," Henry said.

I had no intention of doing so! We were as doomed as the intended passengers of this slave ship if we got captured, sure to be clapped in irons and tossed overboard once the ship was out to sea.

We turned and ran a few paces, and then Henry whirled about. As the guard raised his weapon, Henry flung one of the branding irons at him. The stout metal rod whirred through the air and caught the man full on the shoulder just as he fired the gun. The bullet struck and splintered a spar not a foot above my head.

As we raced sternward we saw another man emerge from the captain's cabin on the quarterdeck with a grappling hook in his hand. We stopped, apparently trapped.

"Up!" Henry cried. "We must go up."

Both of us jumped onto the rigging of the aft mast and scampered upward as a bullet was fired. It whizzed in the air above us and did neither of us harm. We reached the topmost yardarm, as shouts sounded below us. No more shots were fired as we kept the thick mast between the shooter and us.

"What now, Henry?" I said as I looked down at the deck from a height that caused my head to whirl.

"There's nothing for it," Henry calmly said, "but to leap into the water. When you come up stay close to the ship and swim to Cato."

"What if the shots have caused him to flee?"

"That would be most unfortunate," Henry said.

To get beyond the deck below and over the water, we had to slide our feet along a swaying rope under the yardarm whilst we clung to it for balance. Another bullet buzzed through the air past us as we sidled out, Henry leading the way. The other guard was climbing up toward us, growling obscenities and waving the grappling hook.

Henry scurried out to the end of the yardarm, turned to me, and said, "Leap for your life, Adam."

Then he was gone. I moved after him, but a shot from below parted the rope below my feet, and instead of leaping I fell like a sack of potatoes straight downward. I expected to have my head cracked open like a coconut shell against the gunwale, but only my left hand grazed the side of the ship as I tumbled, arms and legs flailing. I hit the water feet first and plunged deep into the bay.

I slowly rose up along the smooth side of the ship to the surface and swam bow-ward. I saw no sign of Henry. When I reached the bow I saw Cato's boat bobbing below the bowsprit. He looked to be alone.

He motioned me toward him, and when I reached him he leaned far over and hauled me up over the side. "Henry?" I gasped.

"Don't see him," Cato whispered.

We waited one, two, three minutes, or was it an eternity? What if Henry had struck a timber floating in the water and been knocked out and drowned? Or been shot? He might well be injured, clinging to the side of the ship, unable to move.

"I must swim back to look for him," I said.

"No call for it," Henry whispered from the water. "Pull me up, Cato."

Henry was smiling broadly, making clear his delight with our adventure. For a man who claims to be most content in quiet contemplation, he surely loves action when it comes his way. He raised the branding iron to show me he had managed to hold on to his evidence. I still had the whip as well.

After Cato got us safely ashore, Henry and I hurried to the home of John P. Coburn, leader of the Boston Vigilant Committee. As a free black man, Mr. Coburn had attained a level of wealth sufficient to own a fine, three-story brick home at the top of Phillips Street on Beacon Hill. I had never met this friend of Henry's, a short, plump man with grizzled side-whiskers, and introductions were quickly made at the door.

"Pray excuse my informal appearance, gentlemen," Coburn said, retying the belt on his velvet smoking jacket, "but I was not expecting visitors."

Politely ignoring our own appearances, for we must have looked like two drowned water rats, he ushered us into his library and invited us to sit down. We hesitated, not wanting to apply our damp posteriors to the horsehair cushions, but he insisted we pay no mind to that.

Henry told Coburn of our discovery of the slave ship, making sure to praise Cato's bravery in putting himself in harm's way to guide and assist us. Coburn listened intently and without interruption, but his eyes expressed his growing horror, and when Henry produced the branding iron and I the whip, Coburn outright shuddered.

"So this evil pollutes even the Boston harbor, despite laws against building slave ships," he said in a voice hoarse with emotion. "Millions upon millions of souls are in bondage, yet ships are still being built to capture *more* slaves! When will it end?"

"As long as slavery remains legal, it will continue to grow," Henry said.

"And for every thousand we help escape to freedom each year on the Railroad," Coburn said, "thousands more are born or sold into slavery."

"We cannot give up," Henry said. "There is victory in every effort." He hefted the branding iron in one hand and the whip in the other. "And at least we have evidence to stop one slave ship from sailing."

"Let us go to the police forthwith," Coburn said.

"What about Pelletier?" I said. "If he receives word from

the guards on his ship that security was breached, he will likely flee the country."

I volunteered to go back to Plumford to prevent him from leaving before authorities came to arrest him, and Coburn supplied me with a change of dry clothes and a horse from his stable.

JULIA

Monday, May 22

I was left in a limbo between hope and despair after Adam and Henry departed for Boston—hope that they would be able to put a halt to Pelletier's criminal plans; despair that nothing could stop Pelletier from *any* of his evil intentions. My spirit rose one moment and plunged the next, and to calm myself I took the best cure I knew. I went for a walk. Unfortunately, I had become the town's Unrespectable Spectacle, so rather than have people silently glare at me on the Green or public byways, I limited my stroll to my own long backyard. Up and down it I paced, the late afternoon sun warming my back and the breeze cooling my face. My inward musings turned to an outward awareness of my surroundings, and for a while I felt at peace with myself and the world around me. The wisteria and iris were blooming, the aspens were shimmering, the warblers were warbling, and the air was redolent with the scent of honeysuckle. How good Mother Nature was, how gentle and bountiful!

But then plangent squawking and screeching broke my short-lived peace, and from a nearby mountain laurel burst a Cooper's hawk, clutching in its talons a piteously peeping robin hatchling, still naked, its stubby wings barely formed. Two adult robins, screaming madly, made a valiant attempt to save their baby by pecking at the hawk's back, but they could not stop it. The hawk disappeared into the dense leaves of a sycamore with its helpless victim, leaving the parents to circle aimlessly in the sky.

I buried my face in my hands and wept for them. In my overwrought mind I could not help but think of the hawk as my avenging husband and the hatchling as Adam's and my child. I did not allow this maudlin notion to overcome me for long. After a moment I took a deep breath and wiped the tears from my face. This was not the right time for self-pity. Indeed, there is never a right time for such an indulgence as that.

I returned to the house and went up to the attic to see if Tansy needed anything. She was lying on the makeshift bed, staring up at the rafters. "I'm getting mighty twitchy to move on," she told me. "My whole life seems to be at a standstill."

I sympathized. There is nothing more frustrating than having one's life put on hold for reasons out of one's control. "You must try to be patient," I said. How much easier to give that advice than take it.

"I don't mean to sound ungrateful, Julia. I do appreciate having a safe place to hide out. And I thank you for putting me up for so long."

"It's only been three days. How long did you stay with the Tripps?"

"Only a day. But that was long enough to see something I wish I hadn't."

"What was that?"

"Never mind. I shouldn't have mentioned it."

"Whatever you saw might help us find Mr. Tripp's killer, Tansy."

"This has nothing to do with his murder. And I do not wish to talk against the man who lost his life because he was helping me."

I debated whether or not to tell Tansy about the other Conductor who had been killed the same night. Would knowing that Mr. Vogel hadn't been transporting a runaway when he was murdered appease her guilt? Or would learning that there was an assassin out there bent on killing UGRR Conductors make Tansy think it would be safer to strike out on her own? Surely Prouty would catch her if she did.

I decided to hold back telling Tansy about the assassin. I also held back from questioning her further about what she saw regarding Mr. Tripp. It had been my experience with Tansy that she would only divulge information in her own good time. Unbidden, she often talked about Prouty, and I knew more about the man than I really cared to, such as his preference for beets over okra, and his extraordinary ability to smell rain coming. But whenever I tried to ascertain Tansy's true feelings for him, she would just press her lips together and shake her head.

"I wager a change of scenery would cheer you up," I told her. "We can't chance having someone catch sight of you through a first-story window, but if you stay upstairs you'll be safe enough from prying eyes."

"What if your housekeeper comes upstairs?"

"That's no longer a concern," I said. "Molly didn't come today, and neither do I expect any visitors. Indeed, I would much appreciate your company, Tansy."

We settled at a card table in my bedchamber, and I taught her how to play the French card game écarté. She learned the game quickly but soon grew bored with it and suggested that we read to each other instead. I immediately went to my bed stand and picked up the book atop it.

"What about this?" I said. "It's a novel I recently ordered

from London that I am most eager to read. It's said to be rather radical."

Tansy looked interested. "Who wrote it?"

"Currer Bell. But that's probably a pen name. Rumor has it a woman wrote this novel. It's called *Jane Eyre: An Autobiography.*"

Tansy's interest appeared to wane. "That doesn't sound very radical."

"Apparently male critics find the book so. In their opinion the character Jane Eyre is far too independent and rebellious in her thinking."

"Then let us read her autobiography by all means!" Tansy said.

We spent the rest of the afternoon reading aloud to each other, our voices growing more intense as the story's excitement built and the characters' emotions deepened. At dusk I brought up a pot of tea and a tin of biscuits, along with the Argand lamp from the parlor. Before I lit the lamp I drew the curtains tightly closed, for my bedchamber windows face the Green. The tea was weak and tepid, the biscuits were stale, but what did that matter? The writing was strong and fresh, the story both heartrending and inspiring, and another few hours flew by.

And then, as evening fell, there was a sharp rapping on the front entrance door. Tansy stopped reading mid-sentence and stared at me, wide-eyed. "Who might that be?"

I knew exactly who it was, for I recognized the staccato rhythm of Pelletier's cane. I considered ignoring his rap but feared that would only provoke him to defame me publicly again with vile insults shouted on my doorstep.

"I must deal with this visitor," I told Tansy.

"Should I go up to the attic?"

"Yes, that would be safest."

I picked up the lamp, and we went down the hall together. We paused at the attic doorway, and I cautioned Tansy to take care going up the stairs in the dark and to not make a sound. I then proceeded downstairs to open the door to Pelletier.

"What do you want?" I asked him.

"Aren't you going to invite me in?"

"We have nothing further to discuss."

"What took you so long to answer the door? Is your lover with you?"

"I am quite alone and wish to remain so."

Pelletier pushed his way past me into the hallway and snatched the lamp from my hand. "I would like to verify how alone you are, faithless wife."

Off he went searching from room to room as I followed close at his heels. "Get out of my house, Jacques!"

"*Our* house, my spouse."

After looking into all the downstairs rooms, he headed up the stairs with me right behind him. I prayed that he would not get it into his head to inspect the attic, too.

He did not. After looking into all the other bedchambers, he got to mine and glared at the two teacups on the table. He even took the liberty of sticking his finger into one of them. "He was here with you just a little while ago, wasn't he, my dear?"

My husband's voice was as smooth as silk, and his eyes were as hard as stones. Those were warning signs I was regrettably familiar with, and I moved as fast as I could to get out of his reach. 'Twas not fast enough to get out of the reach of his cane, however. He managed to give me a glancing blow on my forehead with it. Dazed, I stumbled against the table. The china teapot fell to the floor and shattered as I dropped to my knees.

"I could beat you to death and be pardoned for it," he said, standing over me with his cane raised.

Before he could strike me with it again, I picked up a porcelain shard and plunged it into his thigh. He yelped like a dog and dropped his cane. I tried to rise to my feet, but he hit me again, this time a punch to the eye with his fist. That sent me right down on my back. He was on top of me in the next instant. I still had the sharp teapot fragment in hand, and I meant to plunge it into his chest this time, but he caught my wrist and twisted it until my china weapon fell from my grasp. He hit me a few more times in the face, but not as hard as the first punch. He was panting, and I sensed he was growing weak fast. I believed I still stood a chance of getting the better of him before he raped me, for I was sure that was his intention. But then I felt his hands around my neck and realized he intended to throttle me instead. What strength he had left was directed into that grasp. My vision dimmed, but I clearly heard the sound of insane laughter. It did not seem to be coming out of Pelletier's grimacing mouth.

A thwacking sound followed, and I saw that Pelletier was being attacked from behind by a shrouded creature that continued to howl with laughter as it used Pelletier's own cane to beat him about the back and shoulders. When he took his hands from my throat the beating stopped. He pushed himself up and stood. His attacker and he were of equal height, but he did not attempt to take on the deranged creature. Instead, he stumbled out of the room and down the stairs without looking back. The creature threw his cane over the banister after him, and it clattered on the floor. I scrambled upright, found his hat on the floor, and threw that over the banister too. A moment later the front door slammed shut. The creature flew to the window and peeked through a slit in the curtain.

"There he goes. Looks to be limping toward the tavern. Good thing I threw him back his hateful cane. Don't think he could have walked away without it. I could have done him worse injury, but feared I would kill him if I hit him on the head. I didn't want to get myself hanged for killing a white man."

"He might well have killed *me* if you hadn't come down from the attic and scared him off," I said.

The creature turned to me and let the sheet shroud drop away. "Mrs. Rochester at your service." Tansy curtsied.

And I applauded. But then I had to hold on to the bedpost to steady myself. I was quite shaken up. "It was brave of you to come to my aid, and I thank you, Tansy."

"Who was that nasty old man anyway?"

"My husband."

"No!" Tansy's eyes widened. "I drove off Satan himself!"

"But he may come back."

"I'll keep watch," Tansy said. "You best lie down, Julia. You don't look so good."

I took up the looking glass on my dresser to see for myself and near fainted. "Dear God help me," I said.

"Dear God help us both!" Tansy said as she peered out the window. "A monster even more fearsome than Satan is coming toward the house. He is as black as the night and as tall as a mountain."

A moment later there was pounding on the door. "Will you go down and let him in, Tansy? I feel too dizzy to manage it."

"Let him in? Are you plumb crazy?" She did not move a muscle.

Mawuli let himself in, for neither Tansy nor I had thought to bolt the door. He stood in the hall and shouted my name.

"He's come to get you, Julia!" Tansy said.

"No, he's come to help me."

I called back to Mawuli to come upstairs. Tansy gasped at first sight of him, no doubt because of his scars, but Mawuli showed no reaction when he took in my battered face.

"I knew Monsieur had done evil when he returned to the Sun," he said in an even tone. "I came here to make sure you were still alive. Where is Dr. Walker?"

"He went to Boston with Henry Thoreau."

"To the shipyards?"

I nodded. "If you know that, Mawuli, you must also know their reason for going there. You know that Pelletier is having a slave ship built."

His expression remained inscrutable. "Go to bed, Madame. You look like you have had a very hard time of it."

ADAM

Early Tuesday morning, May 23

It was well past midnight when I rode into Plumford, but I was not surprised to see light through the drawn curtains of Julia's bedchamber windows. I had expected her to wait up for me. I let myself in and bounded up the stairs, eager to tell her that our mission had been successful and Pelletier would soon be arrested. I found her in bed, propped up by pillows, a cloth over her face. Tansy was sitting beside her, holding her hand.

"What happened?" I said, rushing to Julia's side.

Julia removed the cloth from her face, and I saw that she had contusions over her left brow and right cheek, an ecchymosis of the left eye, and a split lip. Most horrifying of all were the purple finger marks on her smooth white neck, for they might have resulted in death by strangulation.

"I'm going to be just fine," she told me softly. "Tansy has been taking good care of me."

"I've been applying a cabbage leaf poultice to her bruises," Tansy said. "It helps them heal faster. One time Prouty got himself kicked by a mule and—"

"Did Pelletier do this to you?" I asked Julia.

"Who else?" a deep voice inquired. I whirled around and

saw Mawuli enter the room. He was carrying a coffee pot, which he set upon the card table. "Shall I bring you a cup, Dr. Walker?"

I brushed past him without bothering to reply and made my way out of the room, blind with rage.

"Don't go to the Sun, Adam!" Julia called after me as I dashed down the stairs.

I could hear Mawuli's tread right behind me, and he grabbed my arm when I reached the front gate. "Leave the old man alone," he said.

"Why do you want to protect Pelletier, Mawuli? He's still a slaver, damn it! I saw his new ship with my own eyes tonight."

Mawuli had nothing to say to that. His countenance was impassive as he continued to grip my arm. He was a good foot taller than me, but also a good forty years older, so I reckoned I could take him on.

"Let go my arm or I will fight you," I said.

He released his hold immediately, and without another word he returned to the house. I continued on to the tavern. Fueled by rage, I was there in what seemed seconds.

I did not know what I intended to do to Pelletier when I entered the Sun. Do him bodily harm, most certainly. Kill him? Possibly. I was too incensed to have formed a lucid plan in my fervid mind. I glanced around the taproom to see if Pelletier might be lurking there, but the only customers at this late hour were Beers and a drinking crony. They were playing a desultory game of dominoes whilst Ruggles wiped down the bar. The three men all looked back at me warily. My countenance must have reflected my fulminating emotions.

"I was getting ready to close up, Adam," Ruggles said in a cautious tone. "But I'll be happy to serve you up a drink on the house. You look like you are in need of one."

"Not at all," I said as coolly as I could manage. "I have come to check on my patient Haven."

"Odd time to be doing that," Ruggles said.

"Such are a doctor's hours."

With as much control as I could muster, I proceeded to mount the stairs leading to the inn's bedchambers. The first room, I knew, was occupied by Haven, and I walked right past it. I tried the door of the next one. It was unlocked, and I peered inside. No one was within, and the narrow bed was neatly made. A leather carpenter's apron hung on a peg, and I guessed it was Henry's temporary living quarters. It occurred to me that if Henry had returned to Plumford with me, he might have talked me out of what I intended to do. But *what* did I intend to do? I still had not admitted to myself that my intention was murder.

The next door I opened revealed an unoccupied sitting room lit by a sputtering oil lamp on the wall. I recognized Pelletier's cane leaning against a chair and his top hat upon it. There was a small table covered with a white cloth in the middle of the room, and on it was a full carafe of wine, an empty glass, a fork beside a folded napkin, and a thick piece of steak on a plate, the blood and juice around it congealed. Despite my raging emotions, I paid careful attention to all this in order to ascertain if Pelletier was alone behind the closed door across the sitting room, which I assumed led to the bedchamber. I had no wish to harm anyone but him. There were no signs that he had company, so I threw open the door.

Pelletier was indeed alone, laid out on his back in the bed, fully clothed. He did not acknowledge my sudden presence. I would have thought him in deep, peaceful slumber but for the knife buried in his chest. I pulled it out and observed wet, slick blood on the blade. There was no blood on his pale silk waistcoat until a drop or two dripped upon it from the withdrawn knife. With my free hand I felt his forehead. It was cold. I moved his jaw from side to side with difficulty. I picked up his arm by the wrist and noticed definite stiffening in the shoulder joint. There was no question rigor mortis had commenced, and I estimated he had died at least five or six hours ago.

I became aware of footsteps and looked out the doorway to see Beers and Ruggles enter the sitting room. I stood frozen over the body as they rushed toward me.

"Good Lord, Adam, what have you done?" Ruggles said, pausing at the bedchamber threshold.

"Put down your knife," Beers ordered, standing behind Ruggles.

"It's not my knife. I found it already plunged into his heart when I came in. But I don't think it killed him."

"Of course it did!" Beers said. "A knife in the heart is always fatal. And I will ask you one last time to put down your murder weapon, Walker. You are under arrest."

"Don't be an idiot, Beers!" I yelled in frustration, brushing past Ruggles to speak directly to the constable. "Just listen to what I am trying to explain to you. This is *not* the murder weapon." I waved the knife in front of his bleary eyes.

Beers backed away from me and blundered against a chair in the sitting room. "Help me, Ruggles!" he said.

I turned to look at Ruggles, still standing at the threshold. He was white as a sheet from the shock of seeing a dead man in one of the Sun's bedchambers. "Best you drop the knife, Adam," he said softly.

In the next instant I caught a glimpse of the heavy silver head of Pelletier's cane come flashing at me. It hit the side of my head before I could duck. I dropped the knife and pressed my hand to my ear, cupping blood. Stunned, I stared at Beers.

He drew back the cane again, his fat face looking frightened yet eager to deliver another blow. This one landed on my crown, and I lost consciousness the next instant.

JULIA

Tuesday, May 23

I was greeted by a sound like a beehive stirred up with a stick when I entered the Meetinghouse for the Hearing this afternoon. The pews were packed, and all heads turned to watch me walk down the aisle. How grateful I was to have Henry's strong arm for support, for I was weak from shock and lack of sleep. I ignored the hissing whispers and buzzing murmurs my arrival had incited and looked to neither left nor right. My visage was covered with a black mourning veil that Tansy had found for me in an attic trunk. 'Twas not from shame that I hid my face although I am sure that was what people thought. I would have preferred to stare each and every one of these sensation seekers down, but I wanted to keep my facial injuries hidden from view. If Justice Phyfe saw the damage Pelletier had done to me, he would likely conclude that the beating had incited Adam to murder my husband.

Had it? My heart cried *no!* The man I love is a healer, not a murderer. But neither do I think myself capable of murder, yet I had wanted to plunge my shard of porcelain into Pelletier's heart whilst he was attacking me.

I'd not been allowed to see Adam before the Hearing. But I'd been required to view my husband's body. The police officer Henry had brought from Boston to arrest Jacques Pelletier needed me to officially identify him. They brought me into the chamber where he'd been murdered, and as I looked down at the corpse in the bed, I felt no hatred. Only relief.

Henry and I sat in the front pew that had been designated for those whom Justice Phyfe intended to question. The Hearing had been called to establish if there was reason enough to hold Adam on suspicion of murder. If Phyfe concluded that there was, the next step would be a grand jury investigation presided over by the State's Attorney General. If indicted for murder by the grand jury, Adam would be jailed until his trial. And then, if a trial jury found him guilty, he would be hanged. No! I would not allow myself to think that possible. Adam would be set free, if not this very afternoon, then no more than a year from now, when this ordeal came to an end with a verdict that found him innocent.

Was he? Again, that worm of doubt slithered in my breast. If only I had been able to talk to Adam earlier. I longed with every fiber of my being to see him again.

And in the next moment I did, as he was led down the aisle by Constable Beers to stand in front of the deacons' table at the front of the Meetinghouse. Beers kept a firm hold of Adam's arm, as if his prisoner would try to escape. And run where? Everything in this world that Adam cared about—his relatives, his patients, his friends, his farm, and yes, me—were right here in Plumford.

He turned to look at me, and I lifted my veil so that he could see the love in my eyes. He was hatless, and there was a nasty bruise on his temple. He managed a small smile, but I could not manage one in return, for my lips were trembling.

Justice Phyfe entered through the minister's door at the front of the Meetinghouse, and I dropped my veil.

Phyfe went to the deacons' table and knocked his gavel upon it, an unnecessary gesture of authority since everyone had fallen silent as soon as he'd made his appearance. "Adam Walker, you have been brought in front of me today by Constable Beers, who has charged and arrested you for the murder of Jacques Pelletier, husband of Julia Bell Pelletier." Phyfe regarded Adam with more disappointment than disapproval. Although they'd had strong differences in the past, Phyfe had always respected Adam's dedication to his profession. "Do you claim yourself innocent or guilty as charged, Doctor?"

"I am innocent, your honor. Allow me to explain what—"

Phyfe banged his gavel. "In due course." He seated himself behind the table. "First, I would like to hear from Constable Beers. Why did you arrest Dr. Walker for Mr. Pelletier's murder, Constable?"

"Because he did it!"

"Did you witness him kill Pelletier?"

"Well, I nearly did."

Beers went on to state that he had suspected that Dr. Walker was up to no good the moment he entered the tavern. He had blatantly lied about going upstairs to see to a patient, but Beers wasn't having it. Being a diligent constable, he decided to investigate what Walker was really up to. He found the doctor standing over Pelletier's body with a bloody knife in his hand. Beers demanded that Walker put down the knife, but instead Walker proceeded to attack him with it. Beers had staunchly held his ground, however, and overpowered Walker, subduing and then arresting him.

"No one can say that I do not do my duty as the constable of this town," Beers concluded, glaring at Adam.

Mr. Ruggles was then asked to testify, and he more or less

verified what Beers had said. "But I do not think Dr. Walker intended to stab Constable Beers," he added.

"Was he still holding the knife as he went toward the constable?" Phyfe asked Ruggles.

"Well, yes."

"I made sure to bring the murder weapon with me, sir," Beers said. He pulled the knife, wrapped in his soiled handkerchief, out of his jacket pocket and laid it on the table.

Phyfe looked down at the knife. It was about ten inches long, with a heavy walnut handle. The blade was streaked with dried blood. "Is this your knife, Dr. Walker?"

"No, it's the knife I found implanted in the victim's chest. May I explain now how—"

"In due course," Phyfe said again. "I would first like to ascertain whose knife this is."

"Mine," Ruggles said. "One of a dozen I had specially forged of the best steel for the Sun Tavern. It was brought up to Mr. Pelletier with the steak he requested to be served to him at midnight. Along with a fork, of course."

"Did you deliver the steak to him?"

"No, sir. My wife did. He wanted it fetched up straight from the kitchen by the cook."

"Is your wife here?"

"She's sitting in the back."

"I would like to question her," Phyfe said.

Ruggles leaned across the table toward him and spoke in a low voice. "Edda's English is not so good, sir."

"No matter. I am sure we will manage to understand each other," Phyfe said.

Ruggles looked over the heads of the spectators, and when he spotted his wife he motioned her to come forward. I did not turn around to see her reaction, but apparently she did not want to oblige him, for Ruggles motioned again, with a broader gesture and an impatient expression. Finally Justice Phyfe called out. "Mrs. Ruggles, come up here. Now!"

She hurried to the front of the Meetinghouse, fussily readjusting her shawl around her shoulders and her bonnet on her head. Phyfe asked her to take a seat across from him.

"When you brought up Mr. Pelletier's steak, did you talk with him, Mrs. Ruggles?"

"About what?"

"About anything. Did you converse with him at all?"

She shrugged. "A little. Not so much. He is a stranger to me."

"Did he by any chance mention that he was expecting a visitor later?"

She shook her head vehemently. "We do not allow prostitutes into the Sun."

"I should think not!" Phyfe looked most dismayed. "I meant a gentleman visitor."

"Oh. No."

"No what?"

"No mention."

"Did Mr. Pelletier act in any way differently than he normally did?"

"How do I know? I told you he is a stranger to me. I only meet him two days ago."

Phyfe appeared to have grown bored with her testimony. "Thank you, Mrs. Ruggles. That will be all."

She practically jumped out of her chair, dropping her reticule in the process. It fell near Henry's feet, and he picked it up for her. When she took it from him I saw that her hand was shaking. Poor Edda. She had so wanted Pelletier out of the Sun. Instead, he had ended up dead there. She would not look at me. No doubt she thought it was all my fault. No doubt everyone did.

"Mrs. Pelletier, I would like to question you now," Phyfe said.

I reluctantly rose and went to the table. Phyfe did not invite me to take the seat across from him, but I did so anyway, for I was not very steady on my feet. He regarded me as patronizingly as he had when he'd been the Plumford schoolmaster and I was a saucy girl who did not know her proper place.

"Pray remove your veil, Mrs. Pelletier."

"I am in mourning, sir." Did I hear titters behind me?

"Of course you are," Phyfe said condescendingly. "And I offer you my condolences for the passing of your husband, madam. But I want to see your eyes when I question you."

"If you insist." I threw the veil over the back of my bonnet.

Phyfe winced at the sight of my face. "Julia," he said softly, and for an instant compassion tempered his haughty expression. "Who beat you?"

I made no reply.

"Was it Dr. Walker?"

"Of course not."

"No, I don't suppose he had cause to," Phyfe said.

"No man has cause to beat a woman."

"Some would say your husband had cause, madam." Phyfe's pronouncement got a few murmurs of approval from some manly voices in the audience.

I glared at him. "Is this a session to hear facts or to share gossip, sir?"

Phyfe blanched, just as he used to when I talked back to him as a girl. *When will you ever learn, Julia?* That was what Phyfe would ask me right before he rapped my knuckles with a ferule.

Now he banged the table with his gavel. "I shall ask the questions, madam! And you must truthfully answer them. Now tell me. Was it your husband who beat you?"

"Yes," I hissed.

"When?"

"Last evening."

"And did Dr. Walker see you last evening?"

"No," I said. It was not a lie. Adam had seen me in the early hours of this morning.

Phyfe looked at me long and hard. "You are dismissed, Mrs. Pelletier."

I pulled the veil back over my face and returned to the pew. I dared not look at Adam. Henry took my icy hand and gave it a good, hard, comforting squeeze. He then stood up and requested to testify.

"Were you present when Mr. Pelletier was murdered, Mr. Thoreau?" Phyfe asked him in a cold voice. They had locked horns over court procedures before.

"I was not."

"Then sit down."

"I will not."

"I can damn well make him sit," Beers offered.

"No profanity in court, Constable," Phyfe chastised. "Very well, Mr. Thoreau. Have your say and be done with it. But pray remember this is not the time nor the place for one of your lyceum lectures."

"I have only two statements to make. Firstly, Jacques Pelletier was a slave trader and was having an illegal ship built and equipped in the Boston shipyards to transport captured Africans across the Atlantic to be sold."

That stirred up loud murmurs in the beehive, and to his credit, Justice Phyfe looked both shocked and outraged. But then he banged his gavel and spoke. "Are you saying, Mr. Thoreau, that because Pelletier was a slaver he deserved to be murdered by Dr. Walker?"

"No! I am saying that Dr. Walker had no motive to kill

him, for Dr. Walker knew that Pelletier was soon to be arrested for his crime. In fact, I arrived in Plumford this morning with a Boston police officer who intended to do just that."

Phyfe thought upon this for a moment. "Perhaps Dr. Walker did not want to lose the opportunity to kill Mrs. Pelletier's husband before he was incarcerated."

"Such a supposition as that demonstrates your prejudice against Dr. Walker," Henry said.

"I have no prejudice against Plumford's only doctor. Indeed, it pains me to order him imprisoned on suspicion of murder. But what choice do I have when both the town constable and our respected publican saw him standing over Pelletier's body with the murder weapon in hand, still dripping blood?"

"Pelletier was dead long before I saw him," Adam said. "Rigor mortis was at an advanced stage."

"Unfortunately, there is no one to back up your statement," Phyfe said. "Under normal circumstances in such an investigation I would call for a doctor's opinion concerning the state of the deceased, but since the doctor I would call is in fact the accused murderer, I cannot very well trust his testimony."

Henry groaned. "I have never heard such specious reasoning."

"Silence, Thoreau!" Phyfe said. "Or I will have you arrested for contempt."

"If it is a crime to have contempt for pompous town officials who ask all the wrong questions, then I plead guilty."

Phyfe chose to ignore Henry this time and looked straight at Adam with a grim, implacable expression. "Dr. Walker, I order you to remain in custody at the Sun Tavern until arrangements are made to transfer you to the Concord jail tomorrow."

"I request to be released on my own recognizance so that I may be at liberty to care for my patients," Adam said.

"Request denied," Phyfe replied with a bang of his gavel.

"Murder is too serious a crime to give you, the one and only suspect, such freedom as that. Take your prisoner back to his cell, Constable."

As I watched Adam being marched out of the Meeting-house, I noticed the hair on the crown of his head was clotted with blood. Yet he held his head high, and his stride was strong. Battered and bruised though he was, he remained unbowed. And I resolved that I would remain so, too. For his sake and our child's.

ADAM

Tuesday, May 23

Beers must have delighted in strutting the length of the Green with me in tow as his prisoner. His beefy paw gripped my arm like a vise, but at least I was spared the humiliation of wearing manacles. Shrewd politician that he is, Justice Phyfe must have instructed Beers not to shackle me. That would not have gone down well with the townspeople we passed on our march from the Meetinghouse to the Sun Tavern. Most of them regarded me with sympathy rather than censure. I had been to their homes to minister to the sick, to stitch and plaster, to splint broken limbs, to help bring their babies into this world, to relieve the pain of the dying, and to grieve with the bereaved. And Beers, who wanted to be reelected to the lucrative office of Town Constable, kept his hatred for me tightly corked whilst we were in public. No smirks, no snickers, no unnecessary bashing upon my head with a cane. Indeed, his conduct was beyond reproach.

Once we went down to the Sun cellar, however, his demeanor changed from peacemaker to bully. He shoved me into my cell so hard I almost fell to my knees, but I kept my balance and my temper. Trouncing the town's one and only law enforcer would only make matters worse for me. If indeed that were possible.

Plumford had no jail, and my cell was just a damp corner of the cellar that Ruggles had walled off with rough boards. He used the space to store his kegs of cider, barrels of beer, and boxes of bottled spirits, and thanks to a padlock on the crooked door, it was just secure enough to keep out a thirsty inebriate. Or to keep in a supposedly murderous doctor, at least temporarily.

"You will soon be wearing a hempen cravat, Walker," Beers said with his familiar but hardly endearing sneer. "And when they hang you, I will be right there to watch you dance a hornpipe in the air." With that last witticism he slammed shut the door and padlocked it. I confess I was not sorry to see him go.

I sat myself upon the narrow rope bed Ruggles had brought down last night for me. Dim light leaked through one small cellar window, and mice squeaked in the fieldstone foundation. From the huge timbers that supported the floor above there issued the smell of punky wood and dry rot. My head still ached from Beers's cane battering, and my heart ached for Julia. How long would we have to endure being separated? It seemed likely that she would have to go through her pregnancy and bear our child without me there to support her. And she would have to raise the child without me too if I were hanged for Pelletier's murder.

With that dire possibility in mind, I began plotting my escape. It would have to be tonight, for tomorrow I would be removed to the Concord jail, a solid stone structure said to be as secure as a fortress. Not so this makeshift cell. The horizontal wall boards were spaced a few inches apart, and I slid my hands beneath one of them and gave it a tug to test how difficult it would be to dislodge. I felt it give enough to make me conclude that I could manage it. Once out, I would go to my office and take what money and valuables I had there. Would then ride Coburn's horse back to Boston and get on the first ship leaving on the next tide. Destination wouldn't matter. From wherever I landed I would contact Julia to join me. A vague plan, yes. But a damn sight better one than waiting around to be hanged.

I heard footsteps coming down the stairs and looked through a gap between the boards to see Julia and Henry approaching. I had not been given the opportunity to talk to either of them before the Hearing. Julia threw back her veil, and I pushed my hands through the gap to gently touch her face, so beautiful despite the injuries to it. To give us privacy, Henry moved to the area of the cellar where he was constructing the dumbwaiter and pretended to examine his work.

"You are not allowed visitors," she said, "but Mr. Ruggles kindly looked the other way when Henry escorted me past him." She brought my hand to her lips and kissed it. "I cannot bear to see you locked up like this, my darling."

"I intend to escape from here tonight," I told her sotto voce. "I will get word to you as soon as I can."

"No, no, no," she protested in a rasping whisper, golden eyes wide with alarm. "They will hunt you down, Adam. You might be shot dead. Don't put your life in jeopardy!"

"My life is already in jeopardy. You heard the testimony from Ruggles and Beers. That was enough to convince Justice Phyfe I killed Pelletier, and it will be enough to convince a jury I should hang for it."

"*Did* you kill him?"

"No, Julia. But the only doctor who can attest to my innocence with medical evidence is myself. And who would believe me?"

"Julia and I will believe you," Henry said, coming forward.

I had forgotten he could hear like an owl. "Tell us what this evidence is, Adam."

"As I attempted to explain to Justice Phyfe, Pelletier was dead hours before I came upon his body, for rigor mortis had set in," I said. "And what's more, I think he was dead before the knife was plunged into his chest. When a beating heart is stabbed, it pumps out a great quantity of blood, internally and externally. There was no blood whatever to be seen; only the few drops on his shirt where I drew out the blade."

"But why would someone stab a dead man?" Henry said.

"Perhaps as some sort of ritual," Julia said and took in a sharp breath. "Did Mawuli kill Pelletier?"

"If he knew about the slave ship, he certainly had motive enough," I said.

"But no opportunity," Henry countered. "I've already questioned Ruggles and a few others who were at the tavern last evening. They observed Mawuli and Pelletier in conversation on the porch around nine o'clock. Then Pelletier went up to his rooms. Mawuli did not follow him upstairs. Instead, he left the tavern and walked toward Julia's house."

"Yes," Julia said. "Mawuli came to my house to see if I was all right. He was with me all evening. He was still there when Adam came back from Boston."

"And what time was that?" Henry said.

"Two in the morning," I said. "When I saw the injuries Pelletier had inflicted on Julia, I went directly to the Sun to confront him. I admit that I was enraged enough to have killed him, but instead I found him already dead."

"For how long do you estimate?" Henry said.

"At least five hours. His jaw and limbs had stiffened."

"But at the Hearing," Henry said, "Mrs. Ruggles testified that Pelletier was alive at midnight when she brought up his beefsteak. Why did she lie?"

"To protect her husband!" Julia cried and then looked toward the stairway to see if Ruggles was lurking in the shadows. "He killed Pelletier."

"What motive would Ruggles have had for killing Pelletier?" Henry said. "Had they known each other before?"

"It does not seem likely," Julia said. "But anything is possible."

"I cannot see Ruggles as a murderer," I said.

"He was quick enough to see you as one, though," Henry said. "Perhaps he needed a scapegoat. It would have been easy enough for Ruggles to poison Pelletier."

"The steak I saw on the table in Pelletier's suite was uneaten," I said. "There was also a full carafe of wine and a clean glass."

"The carafe could have been refilled, and the glass rinsed," Julia said.

"Or replaced," Henry said.

"If Pelletier had indeed ingested a poison," I said, "I would find traces of it in his stomach. Unfortunately, I am not free to perform an autopsy."

"Another doctor must perform one as soon as possible," Henry said. "Whom do you want me to contact, Adam?"

"Dr. Holmes at Massachusetts General Hospital," I said. "I expect he will come as soon as he learns I'm in trouble. I was one of his favorite medical students, and he always predicted I would make a name for myself. Alas, not as a murderer."

We all stopped talking when we heard a heavy tread upon the stairs. It was Ruggles, carrying a bowl of soup. "I am sorry, Mrs. Pelletier, but you must leave now. If Beers catches you down here, we'll all be in trouble. Henry can remain, though, since he has the excuse of doing work down here."

Julia gave me one last look, kissed my hand again, and left without a word of protest. That was so unlike her that I knew she must be up to something.

Ruggles asked Henry to hold the bowl for him whilst he

dug a key chain out of his apron pocket. It held many keys, including the one to the padlock. He opened the door, took the bowl from Henry, stepped into the cell, and set it on a cider keg, along with a spoon and a starched white linen napkin. "Edda cooked up some oxtail soup special for you, Adam."

"Did she cook up that lie at the Hearing special for me too?" I could not help but ask.

Ruggles stared at me. He looked genuinely stunned. And then exceedingly angry. "What the hell do you mean by that?"

Before I could reply, there was another tramp of footsteps down the stairs. I thought for sure it was Beers, but it turned out to be Rusty the daguerreotypist.

"You are not allowed down here!" Ruggles shouted at him. He quickly closed and padlocked the door to my cell.

"I just want to shake the hand of the man who killed a slave trader," Rusty said, smiling back at me as I looked at him between the boards.

"As much as I disdained Pelletier for his trade," I told him, "I did not kill him."

"Of course you didn't." Rusty's smile broadened. "But I congratulate you all the same."

I was not about to put out my hand for Rusty to shake. "I did not kill the man," I repeated wearily.

Ruggles gave me a woeful look and shook his great globe of a head. "I understand why you must lie to save your own skin, Adam, but do not accuse others of lying to save it."

I looked him in the eye and said, "Sam, we both know what the truth is, don't we? And so does your wife."

"Enough!" he roared back at me. "I will not play along with this game of yours, especially in front of others." He turned to Rusty. "Let's go, young man. You have no business down here."

Rusty made a show of saluting me before he departed with Ruggles.

"Your incarceration is most ill-timed, my friend," Henry said after they left. "Why did you get yourself arrested for one murder whilst we were in the middle of investigating two others? It further complicates an already complicated situation."

"My apologies, Henry. I know how you like to keep things simple."

He nodded. "It is indeed my mantra."

"Perhaps Rusty can assist you," I suggested. "He should be most eager to help you capture the man who assassinated his fellow Underground Railroad Conductors."

"Rusty already volunteered to help," Henry said. "He suspects the Quaker as much as I do and keeps an eye on him when I cannot. But Rusty doesn't seem to take the matter as seriously as he should, considering that he too is in danger."

"From what we've heard regarding the dashing daguerreotypist, he's used to danger," I said.

"Yes, Rusty has certainly had his share of close calls," Henry said. "I reckon that's why he's developed such a cavalier attitude about life."

"About death too," I said. "Else why would he express admiration for someone he presumes to be a cold-blooded killer?"

"Methinks Rusty was just trying to express what an avid abolitionist he is," Henry said.

"Nonetheless, it seems rather callous to want to shake my hand because he thinks it plunged a knife into another man's heart."

"We will disprove that notion soon enough with an autopsy," Henry said. "I will send a note to Dr. Holmes forthwith. But before I leave you, I want you to promise me that you will not attempt to escape from here tonight, Adam."

"So you overheard me tell Julia I plan to."

"I also heard her warning you not to do it. She's right, Adam. You'd be putting your life in grave danger."

"Do not concern yourself," I told him. "I will not take off now that I have hope that an autopsy will prove Pelletier was poisoned."

"Will you give me your hand and shake on that?"

I stuck my arm out between the boards. "*Your* hand I will gladly shake, Henry."

JULIA

Determined to question Edda Ruggles about her false testimony at the Hearing, I went looking for her immediately upon leaving the tavern cellar. I did not find her in the kitchen or the taproom or the ladies' parlor or the porch, so I went upstairs and knocked on the door to the Ruggleses' private suite, calling her name. I received no response, but the door was ajar, and I took that as invitation enough to let myself in. There was no one in the sitting room. Yet the rocking chair was still rocking.

"Mrs. Ruggles!" I called. Silence. I imagined her cringing behind one of the closed doors. "Edda, pray come forth. We must talk." I listened a moment, but heard not a sound. "I will not go away, I assure you, until you explain why you lied to Justice Phyfe. Either come out, or I will hunt you out."

She did not come out. Therefore, a-hunting I did go. The door I opened led to a bedchamber. Mr. Ruggles's night shirt was neatly folded on a plump pillow of the high, wide bed, and Mrs. Ruggles's diaphanous nightdress hung from the bedpost like a frilly flag. I had intruded into their private inner sanctum and did not care a whit. I wanted answers.

"Mrs. Ruggles!" I called again. "Where are you?" As I considered looking under the bed I heard a rustle of movement in the massive mahogany wardrobe wedged in the far corner of the room. "I know you are hiding in the wardrobe, Edda. You are behaving like a child."

I waited a moment to give Mrs. Ruggles the chance to regain a portion of her dignity by coming out on her own. When she did not, there was nothing for it but to cross the room and throw open the double doors of the wardrobe. All hell let loose when I did. A raucous screech pierced my ears, and Edda's parrot flew out of the dark space and into my face, knocking me down. The bird then began to attack me.

I rolled over onto my stomach and covered my head with my arms as Roos dove at me again and again. Her claws and beak tore through the thin cloth of my frock but could not, thank God, pierce through my steel and baleen corset. I was getting scratched and bitten on my upper back and arms and hands, however, and could not very well just lie there like carrion. I pushed myself up on my knees, and, keeping my head down and shielded by my arms, I crawled toward the bed for protection. When I slid under it I found that I had company. Edda Ruggles. How I wished I had looked there for her before looking in the wardrobe!

Edda and I stared at each other, our faces inches apart, as the parrot continued to flap around the room, screeching. "You frighten Roos," Edda said to me. In an accusatory tone, no less! "The wardrobe is her secret nesting place."

"And under the bed is yours?" I said.

My sarcasm escaped her. "You frighten me too," she said. "I thought you was a burglar."

"Nonsense. You just didn't want to talk to me."

"Go away," she said.

"I'm staying put right here until you contain your vicious parrot."

Edda crawled out from her hiding place, and I heard her cooing to her pet. The screeching stopped, replaced by a stream of crude curses in the parrot's little girl voice. Roos was cursing in French! And Edda spoke back to her in French, entreating Roos to come to her. But the bird was too riled up to comply and continued to spew out French gutter talk. Her repertoire was quite impressive. Finally, Roos fell silent. When I heard Edda close the wardrobe door, I stuck my head out for a peek. Roos was nowhere to be seen, and Edda was sitting on a chaise longue silently weeping.

I left my shelter and went over to her. "How long did you work in a French brothel, Edda?" I asked her right off, for I could think of no better place for Roos to have picked up such language.

Edda did not bother to deny my assumption. "Too long," she replied.

"And how well did you know Jacques Pelletier?"

"I do not even remember him from there. But he remembers me because of my parrot."

"Did he threaten to tell your husband of your past?"

"Yah. He torments me. And I know he will make good his threat. Just to hurt us."

"Yes," I said. "Jacques Pelletier was a very cruel man."

"I am not sorry he is dead."

"But surely you must be sorry that an innocent man, a *good* man, is being charged with his murder," I said.

She nodded again and looked down at her hands. Tears fell from her eyes onto her lap.

"Did you poison Pelletier, Edda?"

She looked up at me with wide, wet eyes. "No."

My heart sank. I thought she had been ready to confess. Rather than continue to stand over her like the Grand Inquisitor, I sat down beside her on the chaise and spoke more gently, hoping to slowly lead her into admitting the truth.

"Wasn't Pelletier already dead when Adam found him, Edda?"

She took a deep breath. "Yah."

"And didn't you lie when you testified that you talked to Pelletier at midnight?"

"Yah. When I come up to his suite with his beefsteak he is asleep."

"Asleep? But you just admitted to me that he was dead."

"Not yet." Edda took another deep breath. "He is fast asleep in his bed, and I know this is my only chance to kill him. So I tiptoe into the bedchamber with the steak knife and stab him right in his black heart! And I am not sorry for it. But I do not want to hang for it."

"You won't," I said after a stunned moment. "You can't be hanged for stabbing a dead man."

Edda looked at me, confused, and I explained to her why Adam was sure Pelletier had died hours before midnight.

"So I do not kill that bastard after all," she said. She sounded relieved. But she looked somewhat disappointed.

ADAM

The afternoon was stifling hot as Henry and I waited at the Concord station for Dr. Holmes. I was glad Pelletier's body lay in the cold of the Plumford icehouse, for the rate of putrefaction in summer heat can be explosive. An autopsy viewed by my inexperienced fellow townsmen would be hard enough for them to stomach without the stench we doctors are habituated to endure in such weather.

It was easy to spot my professor as he descended from the cars. He was carrying a black leather medical bag and dressed as the elegant Boston Brahmin he indeed was. His tall, black silk top hat helped to extend his short stature, and beneath the hat's narrow rim his features looked most patrician. Despite his formality of dress and demeanor, he is much loved by the medical students who attend his stimulating lectures. He is an extraordinary teacher, enthusiastic and original, and students cheer when he steps up to the podium or enters a dissection class. They even laugh at his terrible puns.

He stopped in surprise at seeing me at Henry's side. "Did you break out of jail, Adam?" he asked me drolly as he shook my hand.

"I was released from custody," I told him, "when the taverner's wife confessed to stabbing the man I'd been arrested for murdering."

"And is this the taverner?" Dr. Holmes asked, gesturing toward Henry.

"No, this is my friend Henry Thoreau. He wrote to you on my behalf yesterday."

"And a most thorough message it was, Mr. Thoreau," Dr. Holmes said, unable to resist the pun on Henry's name as they shook hands. "But it appears the situation was not as urgent as you indicated, and I need not have canceled all my appointments to come save Dr. Walker from hanging."

"The situation has indeed changed," Henry said, "but it remains urgent. You can help us save the taverner's wife from such a fate, Doctor."

"A woman I do not even know," Dr. Holmes pointed out sharply.

"It should prove to be a most interesting autopsy, sir," I said and explained how I had found the victim at a stage of rigor mortis that did not correspond to the time Mrs. Ruggles stated she'd stabbed him.

Although Dr. Holmes must be nearing forty, he still has the curiosity of a first-year medical student, and this trait overcame his pique. "Let us open up the fellow and see what we can see!" he said after hearing me out. "I propose you conduct the autopsy whilst I watch, Dr. Walker. I have always taken pleasure in observing your skill with the scalpel."

I readily agreed, for I was most eager to slice into Pelletier.

We climbed into the gig and headed for Plumford. Though Henry had not studied medicine under Dr. Holmes at Harvard, he was familiar with his work in another field of endeavor—namely poetry—and a good portion of the short trip was taken up with a discussion of the power of words to influence actions. Henry stated that he only hoped that when his latest essay, entitled "Resistance to Civil Government," was published, it would influence the general population as much as Dr. Holmes's poem "Old Ironsides" had. Dr. Holmes made it clear he was not in favor of anyone advocating resistance to government, and an argument would have ensued if I had not eased the conversation onto more neutral ground.

"Did you know, Henry, that it was Dr. Holmes who invented the word *anaesthesia* for the state of insensibility produced by ether?"

"From the Greek word *anaisthesia*," Holmes added.

"Which means lack of sensation," Henry said. "Therefore the patient is said to be in the state of anaesthesia."

"That's correct," Dr. Holmes said. "It appears you know your Greek, Mr. Thoreau."

"Well enough," Henry said modestly, without mentioning that he too could claim a Harvard education.

Dr. Holmes turned his attention to me. "When do you plan to return to Boston and take up your career as a surgeon, young man?" He did not wait for me to reply. "I am certain that you have your reasons for planting yourself out here in the countryside, but I am even more certain I will find them entirely inadequate. How can you justify hiding your talents under a farmer's straw hat, Adam? Your skills would be greatly valued in the Ether Dome of Massachusetts General Hospital. Have I not told you more than once that you have a rare talent for surgery? That was proven by the extraordinary delicacy, I even call it artistry, with which you repaired that young boy's harelip a few months ago."

"I found great satisfaction in performing the surgery you allude to with such kind words, sir," I replied. "But I also find satisfaction ministering to folks in more humble ways. Besides, I have had obligations to meet over the last few years. I felt duty-bound to take up my Grandfather Walker's practice when he fell

ill, and when he died there came to our small town a Consumption epidemic that I could not just walk away from. Now
my Grandmother Tuttle, who raised me up on her farm, is on
her deathbed, and I want to see her through to the end."

"That is all well and good," Dr. Holmes said. "Yet for one
who has such noble intentions, you seem to get yourself into a
lot of fine messes, Adam. I recall intervening a year or so ago to
prevent a police officer from arresting you on a Boston street."

"That was a misunderstanding that can be easily explained."

"Well, do not take the time to explain it to me now. What
I would like to know is how you managed to get yourself arrested for murder. Who was the victim?"

"His name was Jacques Pelletier, and he was . . ." I could
not very well tell Dr. Holmes that Pelletier was my lover's husband.

"He was what?" Holmes pressed.

"A slave trader," Henry put in.

Dr. Holmes's refined countenance stiffened with revulsion.
"Is that why he was murdered?"

"It would be reason enough, I reckon," Henry said.

"I suggest we say nothing more about the victim, Dr.
Holmes," I said. "That way you can observe the autopsy with
an objective eye."

Holmes nodded. "I am a great proponent of scientific ob-
jectivity."

"Yet there is no such thing as pure objective observation,"
Henry said.

"I beg to differ," Holmes said.

And off they went on a philosophical discussion that I was
far too anxious to follow. As we neared the icehouse, situated
on the Assabet River, my only concern was proving my hypothesis that Pelletier did not die of a knife thrust to the heart,
for I did not want my friend Sam Ruggles to suffer through

the trial and execution of his beloved wife. She was being held under house arrest in the Ruggleses' rooms at the Sun until the Coroner's Jury determined the cause of Pelletier's death.

The owner of that icehouse, Undertaker Jackson, greeted us outside the large wooden structure, and a boy was sent to fetch Coroner Daggett and the six members of his jury awaiting our arrival at Daggett's store.

Jackson led us into his storage facility. Hundred-pound blocks of cut ice, covered with sawdust and straw, were stacked almost up to the roof on three sides of the cavernous room. Jackson informed us that it would be a lot colder and more jam-packed inside had not a good portion of the winter ice harvest already been sold off and removed by rail to Boston and from thence by ship to warm climes all over the world.

It was still plenty cold enough to make us all button up our frock coats, and I appreciated having enough space to conduct the autopsy. Jackson had followed my instructions to the letter. Pelletier's sheet-shrouded body had been laid upon a yard-high stack of ice blocks covered with canvas. A collection of lanterns had been placed on crates and ice blocks all around.

"Let us light the lanterns and begin," I said when the Coroner's Jury filed in.

The six men whom Coroner Daggett had selected for his jury, I was relieved to see, were as stalwart a collection of laymen as I could hope for. Along with Jackson the undertaker and Munger the butcher, four stout and hardy farmers arranged themselves around the table. I credited them all with stomachs strong enough to observe an autopsy. Justice Phyfe and Constable Beers were also in attendance.

"I wager Beers lasts ten minutes before puking," I told Henry in a low voice.

"Five," he replied.

As Henry and I lit the lanterns, Dr. Holmes arranged the

surgical instruments on the improvised operating table. He looked most eager for the procedure to commence. "All is ready for you, Doctor," he told me and stepped aside.

I took my place before the body and was about to pull back the sheet when the icehouse door opened. Everyone's attention was drawn from the body to the towering figure approaching us. Mawuli.

"You are not allowed in here," Beers told him.

"Why shouldn't he be allowed?" Henry said. "There is no law against it."

Beers looked to Phyfe. Phyfe looked up at Mawuli, considering how best to handle the situation.

"I have come at the request of Madame Pelletier," Mawuli told Phyfe. "Does she not have a right to know the cause of her husband's death? If you send me away, I am sure she will come herself."

Upon hearing this alternative, Phyfe made his decision. "You may stay," he told Mawuli.

Mawuli gave him a slight bow and turned to me. "May I assist you, Doctor?"

I confess I found his offer presumptuous. "Performing an autopsy requires specific training," I replied a bit huffily.

Mawuli smiled. "But holding a lantern does not. My height should be to your advantage." He took a lantern off a crate and held it directly over the body, providing excellent illumination.

"I thank you," I said more humbly. I then introduced Dr. Holmes and provided the jurors with his impressive credentials.

"We will certainly heed the opinion of such a respected doctor," Coroner Daggett said. "Do you have anything you would like to tell us beforehand, Dr. Holmes?"

"Only one thing, which I tell all my first-year medical students. If any of you become nauseated, please step as far away as you can from the proceedings before vomiting. Now, Walker, please proceed."

I drew back the sheet. Pelletier was still fully dressed. I'd asked Jackson not to remove his clothes so that the jurors could see how little blood was upon them. I explained that the three small blood spots on the waistcoat had dripped from the knife when I'd extracted it. I then undressed the body. As rigor mortis had long ago faded from it, I had little trouble doing so. Pelletier was now just a corpse, scarcely resembling the man so recently brimful of evil intent. The energy that had animated him had gone elsewhere, be it to hell or some other timeless void. Nonetheless, I covered his face with a handkerchief. I did so out of respect for the living more than the dead, for an autopsy is far easier to view when the corpse's countenance is hidden.

I first described how I had seen the knife buried to the hilt in Pelletier's chest, then pointed out the wound on the body just below the right nipple, where the knife had penetrated between two ribs and angled into the chest cavity.

I picked up a scalpel and looked at the pale, intense faces around me, and then Mawuli's dark face a good foot above them. Light from the lanterns bounded off the gleaming ice and gave the scene a dreamlike or painterly quality. I looked back at the corpse and swiftly cut the characteristic Y-shaped incision across the entire front of the body, one cut starting at each shoulder and then both meeting over the sternum and then continuing as one incision down and round the umbilicus, and ending at the pubic bone. I took care to cut only through the skin, subcutaneous tissue, musculature, and the peritoneum but no farther, the intent being simply to open the body cavity to expose the organs. If the abdominal organs are nicked or sliced, then the bloated gas contained escapes, generating not just a powerful stink but a mess of digestive juices and partially digested food. Such gases are the reason so many medical students take up smoking heavy cigars—the powerful tobacco smoke at least partially masks the inevitable stench. I pulled back the flaps of skin on each side, cutting the flesh away to expose the chest, ribs, and lower organs.

This simple, initial procedure brought gasps of horror, for to perform such a violation of a human body is quite akin to slaughtering an animal. I heard the retreating clomp of boots and then retching. I didn't bother to look up. I knew it was Beers. The man simply did not have the stomach for his job.

I picked up a saw and heard a few groans. I used the saw to cut through each rib and the chest plate and pulled them to the side and up and away so as to reveal the organs in all their complex glory. I removed the organ block from tongue down to anus in one group, which brought a nod of approval from Dr. Holmes. I glanced up to see one of the sturdy farmers keel over backwards. Jackson caught him and laid him out behind the group. Justice Phyfe was paler than a ghost but kept his eyes on the body. He is a tough bird. I give him that much.

"The insides of a man look not so very different from a pig's, I am sorry to say," Munger muttered.

His remark brought to my mind the time he was slaughtering a huge boar that had been gored and trampled by a bull and we had shared a fire-seared, crispy pig's ear together.

After an examination of the throat and lungs, where I found nothing out of the ordinary, I turned to the heart. I thrust my hand behind the organ of life and cut it loose from its arteries and veins. I felt a rush of relief at what I saw, for Edda Ruggles's sake.

"Please observe," I said, glancing at the jury, "the pericardium, which is this whitish sac that surrounds and holds the heart." I pointed to the inch-wide opening in the pericardium through which the knife blade had sliced and continued into the heart. "If the heart had been beating at the time the injury was sustained, the pericardium would be swollen with blood, as such an injury would cause the victim's heart to flood the entire area with blood as it pumped. Doctor Holmes, do you agree with this observation?"

"I will speak after you have dissected the heart," Dr. Holmes said.

I sliced into and then pulled away the pericardium as one would a layer of protective skin. I then cut into the right atrium and pointed to where the blade had cut into and across the atrium and punctured the aorta. This was a slippery business, and I have seen fellow medical students try to hold the heart, lose grip, and send the organ off the table and slithering across the floor. I took care not to have that happen.

"As you see," I said, "there is no evidence of any bleeding from the penetration of the knife directly into the heart muscle and tissue. Dr. Holmes?"

"What we see," he said, "is irrefutable evidence that the heart was not beating at the time of the attack."

He then delivered a somewhat prolonged explanation of what the jury would be seeing if in fact the subject had been alive at the time with a normally beating heart. His description of the amount of blood that would be pumped was near as graphic as the autopsy itself.

"If the knife did not kill the victim, what did?" Coroner Daggett asked in a weak voice.

"We shall hopefully see," Dr. Holmes said. "Proceed, Dr. Walker."

I cut the stomach free of the esophagus and small intestine, lifted and placed the organ on the table. I made an incision of perhaps three inches and through it inserted a small ladle with which I spooned out the contents of the stomach into a high-lipped dish. I saw only normal digestive fluids and detected no smell of almonds, a sure sign of cyanide poisoning. I poured a portion of the contents into a vial to be tested in the hospital laboratory for arsenic if it proved necessary.

I then sliced the stomach in half so its insides could be observed. The stomach lining was raw and inflamed, and an enormous ulcer extended from the stomach entrance to the exit into the intestines.

"This man did not die of poison," Dr. Holmes said, reaching past my hands to point at a large hole in the ulcer that had penetrated through the stomach wall. "He suffered severely from cancer of the stomach. This massive perforated ulcer was the immediate cause of death. No known poison can produce this condition."

I glanced up at Mawuli, who met my eyes and then returned his calm gaze to the body of his former master. Was there a sliver of a smile upon his lips?

"My good gentlemen, allow me to summarize our conclusions for you," Dr. Holmes told the jurors. "The heart of the corpse before us was indeed penetrated with the point and body of a knife. However, since no bleeding resulted from that penetration, I can only conclude the heart had stopped before that event occurred. In other words, this man was already dead when he was attacked with the knife. It is crystal clear that he died from a perforated ulcer in his cancerous stomach. There can be no other conclusion from what we have just witnessed under the examining hands of Doctor Walker."

Coroner Daggett gathered up his jurors, and they went to huddle in a corner together. After a moment they returned but kept their distance from the corpse.

"It is the conclusion of this jury," Daggett said, "after hearing the expert testimony of Dr. Holmes, that Mr. Pelletier died of natural causes. Therefore, no act of murder was committed. The body can be turned over to his wife for burial."

Justice Phyfe thanked Daggett and his jurors for performing a most difficult and demanding civic duty in the pursuit of justice. And Daggett informed him that he did not wish to be appointed Town Coroner again.

Daggett then hurriedly left the icehouse with the jurors. Phyfe and the still green Beers followed right after them. Henry, Dr. Holmes, Mawuli, and Mr. Jackson remained whilst I returned Pelletier's body parts, somewhat helter-skelter since they no longer needed to perform their functions in proper order, into his body cavity and sewed him up with good thick catgut. We all together maneuvered ice blocks so they formed a tight and cold sepulcher for the old scoundrel until Julia decided what to do with him.

JULIA

"We are all free to get on with our lives now," I said to Mawuli after he told me the Coroner Jury's verdict. We were sitting on a bench in my garden, amidst blooming Sweet William.

"I shall return to France on the next boat," Mawuli said. "With your permission, I'll take Monsieur's body with me. He would want to be put to rest in French ground rather than American."

"Of course you have my permission. It is exceedingly kind of you to take him home, Mawuli."

"Ah, well. It is the least I can do, considering I killed him."

"You just told me that Adam and Dr. Holmes proved that he died of natural causes."

"What do Western doctors know of Vodun poison?" Mawuli replied serenely. "It is a poison that cannot be detected, for it is produced from within. I had no need to taint Monsieur's food or drink. Instead, I put a powerful spell on him so that everything he ingested turned foul in his stomach, corroding the organ."

"You think it was your spell that killed him?"

"I know it was." Mawuli looked at me closely. "You do not believe it possible, do you, Madame?"

"I am just relieved that no one will be charged with his murder. Whatever you claim you did is not considered a crime, after all."

"It should be considered a blessing," Mawuli said. "The Spirits I called up were evil, to be sure, but I used them to put an end to a greater evil. I decided that Monsieur must die when we arrived in Boston and I discovered he had commissioned a slave ship."

"Why did he decide to go back to the slave trade? Surely he was rich enough."

"No one who is rich is ever rich enough, Madame. Besides, he lost nearly all of his fortune in the banking collapse in France. What money was left he invested in that infernal ship. Jacques Pelletier went back to being a slave trader because such a trade was his natural inclination. A leopard cannot change his spots any more than I can change the color of my skin." Mawuli smiled. "Or so the Bible tells us."

"What made him think he could keep this from you, Mawuli?"

"Hubris combined with selfishness. Monsieur would have been wiser to leave me in France, of course. But he wanted me by his side during the voyage to America in case he became ill. He trusted my healing powers." Mawuli laughed softly at that. "He also hoped I might help influence you to return to France with him. He told me that winning you back was the purpose of his journey. So that is why I accompanied him."

"To *help* him?"

"No, Madame. To help *you*. I wanted to protect you from him." Mawuli lightly touched a bruise on my face with his fingertip. "Forgive me for failing you. I thought Monsieur would die sooner from my spell. I did not think he would even make it to Plumford. I am only thankful he did not kill you. I feared that was his intention if you refused to come back with him. Such was the fate of his first two wives."

I stared back at Mawuli, horrified. "He murdered them?"

"I have no proof of it," Mawuli said. "Only suspicions. That's why I never told you of his past as a slave trader. I knew that you would leave him if you found out, and then your life would be in danger. Monsieur would not have allowed you to exist apart from him. But you have survived him." Mawuli patted my hand. "And as his legal wife, you will inherit what remains of his estate."

"I want nothing! Whatever I get I will donate to the abolitionist cause. And I want to repay you, Mawuli. Jacques told me my diamond ring was only paste, so you must have given me your own money to pay for my escape."

"Since you would have fled with or without money, I thought it best you had some," he said. "Donate whatever I gave you to the cause too. I have more than enough to satisfy my modest needs." He rose to his feet. "Good-bye, Madame. I have had few friends in my long life, and you are one I cherish most deeply. I will not forget you." He bent from the waist to kiss the top of my head. "And do not doubt my great powers, for now they will work to help you." He gave me a flashing smile and turned and walked away.

I stayed in the garden awhile, breathing in the spicy scent of the Sweet William, and saw a wagon stop in front of Adam's office. I recognized Mrs. Tripp and her son and went over to tell them that Dr. Walker had driven a colleague to the Concord train station and should be back shortly. One of the little boy's hands was wrapped up in a bloody rag, and he was crying.

"I hope we don't have to wait too long," Mrs. Tripp said. "Billy has a pretty deep cut on his palm. It won't close, and I think he needs stitches."

I brought them into the house to await Adam's return and sat them down at the kitchen table. Mrs. Tripp applied pressure to her son's palm to staunch his bleeding, and I popped a sugar plum in his mouth to staunch his tears. Whilst he sucked on it Mrs. Tripp and I chatted about inconsequential things, but suddenly her eyes grew wide with astonishment. It could not have been over my remarks concerning the weather, so I turned to look over my shoulder. Tansy was standing in the kitchen doorway, the red neckerchief wrapped around her head like a turban.

"I heard your kind voice," she told Mrs. Tripp, "and I just couldn't help myself. I had to come downstairs to see you again, ma'am."

"My dear lost girl!" Mrs. Tripp said. "I hoped you were in Canada by now."

"I've not made much progress in that direction since we parted, have I?"

"I am sorry for that. But I am not sorry to lay eyes on you again."

They regarded each other with a deep, mutual fondness, and then Tansy turned her attention to Billy. "How did you get hurt, honeychild?"

"I was whittling, and my knife slipped," he said.

Tansy shook a finger at him. "You're too little to play with sharp knives."

"I ain't too little," Billy protested. "Jared don't think so anyways. He give me his bone-handled penknife afore he took off for Ohio."

Tansy looked back at Mrs. Tripp. "Jared went to Ohio?"

"Weeks ago," she replied sharply and glanced at me. "Before you came to Plumford."

Tansy looked confused but said nothing more about it. "Anyways, I am sorry you went and injured yourself like that, Billy. What were you whittling?"

"A gimcrack for Ma."

"Well, that's nice," Tansy said.

The conversation continued in this desultory manner until Adam returned. Billy, most likely to prove to one and all that he was not too little, insisted on going into Adam's office to get sewn up without his mother, so Mrs. Tripp stayed in the kitchen with Tansy and me.

"I like the way you are wearing the neckerchief I gave you," Mrs. Tripp said to Tansy, referring to her turban. "The color does suit you."

"I wear it one way or another every day. I do believe it keeps me safe."

"I pray for your safety every day," Mrs. Tripp said.

"And I pray every day for your forgiveness, ma'am."

"My forgiveness?" Mrs. Tripp said. "For what?"

"For making you a widow."

"You cannot blame yourself for my husband's death, dear."

"But he would be alive today if he had not been driving me to Carlisle that night." Tansy buried her face in her hands and wept.

"You had nothing to do with it, dear!" Mrs. Tripp said. "His time had come, and that is all there is to it." She began to weep too.

Weeping is most contagious, and I have been crying enough of late, so I went out to the back porch and left them alone. They spoke to each other in low murmurs that I could not overhear.

ADAM

Henry came to my office this morning looking mighty concerned. His shaggy hair and shoulders were sprinkled with sawdust from his work on the tavern dumbwaiter.

"It's Ruggles," he said. "The poor man has gotten so drunk I fear he is a hazard to himself. Just now he almost fell into the hole I've cut in the floor behind the bar. I have little experience with inebriated people and don't know how to help him."

"Where is Edda?" I said.

"Gone," Henry said. "I witnessed her departure last night as I was gazing out my window. I could make out her figure in the moonlight as she headed down the road with a satchel. She never looked back. When I came downstairs this morning for breakfast Ruggles was already drinking."

I reached for my bag, and Henry and I headed for the Sun. I noticed, as we neared the tavern, a sweat-lathered horse tied to the hitching post by the door. I felt for the animal, for after a grueling run such as it had just endured, it needed to be walked and watered and rubbed down.

We heard a window on the second story of the tavern being flung open and looked up to see Jerome Haven climbing out of it. He balanced on the sill for a second, and then, in a magnificent show of dexterity, leaped up, grabbed the gutter above him, and vaulted himself onto the roof. Just as he was doing so a man wearing a top hat bearing a gold star leaned far out the window and swiped upward with his hand. He missed catching Haven's boot by an inch.

The man shouted a curse and then noticed us watching. "Hey, you two down there! Keep your eyes on that rogue! I have come to arrest him!" The police officer then drew back from the window rather than climb out and try to pursue Haven by duplicating his acrobatic maneuvers.

Meanwhile, Haven scampered across the shingles of the roof like a spider. He balanced on the edge of the roof peak and, after only an instant's hesitation, leaped across a good ten feet of air to grab hold of a limb of the chestnut tree growing beside the tavern.

I stared up at him in amazement, as I would at a circus performer, but Henry sprang into action, sprinting toward the tree.

Haven swung from the limb, grabbed the tree trunk, and shimmied down it until he reached a thick limb closer to the ground. He fearlessly jumped off the limb, from a height of no less than fifteen feet, and landed on the ground like a weightless cat. As I watched I could not help but be concerned that the stitches I'd sewed in his leg would not hold.

When Haven hit the ground Henry was only a few yards from the tree. Haven broke into a run, and Henry set off after him. As fast as Haven was, Henry was faster and caught up with him. He grabbed Haven's collar to stop him, and Haven twisted round and struggled to wrench free. Combat commenced. Though Henry is modest in height and weight, he is sinewy and tough as an Indian, and he took several blows to the head but hung on. He then delivered a roundhouse punch to the side of Haven's face that drove the man to the ground with a shout of pain. Henry fell atop him like an eagle covering his prey.

This all happened in less than a minute. I dashed toward them just as the law officer emerged from the tavern. Henry rolled off Haven and hauled him to his feet. The law officer handcuffed him and then gave Henry a closer look.

"Why, it is you, Mr. Thoreau!"

"And it is you, Lieutenant Payne." Henry turned to me. "This is Lieutenant Thompson Payne of the Boston police, Adam. He came with me to Plumford to arrest Pelletier Tuesday."

"Couldn't arrest a dead man," the officer said with a shrug.

"But now you can arrest a ruthless murderer." Still puffing from the effort it took to capture Haven, Henry glared at him like a fire-breathing dragon.

"Murderer?" Lieutenant Payne said.

"He garroted one man," Henry said. "And most likely shot another in the heart."

"If I'd known that, I would have brought more men with me," Payne said, but in a light tone, as if he did not believe it. "I am pretty sure this man is the burglar Jack Steeple. That ain't his real name of course. He is called that in the newspapers because he can climb buildings like a steeplejack." Lieutenant Payne pulled a folded sheet from his jacket pocket. "Here's a depiction of him sent to my police station from New York. I brought it for the purpose of identification."

Henry and I looked at the drawing. It did indeed look just like the man we knew as Jerome Haven.

"May I see it?" the prisoner asked softly. We showed him the drawing, and he shook his head. "This does not look a whit like me. My nose is far thinner, and my chin a good deal stronger." He turned to Henry. "Thou thinks me a murderer? Why, I would not harm a fly." He looked sincerely hurt by the accusation. But since when had this man I knew as Quaker Jerome Haven been sincere about anything?

"Let's go inside and sort this out," Payne said.

We went into the taproom. It was empty of even Ruggles's presence. Payne sat his prisoner down roughly and took out another pair of manacles to secure his legs. "Jack Steeple is a wily rascal," Payne told us as we took seats around the table. "Just two weeks ago he was arrested in New York City for stealing jewelry from an upper-story chamber in the Astor Hotel. He was thrown in the clink, but got clean away. How? By getting naked and squirming his way free right between the bars of the jailhouse window, that's how! Not three days later, a guest chamber at the Tremont Hotel in Boston was robbed in the exact same way. The thief climbed through a window on the fourth floor. Made off with the jewelry of some actress. I got the list of the pieces right here." He patted his coat. "The thief got away but not unscathed. Blood was found on a jagged gutter he clambered down and on the alleyway cobblestones beneath it."

"When exactly did this burglary occur?" I said.

"Wednesday morning, the seventeenth, a little after midnight. We are sure of the time because a dolly-mop doing business in the alley saw the thief shimmy down the gutter and then mount a horse and ride away toward Charles Street just after the State House clock chimed midnight. She did not bother to notify the police of course, but she offered up the information later to have a solicitation charge against her dropped."

I turned to Henry. "We know the Waltham printer was killed at midnight. Haven could not be in two places at once. He is not the assassin."

Henry stared at Haven a very long time. Henry appeared to be having trouble giving up his belief that he had captured

Vogel's killer. "How did you manage to track this man you refer to as Jack Steeple to Plumford?" he asked the Boston police officer.

"An open set of eyes and ears is always the policeman's best weapon," Payne replied. "When I came the other day to arrest that Frenchman, I caught a glimpse of Jack Steeple here in the tavern. Would have paid him no mind whatsoever but for the way he tried to hide his face from me. We are trained to notice things like that. And then, at the police station this morning, what should I see posted on the wall but the drawing I just showed you! I rode here as quick as I could."

"I will have the stable boy see to your horse," I said.

Payne didn't bother to acknowledge my offer. It wasn't his horse's fault that he was discourteous, however, so I went off to find the boy. As I walked by the ladies' parlor I saw Ruggles passed out on the cabbage rose carpet. I checked his pulse rate, and it was normal. He was having no difficulty breathing, so I decided to let him sleep it off. It was not yet noon! As I tucked a pillow from the sofa under his head he grabbed my hand and gave it a slobbery kiss. "Edda, Edda, my darling," he muttered and then resumed snoring.

Upon my return from the stable I found Payne interrogating Haven as Henry silently observed. "I'll ask you one more time afore I resort to physical persuasion," Payne was saying. "Where's the loot hid, Jack Steeple?"

Haven shook his head. "Thee must set me free, for I am but a plain man in speech and deed."

Payne's eyes bulged in anger. "How would thee like a punch in thy face, *friend?*" He raised a closed fist.

"No reason to resort to violence, Lieutenant Payne," Henry said. "Let us simply go up and search his room."

"We'll have to pull up the floor boards, I reckon. Got a crowbar and hammer handy?" Payne said.

"In fact I do." Henry went to the back of the bar and down

the hatch to the cellar, returning a moment later with the requested tools.

"The loot is always below the boards," Payne said when we were in Haven's room. He did not even bother to have a look around before he began to energetically pry up the flooring.

Whilst he did so Henry examined the rest of the floor but found nothing there of interest to him and began running his hands along the walls. What he was looking for, I knew not. I got busy and turned the bed over and felt through the mattress and pillow stuffing. Payne continued to tear up the floor with the crowbar. He appeared to be rather enjoying himself.

"Methinks I found something," Henry said after a good long while of Payne's banging and crashing. "Pray halt with that destruction for a moment, Lieutenant Payne, and look up there." He pointed to a corner of the ceiling.

I could see nothing amiss, but apparently Henry had. He pushed a chair to the corner and stood upon it. Reaching up, he slid his fingertips over the area and then pulled a pocketknife from his coat. Slowly and carefully he prized out a six-inch square of plaster with the tip of his blade. I could see that behind the removed square the lathing had also been cut away.

Henry felt with the tips of his fingers into the space and lifted out a fish hook that had been wedged into the plaster. It had a string tied to it. He pulled up the string and at the end of it found attached a leather pouch. "I do believe," he said, "we have here what we seek."

Payne threw down his tools with a clatter. "I'll take that," he said in peremptory fashion. He grabbed the pouch and marched downstairs to the taproom ahead of us. At the sight of the pouch Haven groaned and dropped his head.

"You can't keep anything hidden from my sharp eyes, Jack Steeple," the lieutenant said. He untied the pouch and poured the contents onto the table. We all stared at a glittering array of gems set in rings, earbobs, necklaces, and brooches.

"Well, well, well," Payne said. "Seems that actress who was robbed has her share of wealthy admirers." He pulled out his list. "But where's the most costly piece of the lot? Where's the ruby necklace?"

Henry picked up a heavy gold necklace with an empty center setting. "I wager this piece once sported a ruby."

Payne scowled at his prisoner. "Flicked it out and sold it already, did you?"

I glanced at Haven, and a look of puzzlement flashed across his face.

"I doubt he had time to sell it," Henry said. "Maybe he swallowed it when he heard you charging up the stairs to arrest him."

Payne turned on Haven. "Is that what you did, you thieving sneak?"

Haven stared at the jewels on the table. "Don't know what thee speaks on with such rudeness. Never seen any of that mess of twinkles. As a Friend I care not for such worldly extravagance."

"If he did indeed gulp it down his gullet," Henry said, "you might want to keep those sharp eyes of yours on his chamber pot, Lieutenant Payne."

"I intend to do just that," Payne said, "when he's safe in our Leverett Street Jail." The lieutenant turned to me. "I will need to rent a wagon to haul this man back to Boston."

He seemed to be under the impression that I was somehow connected with the Sun Tavern stable, and I did not bother to correct him. I procured a wagon and even hitched Payne's overworked horse to it. I checked Haven's injured leg one last time before he was carted away. My suturing had held!

Henry and I watched the wagon roll off toward the post road and went back inside the tavern. We found Ruggles at his station behind the bar, looking bleary eyed but sober enough. We began to tell him all that he had missed whilst he lay in a drunken stupor on the parlor rug. He seemed not the least bit interested and took from his breast pocket a folded sheet of paper. He placed it upon the bar for Henry and me to read.

Farewell, Sam. No good here for me now. People know I am whore. Must travel fast. Cannot take Roos. Got me another roos. *So do not worry. I get by fine. You take care. Always I pray for you.*

"Why'd she go and leave me?" Ruggles moaned. "I forgave her the moment she confessed about her past."

Would the Board of Selectmen have forgiven her though, I wondered. If Edda had stayed here with Ruggles, they well might have decided that his tavern was no longer respectable enough and revoked his license. There were plenty of men in town who would have liked to take over Ruggles's profitable business. Constable Beers for one. I did not point this out to Ruggles, of course. It would take him time to see that Edda had done him a favor by leaving him.

"Does *roos* mean red in Dutch?" Henry asked him.

Ruggles nodded. Reminded of the bird, he whistled for her, and a moment later the parrot swooped into the taproom. She settled on Ruggles's shoulder and pressed her bright red head to his cheek.

"Your mama has gone and left you," Ruggles told the bird as tears streamed down his face.

Henry motioned to me to step outside with him. We stood on the porch and stared out at the Green.

"I think Sam's good, generous heart will eventually mend," I said.

"Is that your diagnosis, Doctor?"

"My hope anyway. Sam only knew the woman for two months, and he has long-time friends here to support and comfort him. So the prognosis is good. I'm more worried about poor Edda getting by on her own."

"Not so poor," Henry said. "She didn't leave here empty-handed."

His remark distressed me. "You think she stole money from Sam?"

"No. I think she stole from a thief," Henry said. "She stated in her note to Sam that she has another *roos*. Meaning another red. Rubies are red."

"She found the jewel thief's stash!" I said. If anyone could have found it other than Henry, it would have been Edda. "But why steal only one jewel? Why not the whole lot?"

"I think it was very clever of her not to be greedy," Henry said. "She must have reckoned that if Haven discovered that only the ruby was missing from his stash, he would accept the loss rather than cause trouble. A thief does not want to draw attention to himself by accusing others of thievery, after all. And Edda must have also reckoned that if Haven got caught, the police would assume he had hidden the ruby somewhere. Payne certainly thinks Haven still has it."

"But what if Payne eventually decides someone at the Sun Tavern took the ruby? Sam might fall under suspicion."

"I think not. Don't forget that Edda has already confessed to the crime in her note by alluding to the *roos*. She did that to protect Sam," Henry said. "Besides, I doubt that the ruby will be the only gem missing by the time an official inventory is made at the police station in Boston. And Lieutenant Payne will make sure to caste the blame on Jack Steeple or claim he had an accomplice who made off with the missing pieces."

"Should we tell Sam your theory, Henry?"

"Yes, when he's sober enough to understand. He will be comforted to know that Edda will not be in desperate financial straits. She should get more than enough money for that ruby to set herself up in a new life where nobody knows her."

"So we have seen the last of her," I said. "And the last of our quack Quaker too. I suppose we'll eventually learn Haven's real name when he's put on trial."

"I don't much care what his name is," Henry said. "Indeed, now that I know he is not the assassin, I have no interest in him at all. We must return our attention to finding Tripp's and Vogel's killer, Adam. Before there is yet another Conductor killed."

JULIA

Thursday, May 25

Around noon Tansy and I shared a light luncheon at the card table in my bedchamber rather than in the dining room, where ground floor windows would have made her more likely to be viewed by passersby. I decided to be completely open with her, hoping she would be so with me, and finally told her about the brutal assassination of the Railroad Conductor in Waltham.

"So you see, Tansy, it wasn't necessarily because Mr. Tripp was in the act of transporting you that he was murdered. When Mr. Vogel was killed, he wasn't conducting a fugitive to a Station. He was at his place of business."

"But he was killed because he was helping runaway slaves, wasn't he?"

"Well, yes." It could not be denied.

"As was Mr. Tripp."

"So it seems."

"And you could be killed too, Julia, for sheltering me here!"

Exactly the reaction I feared Tansy would have. "Except for

a few very trusted people, no one knows I'm associated with the Railroad," I told her. "And no one except Adam, Henry, Rusty, and now Mrs. Tripp know you are here. You obviously trust Mrs. Tripp or you wouldn't have shown yourself to her yesterday."

"I did so want to see her again and let her know I was all right," Tansy said. "She was very concerned for my safety when I left for Carlisle with her husband."

"You know, my first impression of Mrs. Tripp was that she wasn't very sympathetic regarding runaways," I said. "But apparently I was completely wrong about her. I wonder why she acted so coldly toward Henry and me."

"Mrs. Tripp isn't cold," Tansy said. "But she is chary. And God knows she had reason to be."

"*Had* reason to be? What was that reason?"

Tansy spooned some hasty pudding into her mouth and chewed awhile. I could tell she was considering how to answer me. "I don't know," she said after she finally swallowed.

But of course she did. "You told me the other day that you didn't want to talk against the man who died helping you, Tansy. That suggests you do indeed have something against him. Did Mr. Tripp molest you?"

"He did not." Tansy must have seen the disbelief in my eyes. "I will go fetch the Bible and swear upon it that he never so much as laid a hand on me."

I believed her then, for I knew that she held the Bible sacrosanct. I tried another approach to find out what she was holding back. "You seemed surprised when Mrs. Tripp told you that Jared had gone off to Ohio."

"Jared? Who might that be?"

"Mrs. Tripp's elder son, as you well know."

"Oh, right. I heard her speak of him."

"It sounded to me like you knew him personally."

Tansy regarded me as if I'd gone off my rocker. "How could I? You heard Mrs. Tripp say that her Jared left for Ohio weeks ago."

"Will you swear on a Bible you never met him?"

"If you do not stop badgering me, Julia, I will just out and out swear!"

But rather than blaspheme, Tansy abruptly left and retreated to the attic. Apparently she preferred that cramped space to my vexing company.

I went down to the kitchen just as Adam and Henry were coming through the back door. "Are you hungry?" I asked them.

"As bears," Adam said.

"Pray have some pudding. I made it myself."

I lifted the cover off the pot on the stove, and they stared at the contents. This being my first try at making a hasty pudding, I thought a few lumps and a bit of scorching forgivable, but these two hungry bears apparently did not and politely refused my offer.

"Perhaps the midday fare at the Sun would suit you better," I suggested a bit huffily.

"Sam has closed the Sun for the rest of the day and taken himself to bed," Henry said.

As he and Adam explained to me why, I brought a wedge of cheese and a tin of crackers from the pantry, and we all settled around the table. That the Quaker had turned out to be a jewel thief in hiding was most surprising, but I was not surprised to hear that Edda had abruptly left Plumford. She had done it for Sam Ruggles's sake, I was sure. His business would have suffered if she had stayed at his side. Those willing to sleep at an inn where the proprietor's wife had stabbed a guest in his bed would be few and far between.

"I have wasted valuable time suspecting the wrong man,"

Henry said. He looked desolate. "What if the two murders are not even connected?"

"They must be," Adam said. "Both men were Underground Railroad Conductors, and the assassin stated in his warning letter that he had been hired to kill Conductors, one after another."

"I have heard you refer to this letter, but I've never seen it," I said.

Henry took a folded sheet from his jacket pocket and gave it to me.

"A most distinct penmanship," I remarked at first glance.

"That spot of brown in the corner of the paper could well be an oil from India," Adam told me. "And the green stain in the fold could be medicinal tobacco powder."

I read the letter with building rage. "These are the sanctimonious ravings of a despicable murderer," I said after I'd finished.

"Do you think the author insane?" Henry asked me.

"I think the institution of slavery insane," I said. "But the man who wrote this letter seems to be in control of his faculties. His intentions are clear enough at any rate. What I don't understand is why he mentions Vogel's murder, but he does not mention Tripp's murder."

"Because he had not yet committed it," Adam said.

"But why would he kill another Conductor only a few hours after assassinating the first one? It seems to defeat his stated purpose," I said and read aloud from the letter. *"May what I did to Vogel serve as a warning for all the others."*

"Read the next sentence aloud," Adam said.

"I will continue to eradicate these Outlaws, until enough are slain for the survivors to see their certain fate at my hands and cease their illegal activities."

"There you have the answer to your question, Julia," Adam

said. "Tripp must have been the next name on the list he mentions, and he simply took the opportunity to eradicate him."

"But how did he know Tripp would be driving down Drover's Lane at that time?"

"That's what I have been pondering," Henry said. "And the conclusion I always reach is one I do not wish to accept. Someone in the Underground Railroad alerted him."

"A spy?" I said in a hushed tone. "Who knew the route Tripp would be taking besides Mrs. Tripp?"

"Only the Station Master who arranged the delivery with Tripp," Henry said.

"Well, who was that?" Adam said.

Henry hesitated. "My mother."

"Oh, Henry, you do not suspect *her!*" I said.

"Of course not. Which means my reasoning must be faulty. Or I am missing a key piece of information. We should talk this over with Rusty. He's been active in the Railroad far longer than I have. Stories concerning his derring-do go back near a decade."

"Does he know you're also a Conductor?" Adam said.

"Well, yes. He made mention to me upon first meeting that we were in the same line of work as Conductors. Weren't you the one who told him, Adam?"

"Not I. In fact, I took care not to. I know how secretive you Railroad people like to keep things."

Henry looked at me, and I shook my head. "Rusty did not hear it from me," I said. "I have spoken to the man only twice. The first time was when he took my likeness."

"He took your likeness?" Adam asked me in a rather sharp tone.

"Yes, and I had no idea he was even connected with the Railroad then," I continued. "The second time we spoke it was but briefly in front of you, Henry."

"I wonder how he found out I was a Conductor then."

"Most likely the same way we found out he was one," Adam said. "There are probably stories circulating up and down the Railroad about your heroics too, Henry."

Henry laughed that off. I discerned a blush beneath the tan of his cheeks.

"I would like to make a copy of this letter straightaway," I told him.

"Certainly," Henry said. "Meanwhile, I'll go fetch Rusty. I'm rather curious to see the inside of his wagon, although I've refused his many invitations to have my likeness taken. I know well enough what I look like."

As soon as Henry left, Adam and I went to my studio. I put the letter on the drawing board and began to copy it whilst Adam gazed out the window.

"There goes Henry across the Green," he said.

"Are there any customers waiting at Rusty's wagon?" I asked.

"No, Rusty is leaning against the side of it with nothing better to do than pose like a coxcomb in those flashy striped pantaloons of his. He thinks himself quite the ladies' gent, doesn't he?"

"I suppose he does."

"Why didn't you tell me he took your likeness, Julia?"

"Because you would have wanted to see it, and I do not care for the way I came out. Rusty insisted that I smile, and the result is quite artificial."

"What right did he have to insist that you smile for him?"

"Adam! You sound downright jealous. If you are, you are being absurd."

His shoulders lifted in a shrug, and he continued to stare out the window. "Henry is talking to Rusty now. They're going inside the wagon." He then turned to face me. "I apologize, Julia. You're right. It's absurd of me to be jealous of Rusty. But I don't like the man."

"I didn't like Rusty the first time I met him, either," I admitted. "But now I understand his brash behavior and silly patter are meant to distract people from his true mission. We cannot forget all he's done over the years to help slaves escape."

"That's certainly to Rusty's credit," Adam said. "If he's been active in the Railroad for so long, he must be older than he looks. I reckon his freckles make him look younger."

The image of Rusty's freckled face flashed in my mind. And then it flashed again. Each image was slightly different. "His freckles changed position!" I said.

"Freckles cannot change position," Adam said.

"Well, his did," I insisted. "I am a portraitist and notice such things. Upon first meeting Rusty, I observed that a pattern of freckles on his right cheek reminded me of the shape of the Big Dipper. But when I saw him a second time, the freckles on that cheek had a different arrangement. In fact, I think *all* his freckles were askew. I paid little attention to it at the time. I just thought he looked slightly different."

"Freckles don't rearrange themselves around someone's face," Adam reiterated.

"Real ones don't," I said. "Rusty's, however, are fake. He paints them on."

"That's hard to believe, Julia. I could understand a man wearing fake whiskers if he's unable to grow his own. But fake freckles? A freckled visage is hardly considered an attribute. In fact, I've treated young ladies who have near ruined their complexions by trying to bleach them away."

"I agree that it makes no sense," I said. "But I am pretty certain his freckles are fake."

Shaking his head over the absurdity of such a notion, Adam turned back to the window. "I see Rusty heading for the Sun stable. To paint fake white patches on his piebald horse perhaps?"

I ignored that. "Didn't Henry say he was going to bring Rusty back here to talk with us?"

"Henry must still be in the wagon. I didn't see him come out."

"I wonder if he let Rusty take his likeness. If so, I would very much like to see it."

"I would very much like to see yours," Adam said.

"It's dreadful! I haven't looked at it myself since I stuck it in my reticule."

"Pray show it to me."

"Oh, very well. But you'd better not laugh." I went searching for my reticule, which as often as not I misplace, and found it under the drawing table. I withdrew from it the daguerreotype, and when I unfolded the gloves I had wrapped around it for protection, I saw green stains smeared on the white cotton and cried out.

"Come now, my love. If it's an image of you, it cannot be that bad."

"Look at my gloves, Adam." I threw them on the drawing table. "They were spotless before I went inside Rusty's wagon."

"The stains on them are the same green color as the powder stain on the assassin's letter," Adam said.

"It's henna powder," I told him. "Made from the ground leaves of the henna plant and so fine it floats in the air and lands on everything. Mixed with lemon and oil it becomes a reddish brown paste. I knew an Indian artist in Paris who applied it as a temporary skin decoration. And I knew a woman who used henna paste to dye her hair red. Just as the imposter who calls himself Rusty does!"

"You believe Rusty is actually the assassin in disguise?" Adam's voice was low and calm.

I, on the other hand, was near ready to start screeching like Roos the parrot. "Yes! What more proof do we need?"

"We need to get a sample of his handwriting to see if it matches the handwriting in the assassin's letter."

"We have one," I said, turning over the daguerreotype. Written upon the pasteboard backing was Rusty's initial and the date. "Look how the capital *R* matches the ones in the letter. And see how the word *May* is formed identically in both the letter and the date Rusty wrote on the board."

"Yes, I do see," Adam said and hurried to the window. "The daguerreotype wagon is gone, Julia!"

We rushed out the front door together and looked up and down the Green. There was no sign of Henry or the wagon. A group of boys were standing by the pump, and we asked them if they saw which direction the wagon went. They all pointed north up the post road.

ADAM

Thursday, May 25

I told Julia to go to my office to fetch my shotgun, and I ran to the barn to saddle my horse. I mounted Napoleon, and Julia handed me up the gun. Her eyes implored me to be careful, but she said not a word. She knew trying to stop me would be futile. If Henry had not yet been assassinated, it was up to me to save him from such a fate.

On the post road I discerned the deeper ruts of Rusty's heavy wagon wheels amongst the confusion of other tracks. I followed them as they turned off the main road and onto Drover's Lane. That Rusty had taken this secluded route did not bode well, and I rode down the rough and rooted lane with an anxious heart. Rounding the curve I saw Rusty's red wagon sitting by the bog. There was no one on the driving seat, and the rear door was flung open. I dismounted, and, shotgun at the ready, I charged into the wagon. Rusty wasn't there. Nor was Henry, but I recognized his sturdy boots on the floor. They were tied together with heavy rope. Puzzled, I stepped out of the wagon and heard shouting on the bog.

I could see no one from the road and ran out onto the sphagnum. My foot poked through the surface, and I pitched forward with such violence my gun flew from my grip and sank into the water. I did not waste time trying to retrieve it. A wet gun wouldn't fire and was of no use to me. My only weapons now were my fists and my wits. I kept my body low as I scuttled through the undergrowth and over the moss and soon came on a desperate scene that brought my heart up into my throat.

Fifty yards ahead I saw Henry, a gag in his mouth and his hands bound behind his back, being pursued by Rusty, who was gripping a bowie knife. The long blade gleamed in the sun. Henry knew how to traverse the quaking sphagnum far better than Rusty, but he was greatly impaired without the use of his arms to give him balance. Rusty caught up with him and shoved him down off his feet. He leaned over Henry, knife raised, and I let out as great and terrifying a bellow as I could manage. Rusty looked my way to assess what sort of danger was approaching, and, seeing I had no weapon in hand, he turned back to Henry. Henry had taken advantage of the distraction to roll onto his back and as Rusty bent over him, knife poised to stab, Henry gave him a powerful kick in the face. Rusty reeled back. Henry jerked himself upright and took off.

I kept pushing across the bog as fast as I could. Although I was not eager to deal with a knife-wielding assassin whilst I myself was unarmed, I was determined to come to Henry's aid. Searching desperately around me for some kind of weapon, I found a water-logged length of wood that felt solid enough to inflict harm. It also helped me better keep my balance as I lurched along.

Rusty recovered from the kick and started after his quarry again. Henry glanced backwards and stumbled, catching his foot on a root. He pitched forward and fell hard. He sat up immediately and tried to stand, but his bare foot was entangled in the tenacious roots. Rusty laughed when he saw Henry's predicament. He was no more than five strides away from reaching his prey now and raised his knife for the kill. With his next step his right foot broke through the sphagnum. He swayed to keep his balance and took another step. His left leg plunged into the bog to his knee. As he tried yanking it free he sank waist deep into the mire.

"Let go!" he cried, stabbing down into the water with his knife. He started to scream. The scream became a gargle, and then his head went under.

Henry managed to pull free his foot, and he crawled to the edge of the sphagnum where Rusty had disappeared. When I reached him he was still gazing down into the water. I yanked off his gag.

"Any sign of Rusty?" I said.

"No," Henry said. "He was pulled under the sphagnum."

"Pulled by what?'

"The phantom," Henry said. He has a wry sense of humor even during times of duress.

I untied his hands, and we each found a long branch to use as a search pole. We crouched down and probed through rents in the moss as far as we could reach. My branch hit against something solid, and I went to a spot ten feet away and broke through the surface with my boot heel, widened the opening, and began to search down with my arm. My fingers passed through what felt like hair.

"Henry, I have him."

I entwined my fingers in Rusty's thick head of hair and slowly pulled his body to the surface. His face emerged. His features were contorted in a frozen expression of horror, eyes bulging out as wide as their sockets would allow. Henry helped me ease him up onto the sphagnum. I checked for any signs of life. There were none. We lay the body across a fallen tree trunk so it would not sink back into the bog.

"How did he manage to get the better of you, Henry?" I could not help but ask.

"He clubbed me from behind as soon as I entered the wagon. I came to with a gag in my mouth as he was tying me up. He took great pleasure telling me how he'd killed the real Rusty and had taken his place in order to infiltrate the Underground Railroad. He thought himself very clever."

"What was he going to do with you?" I said.

"He took great delight in telling me that too," Henry said. "He was going to behead me as he had Mr. Vogel. But he didn't want my blood all over his wagon. He planned to execute me in the woods and send my head in a box to the Vigilant Committee. He said he intended to behead all his victims so there would be no doubt it was the work of the Hand of Justice, as he'd signed his warning letter."

We reached the wagon and went inside. First thing Henry did was untie his boots and put them on. "Good thing I wasn't wearing heavy stockings today or I would have never been able to slip out of these boots," he said. "After I did, I kicked open the door and jumped out of the wagon. I saw I was by the bog and ran onto it. Rusty must have heard the commotion, for he stopped immediately and set off after me."

We searched the wagon thoroughly. Amidst the clutter of developing chemicals we found a pot of green henna powder and a vial of chaulmoogra oil to mix with it. I told Henry how Julia had figured out Rusty was an imposter. We also found a box of stationery that matched that of the letter from the Hand of Justice.

"Now to find the murder weapon he used on Vogel," I said.

"You don't think it was the bowie knife he was going to use on me?" Henry said.

"Oh, I am sure he could have cut off your head with it," I said. "But not so neatly as he sliced off poor Vogel's head."

Henry turned over a small table. On the underside of it, held there by small nails, was a spiral of wire with a wooden handle attached to each end. He detached and unwound it and, gripping the handles, held it taut. "The garrote used on Vogel," he said.

I cast a glance around the wagon and saw the guitar in the corner. I picked it up. The string was still missing. Now I understood why.

"But where's the rifle he used to shoot Tripp?" I said.

"I don't think Rusty shot him," Henry said. "When he was bragging to me about eliminating Conductors, he didn't mention that he'd killed Tripp along with Vogel. And Tripp wasn't beheaded."

"Well, if the imposter Rusty didn't kill Tripp, who did?"

"Whoever it was," Henry said, "has had plenty of time to either hide his tracks or make tracks."

When we left the wagon I put my hand on Henry's shoulder and said, "Rusty drowned. I was riding past, heard him shout for help from the bog, arrived too late to save him, and pulled his body from the water. That is what I intend to report to Constable Beers and the Coroner's Jury, for there is no need to bring you or the Underground Railroad into this."

Henry nodded. "Thank you. The publicity would destroy our secret network completely."

I rode off in one direction, and he walked off in the other.

JULIA

Friday, May 26

Late yesterday afternoon Adam and Henry took the cars to Boston to inform Mr. Coburn that the assassin who killed Mr. Vogel is dead. They also planned to meet with other members of the Vigilant Committee that evening and would spend the night in Boston, since there are no night trains back to Concord.

No doubt the facts of the case will never be made public because of the secret nature of the Underground Railroad. The Plumford Coroner's Jury has declared the daguerreotypist's death an accidental drowning, and there will be no further investigation into the matter. Rusty's body will be buried in the new cemetery with a blank stone to mark it, for no one knows his true name, and his wagon, equipment, and horse will be sold to pay for the burial and his outstanding tab at the Sun Tavern. Any money left over will be donated to the township's fund to help the needy.

"It's enough to make you give up trust in humankind," Tansy said after I told her that the man who had transported her from Boston to Plumford had been the Conductor assassin in disguise.

"The real Rusty was as noble a human being as God makes," I reminded her.

Tansy smiled at me. "I've met more than a few such beings of late. And when I finally get to Canada I will treasure the memory of each and every one of you."

She turned her eyes back to her sewing. She was making me a linen mantelet, and I was sketching her doing so as she sat cross-legged on my bed.

"The assassin admitted to Henry that he killed Mr. Vogel in Waltham," I told her. "Yet he insisted that he did not kill Mr. Tripp." I watched her closely for a reaction.

Tansy's expression remained impassive. She is good at hiding her thoughts and feelings, as I suppose most people born into slavery are. "He could have been lying," she said.

"He had no reason to lie."

"Well, I guess it was somebody else then." Tansy pulled her needle smoothly through the cloth. "Whoever it was, I never saw him."

"Will you tell me again what happened? Try to imagine it from the beginning."

Tansy sighed, put aside her work, and closed her eyes. "It was the middle of the night. Mr. Tripp hitched the horse to the wagon, and I came out of my hiding place in the barn to climb in back. Mr. Tripp got up on the seat and whistled for Ripper. The dog jumped up beside him, I pulled the blanket over me, and off we went."

"You never mentioned before that the dog came along," I said.

Tansy opened her eyes and squinted at me. "Does it matter? Ripper sure isn't going to tell you anything about what happened."

"Never mind. Pray continue."

Tansy closed her eyes again. "So off we went, rolling along on a bumpy road for about ten minutes or so. Then Mr. Tripp stopped the wagon. I reckon the killer had stepped out on the road in front of the wagon. After just a second or two of silence, I heard a rifle go off and Tripp's body thump to the ground. I leaped out of the wagon and started running. I did not look back!" Tansy's eyes flew open, and she glared at me. "I have never been so affrighted in my life, and I wish you would stop making me recall it, Julia."

She went back to her sewing, and I went back to my drawing, and later we both read aloud from *Jane Eyre*. No further mention of Tripp's murder was made.

Upon awakening this morning, however, I went up to the attic to ask Tansy one more question. Her answer was no. I hurriedly dressed and awaited Adam's return from Boston. But then I grew too impatient to wait a moment longer and left him a note. *I have gone to see Mrs. Tripp. I know who killed her husband.*

When I got to the Tripp house I found Ripper dozing in a patch of sunlight on the porch, but good old sentry that he is, he sleepily pushed himself up and began barking at me. I ignored him and knocked on the door. When Mrs. Tripp opened it she looked rather surprised to see me. But she did not look displeased. Since our first meeting ten days ago we had come to like each other. She invited me inside. Billy was in the kitchen packing a straw-filled crate with crockery.

"We're goin' back to Ohio!" he told me.

"I reckon you'll be happy to see Jared again," I said.

"It will be the happiest day of my life," he replied earnestly.

"Mine too," Mrs. Tripp said, wiping a tear from her eye.

"May we talk in private," I whispered to her.

"Go out to the barn and start packing up the tools like a good boy," she told Billy. When he left she asked me to sit down at the table. "I'd offer tea, but the china is all packed up."

"No matter," I said. "I am here to talk to you about Jared."

Her face closed shut. "What about him?"

"He didn't go off to Ohio weeks ago, did he? He left the day your husband was shot."

"Who told you that?"

"It wasn't Tansy. She has done as you asked her to and denies she ever met Jared. But he must have been at the farm the day Rusty delivered Tansy to you because his likeness was taken that day."

"What likeness?"

I glanced around for the daguerreotype of Jared and Billy but did not see it displayed. It was either packed or destroyed. "I have good reason to believe it was Jared who shot your husband, Mrs. Tripp."

She paled. "And what reason would that be?"

"The dog didn't bark."

"What?"

"Ripper always barks at strangers," I said. "And according to Tansy, Mr. Tripp took Ripper along with him on the trip to Carlisle. But when I asked Tansy this morning if the dog barked when Mr. Tripp stopped the wagon, she said no. Therefore Ripper knew who was standing on the road pointing a gun. Not a stranger, but one of the family. It was Jared."

For a moment Mrs. Tripp stared at me open-mouthed, and then she began to laugh hysterically. "The dog didn't bark?" she gasped. "Is that all you have against Jared? The dog didn't bark?" She began laughing again. Or sobbing.

She was right, of course. My evidence against her son amounted to little more than supposition. I saw no point in questioning her further, so when she ordered me out of her house I complied. As I was being escorted down the drive by Ripper, snapping at the hem of my frock, Adam arrived in his gig with Henry. He stopped beside me.

"Why did you come here alone, Julia?" he said. "You should have waited for us. I feared you were in danger."

"Mrs. Tripp would never hurt me."

"But her husband's killer might!"

"Jared is long gone from here," I said. "He took off right after he shot his stepfather."

"How did you reach this conclusion, Julia?" Henry said.

Whilst I related everything Tansy had told me and what I myself had observed and conjectured, Ripper kept up his loud, explosive racket, as if to confirm my hypothesis. Neither Adam nor Henry laughed at me. I jumped in the gig, and we went back to the house. Mrs. Tripp came out and just stared at us as we stepped up onto the porch.

"Is your son Jared still here?" Henry asked her right off. "Are you hiding him?"

"Why would I hide him? He left for Ohio weeks ago. How many times do I have to say it afore you believe me?" She looked ready to drop from exhaustion.

"Mind if we take a walk around the property?" Henry asked her.

"Go ahead if it will make you stop bothering me. You won't find Jared."

Billy came running out of the barn, delighted to see Adam. "You here to take out my stitches, doc?"

"Not yet, son. I just put them in two days ago."

"What's that yonder?" Henry said, pointing to a dead tree standing alone in a field. The trunk was stripped of its bark, and a black circle a foot in diameter was painted on the pale wood.

"That's a shooting target," Billy said.

"Let's go take a look at it," Henry said.

We all trooped over to the tree, including Ripper, who had thankfully stopped barking. The soft, punky wood within the black circle was riddled with holes. Henry pulled out his pocketknife and carefully prized out a bullet. He turned it over several times in his hand as he carefully examined it.

He then took a bullet from his waistcoat pocket. "This bullet killed your husband," he told Mrs. Tripp. "It passed right through his body, and I have kept it." He placed it on his palm along with the one he'd just extracted from the tree trunk. "As you can see, both bullets have a distinctive nick on the side, cut there by a burr in the barrel of the same gun. That gun was the murder weapon."

"It was *my* gun," Mrs. Tripp said. "I shot it at this tree for practice, and then I shot my husband with it."

"May I take a look at it?"

"I threw it into the bog!"

"Ma? You gone plumb crazy?" Billy said. "You don't even got a gun. Jared fired those bullets into the tree with his rifle."

Henry squatted to be at eye level with Billy. "Where's your brother's rifle?"

"He took it with him when he left."

"Do you remember what day he left?"

"I do. It was my birthday, and he give me his pocketknife."

"I wager you were born on May sixteenth," Henry said.

Billy's eyes widened. "How'd you guess that, mister?"

"You look the sort of boy who would be born on exactly that day." Henry stood and patted the boy's head.

"Go back to packing up in the barn, Billy," his mother said.

"I want to stay here."

"If you do as your mother's bidding," Henry said, "I'll give you an arrowhead when I leave." Billy ran off to the barn with Ripper chasing after him.

"What are you going to do with those bullets?" Mrs. Tripp asked Henry.

"I don't know yet," he said.

Mrs. Tripp sank to her knees, clasped her hands, and looked up at him with tears in her eyes. "I implore you not to turn them over to the law."

I have never seen Henry look so uncomfortable. But rather than help Mrs. Tripp to her feet, he sat down beside her on the ground. "Can you tell me why I should not do so?" he asked her.

Mrs. Tripp nodded and began speaking in a low voice. Adam and I also sat upon the ground to hear her better, and the four of us formed a circle in the field as the morning sun warmed our backs.

"Jared was twelve when I married Ezra Tripp," she began, "and Billy only six. Their father had died two years before. I married for their sake more than my own. I did not want them to grow up without a good man's example to guide them. I thought Ezra Tripp a good man. He went to church every Sunday, and he supported my work in the Underground Railroad. We did not have the same sort of relationship my first husband and I had. We shared little intimacy. But that was all right with me. Ezra was kind to the boys. He spent a great deal of time with Jared, teaching him manly skills a mother cannot teach her son, and Jared seemed to worship the ground Ezra walked on. But then, as he grew older, Jared changed toward his stepfather. By the time we moved here last year, he could not bear to be within ten feet of Ezra. They even came to blows in the barn last month. Ezra fell from the hayloft. Do you remember, Dr. Walker?"

"I do," Adam said. "Ezra's shoulder was dislocated."

"After that Jared and he never spoke a word to each other," Mrs. Tripp continued. "Ezra became surly and mean and drank more and more. He'd rant that Jared was old enough to be on his own and he should get out. But he was still kind to Billy. Very kind indeed. Oh, how stupid I was! How blind! It was Tansy who opened my eyes to the manner of man I had married. She espied him fooling with Billy from her hidey hole in the barn. She told me what she had seen, and I told Jared right off. I wanted him to know so he could protect his brother. In truth, I wanted him to run Ezra off the farm now that he was big enough to do it. Instead, he just packed his bag, saddled his horse, and said he was heading back to Ohio. He gave Billy his knife and left. And that's the last I seen or heard of my eldest son."

"Not quite," Henry said. "You heard his gun go off before sunrise the next morning."

"Somebody's gun anyway," she said.

"You must have known it was Jared's or you would have told us about hearing it when we came to talk to you that morning," I said.

"I thought it best to say nothing about anything. I just wanted you gone so I could get on with my mourning."

"For your dead husband?" I said.

"No. For my poor boy. If he killed Ezra I reckon he had reason to. No doubt in my mind that he was mistreated by that monster when he was too little to protest. And he saved his brother Billy from the same fate." She looked at each of us, dry-eyed now, and let her gaze rest last upon Henry. "Should he hang for what he did?"

"It's not for me to judge," Henry said.

"Will Tansy testify she saw Jared kill Ezra?"

"She claims she did not see the shooter," Henry said. "And even if she did, her slave status would prevent her from testifying in a court of law."

"So the only evidence you have is the bullets," Mrs. Tripp said.

Henry opened his hand and dropped the two bullets he held into Mrs. Tripp's lap. "I have no evidence now," he said.

Before we drove off Henry took an arrowhead from his pocket and gave it to Billy as promised. It seems he always has an arrowhead upon his person. He finds them in the ground as easily as pebbles.

ADAM

Friday, May 26

We rode back to town together, and I left the gig in the drive, planning to go on to Tuttle Farm to check on Gran after we told Tansy what we had learned from Mrs. Tripp. Upon entering the kitchen we were astonished to see Shiloh Prouty sitting at the table drinking coffee with Tansy.

"You all calm down now," Tansy told us right off. "If Shiloh wanted to snatch me away, he'd have done it already."

Prouty stood and bowed to Julia. "I apologize for intruding, ma'am."

"Did Tansy let you in of her own free will?"

"Yes, she did, ma'am."

"Then you're not intruding. You are a guest of my guest. Pray be seated."

Henry and I looked at each other. I shrugged, poured myself a cup of coffee, and joined Prouty and Tansy at the table, as did Julia. Henry remained standing in the doorway, leaning against the jamb with his arms folded.

"I peeked out the window and saw Shiloh making a beeline across the Green to this house," Tansy explained, as calm as a millpond. "He called out my name at the front door, so I figured the jig was up and let him in. I reckoned he wasn't going to drag me away, screaming and kicking, in front of all the townspeople on the Green."

"He might have," I said, "without Henry or me around to stop him."

"I wouldn't do no such thing," Prouty said, looking mightily offended.

"You would do no such thing," Tansy corrected him.

"That's right," he said. "I been knowing Tansy was here for days now. And I bided my time till I had a chance to get to her clear of y'all."

"How did you know she was here, Mr. Prouty?" Julia said.

"Rusty told me. He said he wanted the hundred and fifty dollar reward I posted and would cart her back to my farm in Virginia in his wagon instead of taking her north. I was mighty tempted to accept his offer."

"But you didn't," Julia said.

"No, I did not, ma'am. Tansy would have likely put up a fight once she caught on that Rusty had tricked her. And after he brung her to me, she would have likely just run off again. No use getting her back if she ain't going to stay."

"So what are you doing here?" I asked brusquely. Julia, in my opinion, was being too gentle with him. Henry had not said a word and was just observing them all with a slightly bemused expression.

"I am here hoping to talk some sense into my girl," Prouty replied.

"Don't call me that like I was your chattel," Tansy said. "Your horse, your pigs, your dog, your *girl*."

Prouty looked as hurt as if she'd kicked him. "I never can say the right thing to you, can I? I ain't come to lay claim to you as my slave, Tansy."

"So what are you doing here?" I asked him again, my tone even more brusque.

"Mr. Prouty was addressing Tansy, not you, Adam," Julia said. "Perhaps we should all just leave the two of them alone to talk this out in private."

"No need," Tansy said, "for there is nothing further for us to talk out."

"Maybe you will listen to me better than she does, ma'am," Prouty said to Julia. "Tansy come to be my slave as a bequest from my aunt. I know you folks up North don't hold with that, but in Virginia that is the way things are done. And after Tansy come to me, I ain't ashamed to admit I grew mighty fond of her. She knows a heap more than me from book learning, and she's got a heap more sense, too. I'd be proud to have such as her as my lawful wife and helpmeet."

"Then why didn't you just free her and ask her to marry you?" I said. To me it seemed the obvious solution.

"I didn't want to give her up," Prouty said.

"The law in Virginia," Tansy explained, "requires manumitted slaves to leave the state within a year of getting their freedom. So I could not stay there as a freedwoman, even if I married Shiloh."

"That leaves me no choice," Prouty said to her.

"But to keep me your slave?"

"No, honey. I will free you like you want me to. I done made up my mind it's what I got to do to truly keep you. I'll sell my farm, and me and you will go homestead in a free state. That is what I come to tell you. And I do not mind doing so now in front of witnesses."

It seemed like a mighty good plan to me, and I was all set to uncork a bottle of wine and propose a toast. I smiled at Julia. She was regarding Tansy most closely.

"Is that what you want?" Julia asked her.

"I just want my freedom," Tansy said softly.

"Don't you want *me?*" Prouty looked at her beseechingly with his bleached-out blue eyes.

Tansy pressed her lips together and stared back at him. After a long moment, she shook her head.

If that surprised me, it must have stunned Prouty like a blow to the head from a hammer. He did not move a muscle. Did not even blink. The man's world must have turned upside down when he realized that the woman who was his slave did not want him for her husband. Henry and I exchanged a look. If things got out of hand we were both ready to protect Tansy.

"Sell me, Shiloh, I beg you," she said, covering his big sunburnt hand, lying flat and still on the table, with her smooth brown one. "Let my sister buy my freedom from you. Then I can stay in Boston with her. You go back to the farm you love. You'll forget about me soon enough."

"I won't," he said.

"You won't sell me?"

"I won't forget you." Prouty stood up slowly, as if he ached all over. "But I will give you your freedom, Tansy. I said that I would in front of these witnesses, and I will not go back on my word. Before I go home I'll ride into Boston and talk to your sister and her husband."

He bowed to Julia, did not so much as glance at Henry or me, and left, keeping his back straight and his head high for a change.

"He will be better off without me," Tansy said. "I might have been raised up a slave, but I sure wasn't raised up to be a farmer's wife."

"So in truth it is you who will be better off without him," Julia said.

"I always wanted to be a teacher," Tansy said. "My sister

and I have this dream of starting up a school for young ladies of color." Her eyes shined bright with possibilities.

"Here's to your freedom," I said, raising my cup to her.

"Prouty should not be paid for giving it to her, however," Henry said. "Tansy is not rightfully his to sell. No human being can be owned by another."

"Let it be," I told him. "Tansy got what she most wanted, and Prouty left with his dignity intact. That is called compromise, Henry."

He winced, as he always did, at the notion of compromise when it came to slavery, and I hoped he would not dampen Tansy's happiness with further argument. If he had the inclination, he suppressed it, for he was as happy for Tansy as we were.

"You have been through quite an ordeal," he told her, taking both her hands in his. "And I admire your fortitude and spirit."

"If there is any spirit you should admire," she replied, "it is the phantom of the bog. When I ran away from the shooter, she's the one who saved me."

"Did she?" Henry regarded Tansy closely. "How?"

"Each time I broke through the slippery, wobbly bog moss and thought I would disappear for good," Tansy said, "I rose up again as if a hand were lifting me out of the icy waters. When I reached the opposite side and was on solid ground again, I dared turn around to see if the shooter was pursuing me. I did not see him, but I saw *her*."

"And what did she look like?" Henry asked evenly.

"She was silvery and beautiful. She floated above the bog for a moment, smiling at me, and then disappeared into thin air."

"Because she was thin air," I said. "Mist in the moonlight."

Tansy shrugged. "I saw what I saw. And I truly believe she saved me."

"Then she did," Henry said. "I saw her too," he added as casually as if he were remarking on the weather. "Perhaps we see the phenomena of Nature more vividly during times of extreme vulnerability. Indeed, I believe that the woods are choke-full of Spirits."

"When you talk like this, Henry," I said, "it's hard to believe you're the same man who records natural phenomena with meticulous attention and careful measurements."

"Oh, I am that man for certain," he replied. "But my desire for knowledge is intermittent and my desire to bathe my head in atmospheres unknown to my feet is perennial and constant. Nature can be viewed both empirically and mystically, can it not?"

Henry might well have gone on talking in this fashion till the cows came home, but he had more pressing matters to attend to. He left us to go to the Sun and finish constructing the dumbwaiter, for he wanted to move back to Concord as soon as possible. Lidian and her children had returned from their visit to Plymouth.

Tansy asked Julia if she might stay with her a little while longer. She thought it would be best for Prouty to have settled things with her sister and brother-in-law and departed for home before she went back to Boston. Julia agreed, only too happy to have her, and Tansy excused herself to go write Rose a letter.

I invited Julia to come along with me to Tuttle Farm, and we had a long visit with Gran, who was in good spirits. She assured us she did not plan to give up the ghost until she saw us married and held our firstborn babe in her arms come the new year.

Afterward Julia and I went for a walk in the apple orchard. The turf was soft and springy underfoot, and hundreds of apple trees were in full bloom. The clusters of fragrant flowers perfumed the warm breeze as golden sunlight streamed down upon us from the cloudless blue sky.

It seemed as though we were in a heavenly cathedral as we

strolled down a grassy aisle festooned with pink and white petals that had fallen from the canopy of blossom-laden branches above. A choir of humming bees sang all around us. I knew in the deepest part of my being that we would always be together in this life. And that we have been together like this in past lives. And that we would meet and love in future lives.